Books By Luke Smitherd:

Full-Length Novels:

The Physics of the Dead

The Stone Man

A Head Full Of Knives

In The Darkness, That's Where I'll Know You
– The Complete Black Room Story

Serial Novellas

The Black Room, Part One: In The Black
Room

The Black Room, Part Two: The Woman In
The Night

The Black Room, Part Three: The Other
Places

The Black Room, Part Four: The End

<u>Novellas</u>

The Man On Table Ten

Hold On Until Your Fingers Break

My Name Is Mister Grief

He Waits

Do Anything

For an up-to-date list of Luke Smitherd's other books, his blog, YouTube clips and more, visit www.lukesmitherd.com

Weird. Dark.

By Luke Smitherd

Table of Contents

Acknowledgements

At the time of writing, the following people wrote a nice Amazon.com or co.uk review of my most (and very) recent novella *My Name Is Mister Grief* in its original single copy format. It means an immense deal, not only practically— reviews mean people are far, FAR more likely to buy a book—but personally, as disappointments are abundant in the writing game, so any encouragement is amazing to receive, especially from strangers. I'm using here either the name you put in your Amazon review, or a shortened version if you sent me an e-mail. I don't want to ruin any witness protection programmes that might be in progress. And for those of you that have kept reviewing all along, I see your names when they keep coming up. You guys are saints in my book.

Thanks to the following reviewers:

Karen Austin, Amazon Customer, Jason Jones, Swebby, The Fro, QueenTulip, Nita V. Jester-Frantz, Lisa L. Philips, JoanneG, Ryan, BSM, Gwendelyn Turensky, Pooly4, Michelle Kennedy, Mrs Kindle, Ms. J. Kelly, Canis Major, David Plank, Buzzskin, Steve Gatehouse, Angie Hackett, Glennnccc, I.D. Ball, Silversmith, R. Gill, julie6, Neil Tucker, P. Hughes, Mr. Richard James Hustwit, TerryHeth. Daisy, and Lomb.

Thanks to my Patreon subscribers:

Michelle McDonald, Sherry Diehr, Dean Bones, Mike hands, Michelle Kennedy, Marty Brastow, Pete Hughes, K. Edwin Fritz, Kathy Logan, James Phoenix, Barbra Smerz, Richard Carnes, Jeremy Smith, and Barbara Haynes.

Proofreading by Peter Robinson, Denise Smitherd, and Marty Brastow. Major thanks to you.

1. My Name Is Mister Grief

When Robert told Jerry about Mr Grief, he thought he was doing Jerry a favour. At least that's what Jerry always assumed, when he looked back on that day at Mandy's funeral; the two of them standing by the overstocked, hardly-dented buffet and having that weird conversation about Mick Meat the Fine-Meats Man. Whether or not Robert actually *had* done a him a good turn—despite his best intentions—was something that Jerry could never be fully sure about. But it was done now, and could never, ever be changed.

***

"Hey Jerry," said Robert's voice from behind Jerry's ear, soothing and calm and careful, addressing Jerry in the same delicate manner that everyone else had on that long, insanely difficult day. Jerry actually closed his eyes and took a deep breath for a moment before turning around, one hand gripping his paper plate adorned with chinese rolls and chicken skewers, the other halted in the process of reaching for an onion baji. He had no intention of eating any of it—it would be impossible—but Mandy's sisters had done such a superhuman job on preparing a monstrous buffet that so much of it was going to be left over. His girls had even helped. He didn't want them to think people hadn't liked it.

"Hi Robert," said Jerry as he turned, his face wearing a forced smile, but not because he didn't like Robert. He loved him. He was just very tired of all the pleasantries and well-wishes for one day and wanted to be left alone. He hated himself for feeling that way but, today of all days, he cut himself a break. The forced smile, however, gave way to an open mouth. Robert looked *great.*

Not that Robert looking great would have been anything shocking a year ago; Robert had *always* looked great, his olive skin and naturally thick, dark hair making him look almost like a cliché version of the Italian Stallion male of myth, and younger than his forty plus years. His big, easy smile, and imposing height of nearly six feet four had always made him a hit with the ladies. His warm, outgoing manner, sense of humour, and affability made him a hit with the men. On paper, short, pale, awkward and bookish Jerry should have hated Robert's guts when they met, with eighteen year-old Robert an almost custom-made nemesis who possessed all the qualities that eighteen year-old Jerry utterly lacked at the time and so desperately wished for. But university makes for strange acquaintances, and had they met in the student union bar on any other night but their first night there, knowing no-one as they did, maybe they would never have been associates.

But they were. Robert was one of Jerry's best friends in the world. And the last time Jerry had actually seen the man two months previously, Robert had been suicidal.

They'd spoken on the phone since, after they'd gotten Robert help—spoken lots of times, and Jerry had kept offering to come and stay with him—but then Robert had said he was going away for a few months, and did. Whenever Jerry had tried to call him after that, Robert's phone had been switched off.

Then Mandy had died, and Jerry still hadn't heard from Robert, lost as he was in his own pain. Then a text three days before the funeral:

Jerry, I just heard. I've been trying to call you but can't get through. I'll be there on the sixteenth. I have no words to give you that will help in any way, but I am here when you need me.

The day had been such a blur so far that Jerry only realised, when presented with the man, that he hadn't seen Robert so far that day. How could he not have noticed him in the crowd? The transformation was incredible. Robert looked like a movie star again.

"Robert!" gasped Jerry, delight breaking through his own misery. It was so good to see someone doing so well ... even though the sting came with the thought automatically, envying someone that clearly had so little on their mind that they could grin the way Robert's glistening white teeth were.

Don't be an asshole. He looks externally fantastic, but he's covering up the inside very well. Because he does *have something on his mind, doesn't he?*

Jerry knew that Robert did.

Be glad, and hope that you can be doing so well someday too. This is hope, right in front of you. It does *get better. Look at him.*

It was a nice thought, a brave thought, but it didn't make a dent in the future ahead of Jerry as he saw it. A memory of a few nights before flashed before Jerry's eyes; a bottle in one hand, a razor in the other.

Nearly. Nearly. Just get through today. For Mandy.

They hugged, Jerry holding the plate awkwardly behind Robert's back, and when they separated Jerry slapped the taller man on the shoulder.

"You look fantastic, man. Good for you." Robert smiled and nodded, holding his hands up in way that said *I take that compliment humbly, but at the same time, I know. It's good to be back.*

"Well, of course I was going to make the effort today," Robert said, smiling gently. "I was devastated to hear about Mandy, mate. I loved her. Suzie loved her." It was the truth. The four of them had always had such great, boozy times together.

"She loved you guys too," said Jerry, nose wrinkling for the millionth time that day as he dragged back the dam wall that seemed permanently on the edge of breaking. They stood in silence for a moment. "Fucking hell," he added, bitterly. "Aren't *they* supposed to be the ones washing *us* and laying us out for the wake, and all that?" Robert smiled softly, and shook his head.

"I always tried to tell myself that, if nothing else," he said, "that it's good that they *didn't* have to do exactly that. Can you imagine? Knowing that she avoided that always helped me a little bit."

Jerry nodded, trying to think about what Robert was offering but instead struck by a stabbing memory from just a few weeks ago, one of Mandy crying at some soap opera death on TV and looking like a little girl. She'd caught him staring at her and had told him to piss off, laughing through her tears. She'd thrown a sofa cushion at him.

Then they'd gone on holiday. Then Mandy had drowned.

"Yeah," he said, his eyes far away. "She always was the sentimental type. I don't know what this would have done to her."

"I hate funerals," said Robert. "Everyone says that, don't they? But I really do. You know whose I organised, just before I went away?" Jerry was surprised by this. Robert had organized a funeral? There had only been Mandy in his family, no siblings ... perhaps his mother? They didn't speak, as Jerry recalled.

"Whose?"

"Meat's."

"Oh, my God ..."

Mick Meat, the Fine Meats Man. His name actually *was* Mick Meat, a name which had clearly laid out his career path from birth as he'd ended up starting a small chain of butcher's shops. Robert had gotten a job with him straight out of his post-grad course in accounting—a course he took after discovering that a degree in Performing Arts from Coventry University doesn't exactly kick down Spielberg's front door—and Big Mick showed him the ropes. A summer job turned into seven years. The Fine Meats Man had been like a second, sweaty father to him. Robert had then left, amicably, and put his accounting degree into practice, working in the accounts departments of various firms before going freelance a few years back. His first client? Big Mick.

Then the Fine Meats Man had his first stroke. Robert had stepped in and kept the business afloat, free of charge. When Mick got better, they became partners.

"Oh shit. Oh, I'm sorry to hear that Robert," Jerry said. "Why didn't you tell me at the time?" Robert sniffed, and nodded.

"Just wanted to get through it. I was struggling." " And thanks. Tough one to take, that was. Especially so soon after Suzie. Hell of a year, hell of a year," he said, sighing ... but something sounded off to Jerry's ears. He'd heard his own voice being brave enough times. But Robert's didn't sound like that. And Jerry had seen the man with fresh bandages on both wrists just over two months ago.

Don't be a suspicious dick. You're fucked in the head today. Don't take it out on your friends.

"Wait ... does that mean ..."

"Yep. That's the upside."

Robert had been pretty much running the franchise for the last ten years, one that had now had eighteen shops across the region. There was a lot of money in Mick Meat's Fine Meats, and Big Mick had never married, never had any children. He'd always said that he would leave the lot to Robert. And Robert had already been making good money as it was.

"Wow ... well, commiserations and congratulations, I guess," Jerry said, unsure of how to put it.

"Yeah, that's about it. I'm not too bothered about the money side of it— I've been doing well enough—just gutted about Mick, and worried about making sure I don't run his legacy into the ground."

Silence. Robert seemed to be hesitating, like he wanted to say something, and Jerry couldn't handle that. He couldn't handle awkwardness at the best of times, and least of all today.

"How ... how was it?" he asked, weakly.

"Strange," said Robert, almost to himself. "Interesting." He looked up suddenly, realising he'd gone away. "But good. It was good, Jerry."

"Uh ... why good?" asked Jerry, confused. And then he watched as Robert actually did a genuine, old-school movie wiseguy look-right-and-left before leaning closer.

"Look," he said, murmuring and with his eyes darting everywhere as he spoke, never looking at Jerry, "this is the other reason I had for coming here today."

Anger bubbled in Jerry's stomach. Was Robert wanting to talk business at

Mandy's funeral?

You don't know that. Don't overreact.

"Robert ..."

"This is something to help you, ok? *He can help you.*"

What?

Something in Robert's tone made the room go cold. All the other sounds seemed to become very distant and faint, and Robert's earnest stare suddenly seemed very wild indeed.

"Who ... who can help me, Robert?" Jerry muttered. "Help me with what?"

"Not here," Robert said, and looked down, composing himself. "I'm sorry, I didn't want to say anything yet." His normal composure had returned, and the room was normal once more. "I just wanted ... this is gonna be good for you mate, ok? Trust me. Look, I *really* shouldn't have said anything yet. I'll know more in a few months. I just wanted you to know ..." He stopped, and put his hand on Jerry's shoulder. "Just hold on, ok? Don't ... don't do anything silly. I promise you, and this isn't some dumb cliché, this is an actual thing ... help is coming. Okay? You are going to be fine." And Robert looked into Jerry's eyes, and for a crazy moment Jerry felt like Robert *knew* what Jerry had been considering the night before, like his body was made of glass and Robert could see right through him. Then it was just Robert, standing by the buffet and offering what was probably just his way of saying the same old pleasantries. That or, in his time away, Robert had had some kind of religious conversion. At that moment, it didn't matter.

He means well. Just get through the day.

"Sure," said Jerry, reaching up a hand and rubbing his friend's shoulder. Now that the moment had passed, Jerry remembered what Robert had been through. What he was still going through now. "I know. I'll be ok," he lied. To Jerry's surprise, Robert actually smiled indulgently, as if he knew something profound that Jerry didn't.

"I know mate," Robert said, patting Jerry's hand. "Look, I've got to head off now anyway. But I'll see you soon, ok?"

"Of course, of course."

"Great. I'll see you then. You'll be ok?"

"Lots of people here Robert. I'll be fine."

"Ok mate."

And with that, Robert turned and left. For the rest of the day, Jerry forgot about Robert's strange, mysterious statements, distracted both by constant well-wishers and memories of his wife that hammered him like unseen fists. Only when all had left, and his sister was driving his tired body home, did his mind relax enough to think of Robert's strange, insistent stare, and his offer of help. He told himself that they were the words of a man who thought he was coping better than he was, a man who had polished the outside in a misguided attempt to fix the inside.

But the words stayed with him.

He can help you.

***

It wasn't until three months later that Jerry found out what Robert had been talking about.

Jerry had seen Robert, certainly, but every time Jerry brought it up Robert either changed the subject or said that he didn't want to say anything until the right time, and wouldn't be drawn further on it. Meanwhile Jerry trudged through his life as best he could; he had to, he told himself, for the girls. He had to be there for them. But it didn't stop his mind wandering to thoughts of how he would do it, wondering which would be the least painful and the most efficient. He was idly aware that perhaps he should be improving, that the day to day might be impossibly tough but the road ahead should seem a little lighter, but it wasn't. It just seemed longer, and bleaker. Counseling helped for a day or two after each session, but he still lay awake at night all too aware of the huge gaping space on the other side of the bed. During another hysterical phone call to Robert in the middle of the night, Jerry's friend finally said the words:

"Okay. It's time."

"Time?" Jerry croaked, eyes red and squinting at the photo of Mandy in his hand that he could barely see.

"We need to talk about what I mentioned at the funeral," Robert's voice said down the line. It was said with a heavy sigh. "I've been watching your progress Jerry. That's what I've been waiting for. Because there *is* a way that I can get you some help, but it's ... it's pretty drastic. And I didn't want to even give you the option unless you really, really needed it. And you don't seem to be getting any better, so ... well. Please understand that this wasn't something I did lightly, mate. I've not been watching you in pain and just waiting unnecessarily. I had to know that you would be able to cope by yourself. I hoped I wouldn't have to be even telling you about this. And I don't think you *can* cope. This can't go on, three months is enough to know. You'll understand when I tell you. I'll come round tomorrow night. Make sure you have some booze in. We're gonna get you sorted out."

He wouldn't explain any further, but something in his voice made Jerry have the first half decent night's sleep he'd had since Mandy had died.

***

"I noticed him straightaway," Robert said, looking at his hands.

Since he'd started to get around to the heart of the matter, the man hadn't been able to keep still. He'd been wearing a track into the thick carpet in Jerry's living room for the last five minutes already. Jerry stayed silent, and waited for his friend to continue.

He wasn't sure what to expect, and didn't really dare to hope very much that Robert had some genuine help for him. Robert had found some self-help guru that his high-priced shrink had put him onto perhaps, or someone who had taken advantage of Robert's fragile mental state and gotten him hooked on a fresh load of snake-oil horseshit. Jerry tried to tell himself that maybe this would help Robert more than him—and that was a good thing—but dammit, Jerry felt like he should be worrying about himself right now.

And how much good has that been doing you, eh?

He sat on the sofa and listened to Robert talk about what had happened on the day of his own wife's funeral.

"He was hard to miss," Robert continued, squinting, seeing it. "His face was really red, like he'd been in the sun too long. The fact that his hair was thinning as well made his head just look weird. And that big coat. It was roasting in there but he was wearing a big coat." Something occurred to Robert, and he wagged a finger energetically at Jerry. Robert's high energy levels had disappeared when Suzie died, but here in the living room that Jerry's wife had decorated pretty much single-handedly, they were back. "You know who he reminded me of? That lunatic that Suzie was dating. Frank. You remember me telling you about him? The one that turned up at my house that time? I had to drop him on my driveway? The police turned up."

Jerry nodded. He remembered the story.

"Same look in the eyes," said Robert, gesturing to his own with two fingers on one hand. He was dressed very differently today, t-shirt and jeans, his well-trimmed physique looking good in the fitted material. The only sign of his previous breakdown was in the scar on his wrist, the matching one on his other arm covered by a watch. "Just ... on the edge, or already over it. I mean, I *noticed* him, but I had, you know, other things on my mind, obviously. He was standing at the back of the chapel, by himself. I didn't recognize him. At the time, I didn't give a shit if he was just some homeless guy who wanted to stay warm for an hour. But he was hard to miss."

"Who brought him? I mean, which side of the family?"

Robert shook his head.

"No one, Jerry. That was the whole point." He crossed to the sofa and perched on its edge, ready to jump to his feet and regain pacing at any moment. "He wasn't there for the funeral. He'd come to see me."

***

"Mister Terence?" said the voice, speaking so softly that Robert barely heard it all. He did, though; something in it made the hairs on his neck ripple as he nearly jumped out of his skin. There was rasp to it, almost like that of a teenager whose voice was breaking, if that teenager was somehow in his forties.

Robert turned sharply, nearly dropping his cigarette in surprise. He'd thought he was alone, a brief moment of solitude in a seemingly endless day of well-wishers. Not many were left at the wake now—they'd hired the entire pub—only those who had drunk enough to now be reminiscing on any and all matters, and not just those pertaining to Robert's late wife. The tiny smoking area outside the Bull's Head was to the rear of the building, and, with the sun having long dropped below the horizon, Robert had not expected to be disturbed while he pulled on his first cigarette for twelve years.

It was the guy from the chapel. The funny looking one, with the sunburnt face.

"*Jesus*," said Robert, clutching at his chest, theatrically. "Sorry, sorry. Didn't know you were there."

The man smiled slightly, and Robert got a better look at him. If Robert hadn't been so tall himself, he'd have been impressed by the man's height. It was difficult to tell what his build was like due to the big, thick donkey jacket that the man was wearing, but Robert didn't think his new companion was thickset. Something in his stance, the way he shuffled awkwardly on his feet; it gave an impression of *lightness*. Certainly, the painfully gaunt-looking face backed that theory up.

And what a face it was. A low, slightly-jutting brow that made the already deep-set eyes look even more shadowy. The red tint to his skin that made him look like the classic British Abroad after his first day in Spain. And the thin tufts of hair that, along with his pinched facial structure, gave the overall impression of a newborn rat, pink and blinking at its first sight of the sun.

"I saw you in the chapel," Robert said without thinking, distracted for a moment by the man's appearance. There was a pause, and Robert realized that he'd said something slightly blunt and unusual. "I mean—"

"I'm sure you did, Mister Terence," said the stranger, kindly, and there was that soft, rasping voice again, like rough fingers gliding over silk. "I stand out, I know. I tend to be noticed, although I'd really rather not be." There was that sad smile again, and the craziest thought flashed across Robert's brain:

He is full of sorrow. Like no-one you have ever met in your entire life, or ever will.

"Sorry mate, I didn't mean to—"

"No, really, Please, Mister Terence. I'm the last of your concerns today. Don't worry about it."

There was another pause, and Robert remembered social convention and patted at his jacket's pocket.

"Ciggie?" he said, fishing out the packet.

"How do you feel, Mister Terence?"

Robert stopped. Of all the enquiries or words of support he'd heard that day, this was a new one. It was a question with such an obvious answer—*I feel like shit, I just buried the woman I married only two years ago*—that it seemed an almost ridiculous question to ask.

"Robert," was all he could think of to say.

"I'm sorry?"

"Robert. Mister Terrence is my father, and all that," he said, forcing a smile, and he realized that it wasn't just avoiding a weird question. He was avoiding even *considering* the true meaning of the question, the same way he'd been avoiding feeling anything all day long. He was only barely standing as it was.

"Robert. Sorry," the man said, nodding. But he didn't take his eyes *off* Robert.

"I didn't get your name?" Robert said, holding out his hand. The man took it, and Robert cringed slightly as he felt the man's bony fingers between his own. Thin, and brittle. The man wasn't thin. He was emaciated. The coat was his armor.

"I'm afraid I'm not a family friend, Robert," the man said shrugging a little, and staring intently at Robert with those sad, sad eyes. "I didn't know your wife personally, and obviously you and I don't know each other either. You'll have to forgive me, but it was you I wanted to see. I thought that I would wait until I could talk to you briefly, alone."

Robert was confused—his brain wasn't working at anywhere near its full capacity that day, but it could be forgiven in the circumstances—but he bristled nevertheless. This was suddenly weird. He realized that he hadn't seen this man since the ceremony. Had he been in the pub? Hanging back? Waiting? This suddenly sounded suspiciously like a prelude to a business proposition. Or police? Was he police?

"... right," said Robert, finally, but he and the stranger still remained holding hands. "Well ... you'll have to forgive *me*, but I'm not exactly capable right now of having big conversations about anything other than ... well. You know," said Robert, as politely as he could. His hackles continued to rise, though.

Is he some kind of funeral pervert? Who is he?

"So," said Robert, holding up his free hand and looking away from the stranger as that was just somehow easier, "you know, obviously if you could just tell me very quickly what you wanted to talk to me about, and if it's something I actually *want* to talk about, we'll discuss it another time."

You don't know what he wants. He could mean well.

Robert's natural instincts kicked in; he wasn't a rude man. He was just confused, and very tired, and hurting very, very badly.

"Look, I'm sorry ..." he sighed, "this is just a very bad time. Whatever it is ... look, another time, yeah?"

Who is he? What's going on?

The man continued to hold Robert's hand. His faintly-red skin seemed darker where he now stood, having moved out of the direct glow of the security light. It looked deeper, redder.

"My name is Mister Grief, Robert. Well, being totally honest with you, it *isn't* Mister Grief, but that's all you get to know me as, I'm afraid."

Robert nearly exploded at the name. *Mister Grief.* The same way *Mister Whoosh* spritzed out your bin to make it smell fresh, or *Mister Clutch* fixed your car, or *Mister Sheen* put the shine back on your coffee table.

A fucking ambulance chaser. On the day of the funeral.

"*Ohhh ...* " said Robert, his head rolling back on his neck. "Oh ... oh, no. Oh, just fuck off. Just. Fuck. Off." His head came forward again, and he looked Mister Grief dead in the eye. The red-faced man's expression didn't change even a fraction. Normally, Robert would have been screaming by now, but today he was just so damn *tired.* And sad. Here was another part of the world, the horrible, money-grubbing world from which Suzie had been a refuge. That refuge was now gone, and she hadn't been in the ground as much as twenty-four hours before that world was pouring in like toxic sludge. It made him feel so empty that he felt a weight settle into him, turning rage into sad anger. "There's no *blame*, so there's no *claim*, and frankly how dare you come and talk to me about this *today.* Just fuck off, mate. Yeah, it's a job, I get it, you have to make a living, but I don't know how you sleep. Just fuck off pal. Alright?"

Crazily, Robert realized that the man was still holding his hand. He went to pull it free, but without his expression changing one iota, Mister Grief's hand suddenly clamped tightly on Robert's like a steel vice. Grief's other hand came up and over and clamped down on the top of Robert's, the fingers arched and the fingertips pressing like solid rods into the bones of Robert's wrist.

"What the fu—" Robert began to shout, but just as he realized that as tight as Grief's grip was, there was no pain from it, he also realized that his anger had completely disappeared. Robert's entire body relaxed, and the sensation was so surprising that all he could do was stand there with his mouth open.

Once this happened, the man calling himself Mister Grief nodded calmly, and quickly released Robert's hands like they'd burnt him. Robert could only watch as the man lowered his head and wrapped his arms around himself, and then turned his back to Robert, hunching over. He began to let out little gasping sounds, and moved from foot to foot, like someone with a pressing need to piss.

Robert gaped.

After a few moments, Mister Grief straightened, and turned around. His red face looked flushed, making his lightly sunburnt complexion look almost crimson. He breathed slowly but deeply, and that weak smile came back to his face.

"What ... " Robert said, his voice sounding slow and stupid. " ...what was that? What did you do?"

He didn't do anything. You're emotional. This is the hardest day of your life. At best, it was a parlour trick, hypnosis or some shit.

He listened as the protective voice of reason spoke firmly in his mind, and Robert believed it. *Almost.*

You're stood in the smoking area with a lunatic. What are you doing?

"Robert, I'll be blunt," said Mister Grief, sounding tired himself. "I've come here to offer you my help. You will not be the first person I've helped, but if you're not the last you'll be the second to last."

"Help ... me?"

"I'm not going to lie to you," said Grief, straightening some more and arching his back as he regained his composure, "I'm not here for the good of my health, or frankly, yours. I've come because you're a wealthy man, and you can afford to pay me the fee I will charge. Most men couldn't."

"What ... what's going on?" said Robert, feeling his legs start to loosen as it all became too much, the day, Suzie, this guy, everything.

"I can't help you now, Robert," said Mister Grief, almost sighing as he pushed up his coat sleeve to reveal a painfully skinny wrist adorned with a far-too-chunky watch, "I'm not ready. Each job takes several months to prepare, but I'm almost done. I wouldn't be here at all yet if I didn't know that you needed some ... encouragement."

"What?" Robert repeated, giving up on trying to find another word.

"If I rolled up *your* sleeve, Robert, the way I'd just rolled up my own, what would I see?"

Robert felt immediately sick. No-one new about that. No-one knew that he'd *done* that. No-one except the ambulance crew and the doctors, and his mother, who they'd informed as his next of kin. But she would never tell a soul. The old bitch wouldn't want the embarrassment.

"Nothing," Robert lied, on impulse. "Nothing." Grief shrugged in response.

"That might be true," he said. "I don't know. I'm not psychic, or at least in a sense that I can read your thoughts. But you put on a very good act, Robert. Very good. No one knows, do they? They know you're grieving. But they don't know how far it goes. I do. I've been outside your house many nights. Checking. Feeling for it. It comes out of you like screams from a megaphone. And I know what happens to people most of the time if it reaches that point, that peak. I know what they do. So I'm only making an educated guess."

Robert realized that he'd been massaging the fresh scar on his wrist, unconsciously, through the sleeve of his suit jacket. It still ached. He didn't reply. It was his dirty secret. Even in his grief, he was Big Robert. He was *bearing up.* Big Mick had always set him right, like the day he'd found Robert in the meat locker crying into his apron because Alison Courtney had dumped him. *Never let 'em see,* Mick had said, patting Robert's shoulder awkwardly with fingers that looked like the sausages he sold. *You're right to do your crying in here. If you ever show 'em, they'll use it. Never let 'em use it.*

21

"So I thought I should come here today," Grief said, fishing inside his own coat pockets now, "even though I wouldn't normally. I don't like to offer my services until they're ready. But I know that today had every possibility to push you to that peak again, and well ..." He produced a small silver business card case. It was scratched and dull. He opened it, and took out a card. There was only one left in the case now. He saw Robert looking, and gestured to the case and the card. "A good few years old now. I only ever bought one set of blank cards for it," he said. "And I only ever put ten in it. It may be that I never use the tenth. I think there's a good chance you will be the last, but we'll see." He handed Robert a card. Robert took it, expecting it to say something like *Mr Grief, We'll Sort You Out* but the only thing written on the card was a phone number. Written by hand, not printed.

"That number is connected to a pay as you go phone," he said. "I buy one each time I'm about to contact a client, and write the corresponding number on the card. I'm telling you this so you know that you won't find my location or name by that number, I can assure you. If you decide that you wish to use my services, call me. But not for at least another month."

"What services?" Robert asked, blinking like a simpleton.

"I'll take it away, Robert. I'll take all the pain away, permanently." The sad eyes burned into Roberts, and Grief's face was blank. And Robert knew that this man wasn't crazy. Grief could do what he said he could. "Just like that. There are some very minor consequences involved for you that I will explain, but I do have to tell you that the price is high."

"My ... soul?" Robert whispered, unable to help himself. They were the first words that came to mind. There was magic here. He was rapt and lost in Grief's words and stare. This could end? This pain could end? *Just like that?*

"Uh ... no, sorry," said Grief, looking embarrassed. "I should have been more clear. Three hundred thousand pounds, I mean. Quite a high price."

"Oh, right, yes," said Robert, nodding too quickly and turning as red as Grief himself. "Yes, that is a lot."

"Yes, it is rather. But you'll see why," Grief said, kindly, moving on from Robert's faux pas. "If you decide to go ahead. But I'm quite sure that you will. When it becomes too much. When that peak comes again."

Robert remembered that night. When it was done, and he was panicking, calling an ambulance and trying to stem the bleeding. How he hated himself for doing the same as that lunatic Frank had done when *he* lost Suzie, albeit to Robert. *When she goes, she sure leaves carnage behind her,* he thought, and his heart ached even harder.

"Now I know what will happen next anyway," said Grief, looking at his watch again, "because it always does. I've shown you a little of what I can do, and right now you're confused but you believe I can do *something.* As soon as you wake up in the morning, you'll believe it less. You'll think that I'm someone trying to take advantage of you, or whatever. I get that, I really do. There's nothing I can do about that. But do yourself a favour, *don't throw that number away,* because you'll wish you hadn't." He winced slightly, held up a finger. "Sorry, that sounds like a threat. I didn't mean it like that, my apologies. I mean you will wish you hadn't because you'll wish you could call me."

Robert looked at the card, still held in his hand, and then Grief surprised him by putting his hand on Robert's shoulder.

"I know I said I wouldn't be here if it wasn't for the money," said Grief, that quiet raspy voice more quiet than ever, "and that's true. But I *am* sorry for your loss. No-one—*no-one on this planet*—understands how you feel better than I do. If you don't take me up on my offer, I understand and I wish you the very best. But you *should* let me help you, Robert." He took his hand away, and stepped back, awkwardly, perhaps regretting being so forward. "I'll leave now anyway, and I am sorry for bothering you today, I really am. I did it for your sake though, as I say. *Remember* that I said it can end, the next time that you think that there's only one way out."

Mister Grief finished speaking, nodded, and headed away across the nearly empty car park, the back of his pink neck standing out in stark contrast against the black collar of his donkey jacket. Robert stood dumbstruck, watching him go until the red and black were lost to the shadows.

He looked at the card in his hand for a few minutes.

Eventually, he put it inside his wallet. Then he went back inside the pub to get drunk and talk about anything but his wife.

***

The next morning, Grief was right. The conversation of the night before, through the film of a hangover, seemed nonsensical.

But he didn't throw the card away. Instead, he placed it in his bedside drawer.

He couldn't eat breakfast. His sister came round later to do his laundry, and he let her. The distraction was welcome, and the minutes that she was there were more bearable. Then Jerry came round, slightly nervous and awkward around the grieving man, so much so that Robert actually snapped at him and told him to be 'fucking normal'. He felt bad about it, and apologized, and then suddenly broke down in floods of tears that led to him wailing on his knees in Jerry's arms. He could hear Mick in his brain saying *never let 'em see* but he couldn't help it. He just wanted his wife back so much that he wanted to die.

Then there was the next day.

And the next.

And everything the counselors and youtube videos told him never seemed to work; that it was a cliché but he shouldn't think of the future, that he should think of today and only today and that while the pain becomes less and less and never fully goes away, it *does* get better and you can learn to live with it.

He couldn't help but think of the future, and it seemed endless. The pain became manageable? How could it?

Grief's card sat in the drawer, untouched. Robert had convinced himself that it *was* a parlour trick; even through his own grief, business instincts kicked in. He'd never been a sucker. He'd been a success *because* he wasn't a sucker. Big Mick had taught how *not* to be one. And he knew a good scam when he saw it. Three hundred grand? Are you fucking *kidding?* He had it, sure, or the assets to get it, but he wasn't going to be played. Leave that to the doddering widows who could be talked into anything. The thought of what Mister Grief had done made him angry, furious, sometimes.

But he still left the card in the drawer, because even though he didn't admit it, he knew that he could only take so much. And he was taking a lot.

He drank every evening. He stayed awake until dawn most nights. The days became harder, not easier. And in one drunken night, he found himself taking Grief's card out of its resting place.

Something has to give. You're desperate.

And then he realized what grief—grief, not Grief—had made him into, a *sucker* after all. What would Big Mick say?

"Fuck that. Fuck. That," said Robert, his words slurring into *fug tha'* through the fog of whisky, and he screwed up the note and threw it out of the window. Then he passed out onto the bed.

Three days later—after two months of hell—Robert got the call to say that Big Mick had had a second stroke and died. But Robert didn't have Mister Grief's card anymore.

***

"It was my breaking point," said Robert, and then reconsidered, looking at the wrist that was covered by the extra-wide strap of a wristwatch. "Well ... my *next* breaking point, anyway." He was on his feet again now, leaning on the mantelpiece with his left elbow and holding an untouched orange juice in his right hand.

He'd had Jerry's full attention ever since he'd started talking, but there was something else, too. Jerry was at that peak himself. He wasn't as loud and confident a man as Robert, and so his pain was a lot easier for him to conceal. But Robert was now telling Jerry a story about a man that had claimed he could somehow help. Robert had Jerry's full and undivided attention.

"It was like losing my father again," Robert sighed, "and the timing simply could not have been worse. The world just seemed ..." He sighed once more, looked at the glass in his hand, rattled the ice. "I was done. I was checking out. But I realized two horrible things in the same moment."

"What things?" asked Jerry. He hadn't moved since Robert had started talking.

"One was that I couldn't do actually do it again. I'd discovered the reality of it the first time, the actual *knowing* that I would die. That changed everything. Sure, I *thought* I could do it again, that I could go further and make sure I finished the job. I thought all along that I could give it another go, but when I finally decided to do it again ... I just couldn't."

"And the second thing?"

"The second was that I'd thrown the card away, Jerry. I'd thrown it out of the window. A desperate man needs a fallback option, and mine was lost somewhere among the begonias." He sipped at his juice. "You got anything stronger, actually?"

"Sure, sure," said Jerry, standing hurriedly and moving to the liquor cabinet at the other side of the room.

"Thanks," said Robert, continuing. "And I mean literally lost among the begonias. I was on my knees crying with a bottle of whisky in my hand as I rooted through the flowerbeds. The neighbours saw me doing it. I covered that entire garden from top to bottom on my hands and fucking knees. I woke up out there in the morning."

"Jesus, Robert," said Jerry, taking the juice with one hand and passing Robert a bourbon with the other.

"But when I got back inside the house, the phone was ringing," Robert said, earnestly. He was smiling. "It was him. He'd called *me*."

*   *   *

"Robert?"

The pounding headache made it hard to place, but Robert knew that voice. Nobody sounded like that, did they? Was this a wind-up? He couldn't remember ...

"Yeah," he said, tersely. What time was it?

"Robert, do you know who this is?"

No, I don't know who the fuck this is. What do you—

Something clicked, and suddenly Robert knew exactly who it was.

"Mister Grief ..."

"Hello Robert," said the voice. Grief sounded slightly anxious. "I 'd given up on you, to be honest. I thought that perhaps you hadn't listened to my advice, or that you may have lost my card. I don't normally make a habit of chasing up clients, but I heard about your mentor's death. You may be unsurprised to hear that I read a lot of obituaries, especially when I'm in one area for a while."

"No, no, I didn't, well I mean I did," babbled Robert, caught in the unique panic that comes with relief that isn't quite sealed yet. "I got drunk and threw your card out, I'm sorry, sorry, but listen, I'm really glad you called." He could hear the desperation in his own voice. "*God*, I'm so glad ... listen ..." He winced as his head throbbed. Where was his watch? He couldn't see a clock. "What time is it?"

"Eight am," Grief said, quickly, as if he were in a hurry. "Robert, I'll be blunt. I called you because, while all of my clients' stories are painful, yours is more unique given that you have suffered two major losses in such a short time. Of the people that can afford me—that I know about—I think you need me the most right now. I don't say this out of kindness. I was going to visit someone today and offer my services to them, and soon, but with you I think the sales pitch is done. You're ready today, is my meaning. Am I right?"

"Yes," said Robert, slumping into the armchair. "Yes, I really ... look, today. *Now.* As soon as you can. I can't ..."

I can't take this anymore.

"I know, Robert," said Grief, his tone relaxing. "I really do. Alright then. Payment will be made after the job is done. Forgive me for saying this but, given the more clandestine nature of my work, I have to be blunt; non-payment will have dire consequences for you. You understand that I am different to most men, yes?"

"Yes," said Robert, the word almost a whisper. Something about the way Grief had said it—*I am different to most men*—carried weight that Robert couldn't quite describe. And despite the crushing ache in his heart, Robert suddenly wanted to know who Mister Grief was very much.

"I understand," Robert said.

"I know people, Robert. People like me, but unique in other ways. You do not want them to visit you. I am the least of them, the runt of the litter. To put it in context."

Robert's blood chilled.

"I understand. I do."

"Good. Forgive the implication, I hope you understand that I have to make these things clear."

"Yes, yes."

"Alright then," said Grief, his tone brightening slightly. "You're dressed?"

Robert looked down at the clothes he'd been wearing the night before, sprayed with soil and whisky stains.

"Yes, but I don't exactly—"

"You're a five minute drive away from the Formula One hotel, by my reckoning," Grief interrupted, calmly. "You have ten minutes to get here. Any longer than that, and I'll be gone. Tell no one what you're doing. Do you understand?"

"Yes," said Robert, quickly, already looking for his keys but still managing to think *the Formula One? He's staying in that shithole?* The answer came to him quickly, though; Grief *wasn't* staying in that shithole. He'd just gotten himself the cheapest room he could find to do business in, in case Robert didn't take him up on his offer.

He's gonna make three hundred grand on this! He can't afford a decent room, even if I no-show?

But then Robert wondered just how often Grief did this work ... and how frugal he was. What had he said? *You will be my last, or second to last ...* he was planning to retire, perhaps? The guy didn't look that old. He was planning on making that money last if he was.

"I'm leaving right now," he said, spotting his keys on the floor in front of the fireplace, for some reason. "What's the room number?"

"Call me once you arrive," said Grief. "Then I'll tell you the room number. Get a pen and take the number of this mobile. I threw the last one away after I didn't hear from you. "

Robert scrabbled for a pen, hardly daring to believe the lifeline that he'd just been thrown.

***

Grief opened the door to room 237, and Robert was amazed to find that Grief was still wearing his big jacket. As Grief stood to one side without a word and Robert entered the shabby room, the heat swallowed him. It was warm outside, but Grief had still cranked the room's temperature up. The combination made the room like a furnace.

"I have some water," Grief said, as if reading Robert's mind. He crossed to the small counter top in the corner, upon which sat a small bucket of ice containing several bottles of mineral water. Mister Grief pulled one out and crossed back to Robert once more, who took it gratefully. "Here you are. If you would like some more, please help yourself. I understand that the temperatures at which I live aren't comfortable for most people."

Robert said nothing, feeling his heart racing nervously, but he took the water gratefully and unscrewed the cap. His mouth had been dry even before he entered that sweatbox of a room, and he'd been sweating himself as he'd driven like a lunatic across town. He was unsurprised by the standard of the décor; though he'd never stayed in a Formula One, he'd heard the stories. Carpet so thin it may as well be a sheet of linoleum. The aforementioned counter top with a cheap plastic seat beneath it, which Grief was already pulling out for himself, gesturing for Robert to sit on the bed. A plastic dome on the ceiling for a light, dirty looking on the inside. Grey walls that formed a small second room in one corner, accessed by a single door; the bathroom. And an industrial blind for a curtain. It really *was* a shithole.

"Please, take a seat," said Grief, and indeed Robert was already sinking onto the bed, glugging heavily on the bottle of water. "Take a moment to relax. I know you, Robert, and I know I have nothing to fear from you personally in terms of my ... well, my privacy. And I do very much like to get this all done as quickly as possible—especially when I've had to arrange this over the phone— but it's better to give you some time to relax before we begin, as it makes it all easier and saves time in the long run."

"Why?" Robert asked, gasping slightly because he'd been drinking so deeply, getting oxygen back into his lungs. "Why all the cloak and dagger stuff? What are you worried about?" Grief shrugged in response, the shoulders of the huge coat hulking around his skinny neck.

"Maybe nothing," he said. "I was always small potatoes, after all, so I don't worry *that* much. I've not even had any real suggestion that I *should* worry. But wherever I can be careful, I am. Just to be on the safe side. It doesn't affect my life that much. I am nomadic by nature, after all. Give me your wrist."

Robert did so without question, and Mister Grief grasped it gently between his bony fingers. He squeezed for a few moments.

"Your heart rate is up," he said, letting go, "and your pulse is very strong. You'll need a few minutes anyway. Try and slow your breathing, in through the nose and out through the mouth and all that. Yes?"

"But what do you *think* might happen?" Robert insisted. "You didn't give me an answer. You've got to give me *something*."

"I don't *have* to give you anything," Grief said, calmly. "You've come here to avail yourself of my services." He sighed, gently. "But we have some time to kill while you relax a little, I suppose. And there's nothing I can tell you that they wouldn't already know."

He shrugged again, and pushed backwards with his skinny legs, leaning his chair at an angle. He stared at the ceiling and laced his hands over his stomach.

"My life changed the day my brother was sent home from school."

***

There's an old joke about a boy who never spoke.

His parents take him to every doctor under the sun (in the manner of all good jokes) who all say the same thing; there's nothing wrong with him at all. He's just choosing not to speak. By the time he's five, they're used to the fact that he's a mute. He seems happy, and his friends—as children do—have long accepted that this is just the way he is ... so why worry? He'll come around.

"He's fine," his parents say. "It's just a phase. A long, long phase."

By the time he's ten, he still hasn't said a single word, other than to cry out in pain, but the parents don't mind. He's doing well in school and is healthy, and his parents, like the boy's friends before them, have long accepted that this is just the way he is.

One day, eating soup during a family dinner, the boy suddenly puts his spoon down and speaks.

"Not enough salt."

The parents, once they have picked themselves up off the floor, rush to the boy's side.

"Son!" they cry. "Son! You finally spoke! Why now?"

"Well," says the boy, shrugging, "up until *now* everything's been alright."

Mister Grief heard this joke when he was ten years old and thought it was the funniest thing he'd ever heard. He'd laughed until he thought he was going to die unless he could start breathing properly, but he'd *still* laughed, rolling around on his back on the concrete floor of the playground. None of his friends had laughed anywhere near as much—Mark Paley, the joke teller, had looked by turns a bit put out when the joke bombed, relieved when Grief began his hysterics, and finally, like everyone else there, a bit concerned at how long and how hard Mister Grief had been laughing.

That was because none of them really knew about Mister Grief's older brother. None of them really knew about John. That was because John went to a different school than them. It wasn't a school for *crazies*, Mister Grief knew, not like Steve Pinter's brother Will who wasn't allowed to be near people by himself.

No, John went to a school for posh kids. Mister Grief's parents had talked long and hard about it—and argued about it, Mister Grief knew—as it really would be stretching their already meager budget. But Mister Grief's dad took on extra hours, working away from home one week of the month in America because the company paid immense overtime if he did so. Mister Grief's mum went back to work part-time herself, and they just about managed it. Because they believed, whole heartedly, that John needed it, needed a school with not only smaller classes so John could get extra help—not that John was stupid by *any* means—but so John could get the extra attention at school every day to help him *develop.* Not that John was under-developed either, in fact in most ways John was ahead of the pack.

But John hadn't spoken since the day he was born, and none of the therapy or threats or hypnosis or bad soup had changed that.

Like the boy in the joke though, John was happy. He didn't have many friends—not talking limits a great many social opportunities—but the ones he did have, he was close with, and he seemed to prefer time by himself anyway. He didn't play team sports out of school. He didn't attend any youth groups. He was happiest reading, or climbing. He was obedient. He was loved.

One may think that Mister Grief would have been jealous of his brother's seemingly preferential treatment, of the money being spent on his brother and not him because he decided to actually open his mouth and speak, but young Mister Grief didn't care at all. He didn't want to go to the posh school with the posh kids and their stupid posh uniforms. He had a *lot* of friends, despite his strange, permanently-lightly-sunburn skin—or perhaps because of it, learning social excellence as a defence against any mean spirited behavior—and was quite happy where he was. And not only was it hard to argue with a brother that never argued back, but John was so laid back that he was almost, as they saying went, horizontal. If Mister Grief wanted the top bunk, John didn't care. He'd go on the bottom. If Grief wanted the family movie to be *Who Framed Roger Rabbit?* John was happy to go along with the choice. Mister Grief loved his brother.

Then one day John was sent home from school.

Mister Grief never found out exactly what had happened, even in the following decades. He could hazard a rough guess, knowing what he knew about his brother, but he could never say for certain. What he *did* know for certain was this:

Mister Grief had been at home with mild conjunctivitis at the time, much to his delight; he barely felt a thing, but the school had been so terrified of an outbreak that they'd effectively given him a holiday with not only their blessing, but his parents' as well. So he'd been in front of the TV watching *Marshall Bravestarr* when John and his mother exploded through the door, both wearing a wide-eyed expression; his mother's had been confused and concerned. John flickered between rage and shell-shocked, like he didn't quite know where he was but wasn't too happy about it . Mister Grief sat up in surprise, both at the level of energy that they'd entered with and the fact that John was back already—it wasn't long after two o'clock—as well as his mother, who usually didn't leave the office until three to pick John up. Either John had conjunctivitis as well, or his mother had been called in to pick John up for another reason.

It had to be the former. The latter was just unthinkable. John? In trouble for misbehaving at school? Even though John had turned thirteen now, officially a teenager, he'd still been the same hassle-free kid he'd always been (Mister Grief overheard enough of his parents' conversations to know what was expected behavior-wise once the 'terrible teens' began) so it *couldn't* be that.

"Mum?" Young Mister Grief said, not knowing what else to say. His mother looked at him sharply while kicking off her shoes, her face saying *oh yeah, there's you too, now what*. She stared at him for a few seconds before holding up her hands and closing her eyes.

"Not now," she said, as kindly as she could. Then Mister Grief saw John staring at him, squinting. The anger and shell-shock were gone for a second, replaced by a face deep in hard-working thought. John raised a finger, pointed it at Mister Grief. It hung in the air, and John nodded.

"I *know* you," he said.

Mister Grief nearly leapt off the sofa in amazement. John had *spoken*.

"*John,*" his mother snapped, and grabbed John's arm, turning him forcefully to face her. "Leave your brother alone, alright? You go upstairs, and go to your room." Her eyes closed again, correcting herself. "You haven't done anything wrong. *You haven't done anything wrong.* Just go upstairs and ... and wait there. Okay?" John stayed where he was for a second, swaying slightly, and then the shell-shocked face was back. Then he nodded, and went upstairs.

His mother watched him go, and once the sound of John's bedroom door closing had been heard, she ran her hands through her hair and held them there, screwing her eyes up. Mister Grief wanted to ask her again, but he didn't dare. He had to say *something.*

"John's talking," he said, quietly. His Mum opened her eyes, looked at Mister Grief, looked upstairs, looked back at Grief once more. It was as if she didn't realize what he meant. Then it clicked.

"Oh," she said. "Yes, yes he is. Yes, he started talking today. It's … " her sentence hung in the air, her attention gone again. Mister Grief couldn't believe it. That wasn't what this was all about? John was *talking* and there was something else more important than that? Something bigger?

"Why?"

"He just … decided to, by the looks of it," she said, rubbing at her eyes. "Something happened at … are you ok? Do you need anything?"

"No, I'm fine thank you."

"Ok. I have to make a phone call. Just … stay there and watch your programme."

Marshall Bravestarr held little interest after what had just happened, though. Mister Grief pretended to watch, but what he was really trying to do was overhear his mother's phone conversation. All he could get was that, from the snatches of words that he managed to hear and the tone his mother was using, was that she was talking to his dad. Then she hung up and called someone else.

After that, she'd made dinner and brought some to Mister Grief without a word. Then she'd taken a tray up to John's room. It was nearly five pm when the doorbell rang and Doctor Sen was on the doorstep.

Doctor Sen waved at Mister Grief as he came in, and asked briefly about the conjunctivitis—Mister Grief had seen him only the day before—before his Mother had hustled the good doctor into the kitchen. Again the conversation had been lost to Mister Grief's keen pink young ears, but shortly afterwards,

Mister Grief turned to see Doctor Sen and his mother ascending the stairs towards John's room. The door opened, closed, and then all was silent for a while.

Then Mister Grief heard Doctor Sen cry out in surprise.

Shortly after that, his mother started screaming.

Mister Grief jumped off the sofa, and began to run for the stairs himself, when suddenly John's bedroom door burst open and Doctor Sen staggered out. His usually dark brown skin had lightened to a sickly pallor, and his wide eyes mirrored the expression Mister Grief had seen on John's face when he came home. Sen stopped when he saw the young boy on the stairs.

"What ..." he said, and looked back up the stairs behind him as Mister Grief's mother came dashing out of the bedroom as well.

"Please, wait," she pleaded, grabbing at the doctor's arm, "we don't know—"

But Sen was already on the move again, looking about himself rapidly as he went, as if trying to shoo away some maddening bird with his face. He barged past Mister Grief so quickly that he actually knocked the boy aside, and flew into the open living room like a man who had gone temporarily insane. He looked wildly around himself, unable to find the exit, and then plunged towards the door once he saw it.

Grief could only stand and watch as his mother pursued him, getting to the door too late as the sound of Sen's car door slamming shut echoed into the house, shortly followed by the impressive roar of a Mercedes being driven away at speed. His mother stood by the open door for a good ten minutes after that, hand clasped over her mouth, looking like she would fall down if the wind picked up. Eventually, she closed it, and made her way back towards the stairs on brittle legs.

"Go and lie down, son," she said to Mister Grief, as if in a trance. She didn't look at him. "You're not well."

Grief, his small chest rising and falling like there was a piston inside it, did so, not taking his eyes off his mother as she went back up the stairs. To John's room.

The door closed behind her, and the conversation was muffled once more. *If only I had super hearing!* Mister Grief thought with the frustrated logic of youth. Was this some kind of dream? His young brain wasn't capable of even beginning to deal with such madness. *John was talking, having an actual* conversation *with his mum!* Hearing John talk had been like hearing Jesus speak; he'd always imagined it, but had never thought he'd actually *hear* it. He strained his ears, but couldn't get more than the odd sound, until his mother raised her voice. He still couldn't get all of it, but he got enough to make *some* sense:

"What ... doing? Why .... people ? How ... fix it!"

The response wasn't clear, but it was calm yet surprised. Whatever John had done, he hadn't meant to.

His mother screamed the next part in anger, and so her words were perfectly clear.

"Then wipe that stupid smirk off your face!"

"... help it!"

"What have you done, *John?"*

The door burst open once more, and Mister Grief threw himself flat on the sofa, covered by his blanket, as if he'd been watching his *Explorers* video all along. His mother's steps thundered down the stairs, and she was suddenly squatting down to talk to him.

"Don't go up there," she said, her eyes as wild as Doctor Sen's. "Your brother's not well, and it's not safe. You ... " she brushed her medium length hair out of her eyes, a woman in her early forties who didn't look as if she were out of her early thirties. Soon that would change. "I mean, you might catch something. Okay? Don't go in there. And whatever you do, don't ... don't touch your brother. Don't touch him, alright?"

"Alright," said Mister Grief, his voice small and scared. She heard it. She took a deep breath, tried to steel herself.

"It's alright son," she said, and in that moment Mister Grief had one of the epiphanies that all children eventually experience. He realized that even people you loved would lie to you. "He's going to be fine, we're going to fix this."

"What's happened?" he asked, scared to know the answer now.

"I'm not sure," she said. "But your dad's on his way, and I think ..." She dropped her head, breathing heavily again, and Mister Grief couldn't tell if her next words were for him or just her thoughts escaping through her mouth. "Sen will be talking to other people too, already. No way he's not doing that. We're going to have visitors."

"Mum ... what?"

She looked up, her eyes red and teary, still speaking to herself, gone.

"Probably a good thing. Probably a good thing. I don't know what the hell's going on." She bit her lip, and stood up as the phone began to ring. It was Dad again. She took the phone into the cursed other room, and Mister Grief listened to the sobbing coming from upstairs. After a while he realized that it wasn't sobbing. It was muffled laughter.

That night, Mister Grief was sent to bed slightly later than usual. When he asked again what had happened, his Mum had paused by the doorway on her way out of his room, one hand on the light switch, the other holding a small scotch. His mother never really drank.

"Wait until your Dad comes home," she said. "Let me talk to him first, okay? He's flying tonight on the first flight he can get. He'll be back in the morning."

Grief's heart sank even further. There was no way that this was nothing. If Dad was coming all the way back from America *early,* then this wasn't just Sen having a freak out, or a fight at school. This was something life changing.

The next morning, when Dad came home, Mister Grief was having breakfast. He still hadn't seen John, or been allowed to go and see him. His Dad hugged them both, and after a quick chat with Mister Grief about nothing during which his father's smile had been plastered onto his chubby face, his Dad took his Mum for a talk in the other room (Grief fantasizing about walkie talkies, security cameras, hidden microphones glued to the fake orchids in the plant pots.)

"What's happened?" Grief asked quickly, as the pair disappeared into the other room.

"Let me talk to your mother first," his Dad had replied, kindly. Mister Grief thought he was going to burst. When they came out again:

"What's *happened*?" Mister Grief repeated.

"Let me talk to John first, then we'll have a chat" his Dad said maddeningly, his face stern and serious now, making his way towards the stairs with Mum following behind.

"Can I come too?" Grief asked.

"Wait there, and I'll play Carl Lewis with you when I come down," his Dad said over his shoulder. "Get it loaded up, eh?"

Mister Grief did as he was told, and his parents disappeared from sight into John's room.

They didn't come out for two hours. Grief tried to play *Carl Lewis' Olympic Challenge* in single player mode, but it wasn't the same.

That's when the doorbell went.

There was a pause, and then John's bedroom door opened. Mister Grief walked to the bottom of the stairs, looking up at his Dad framed in John's doorway.

"Should I get it?" he asked. His Dad put a finger to his lips in response, and tiptoed down the hallway to look out of the upstairs window, which gave a perfect view of the front step. He stared out of it for a moment or two, then turned to Mister Grief's mother who had moved to join him. Grief watched as his father shrugged sadly, and spread his arms as if to say *do you have any better ideas?* His mother shook her head.

"Something's happened," his father said to her, his voice low but tender.

"I haven't got a clue what to do about it, you don't have a clue, John doesn't have a clue by the sounds of it ... we can't ignore it. *John* is gonna need help. Whatever they are, it's got to lead to *help* eventually. This was never going to go away." They saw him looking, and talked more quietly, quickly, as the doorbell rang again.

They came downstairs together to answer it, and five people came in. Two policemen, and three people— Two men and a woman—in plain clothes ... apart from their hats. Their attire was nothing you wouldn't see in any office in any city, and their ages were as middling as their dress.

But their hats matched, all three of them wearing matching black baseball caps. There was no marking or writing on them, but Grief, who was used to baseball caps on TV and on the cool kids—it was the early eighties, after all— knew that these were somehow different. Their brims were too short for starters, but the main body of the hats themselves just seemed too *thick.* Padded, almost. The policemen stood back while the three shook hands with his parents. Their pleasantries were firm, but kind, the police explaining that these people were from social services, that there was no trouble, just that obviously they needed to discuss a few things. Grief's parents were nodding, unsure whether there really *wouldn't* be any trouble, but put at ease by their tone.

Grief for his part, couldn't take his eyes off the baseball caps. He'd never *seen* anyone from social services before, but he wouldn't have expected any kind of uniform, or at least not one that consisted solely of a hat. He wondered why his parents hadn't mentioned it, but he assumed that it was either that they knew that the caps *were* normal, or that they were too worried to care about what they were wearing, or that they were just being polite.

"Well, let's talk," Grief's dad said, rubbing anxiously at his arms. "Let's uh, let's take a seat in the dining room, that'd be easiest. We can get round the table."

"That sounds like a good idea," the taller of the two men said, warmly. He was very tanned, and despite the lines around his eyes, his hair was very dark too. He grinned, and his teeth were white. "We just want to discuss what's happened, and talk about some options moving forward, that kind of thing. That's why we're here." His smile reminded Mister Grief of Sher Kahn in *The Jungle Book.* He loved that movie.

Grief's Dad led the way, and once his mother came back to make some tea, Grief was gently told to go and tidy his room.

"Let us talk to these people first," she said. Grief wasn't surprised. He tidied his room at lightning fast speed, and was back in front of the TV when the group came out around two hours later. The taller, tanned man was grinning still, but he was the only one that was. His eyes then fell upon Mister Grief, taking him in properly for the first time. The smile disappeared, shrinking like a worm disappearing into a hole.

"Is this him?" he wasn't talking to Grief's parents. He was addressing the other two baseball cap people, and the way he spoke to them sounded like he was in charge. The warmth in his voice was suddenly gone, certainly. It was suddenly as if, as far as tanned man was concerned, Grief's parents weren't even in the room. The other, fatter man and the dark-haired woman stared at Mister Grief, and it struck him suddenly that he'd seen that look before. John had looked at him in the same way when he came home.

"No," the woman said. The taller man turned to the fatter man, waiting.

"Harry?" he said.

" ... no," the man called Harry said eventually, but his face wasn't as certain as the woman's.

"John's upstairs," Mister Grief's mother said, confused now as well as terrified. "It's him you want to talk to." The taller man turned to Grief's mother, the well-practiced smile springing to his tanned face. Even at ten years old, Grief understood what a man practiced in politicizing looked like.

"Of course," he said, his tone soft and perfectly deferential. "Listen to me, talking to these two like we're in the office. I apologise, I normally take care of the logistics from my 'ivory tower' as it were, ha ha, but they asked me to come out personally. Please, lead on." Grief's mum and dad looked uncertain, but did so, as if they were moving in a dream. Once they were in front, the tanned man looked back at Mister Grief. The smile was gone, and his eyes burned into Grief's like embers. Grief suddenly felt naked, pinned on a microscope, and for the briefest moment it felt like something was moving *through* him; *worms,* he would later think. *As if my skin were full of worms, moving and probing and trying to find whatever they can.*

Then the man smiled again, that wide white grin standing out in that varnished face, and he was turning with the others and heading up the stairs to have the conversation that would change Mister Grief's life.

***

"When they all came down, John was with them," Grief said, not looking at Robert and lost in the past. "He just looked ... normal, I suppose. Normal for John anyway. He didn't speak, either. He didn't speak again for a long time after that. Mum and Dad did all the talking that night, either way. They just looked so *beaten.* They said that John was going to the countryside. To a special school in Yorkshire. I thought they meant another private school or something. And they did, in a way. But they said I had to go as well."

Grief sighed, shaking his head.

"I was so *angry,*" he said, his fingers moving as he spoke. "I hadn't *done* anything. I asked what John had done and they wouldn't tell me. I was just shouting and screaming and my parents just sat there, looking at the floor. That was *not* like them, believe me. It was horrible. And that man, the one with the tan. The Headmaster. He just sat there throughout with his arms folded, looking bored. He looked like he'd seen this many times before. I never saw him again after that. I saw the one they called Harry though. I *certainly* saw him. Except when I did, I had to call him Mister Williams. So that night—and I mean that *night,* we had to pack while those three waited for us—we were taken away."

"Did you see your parents again?" Robert asked, rapt. He'd forgotten the heat of the room, although the water bottle was empty."

"Oh yes," Grief said, the way an elderly gentlemen might say when asked *did you ever see an air raid during the war.* "We knew we would going in, it was made very clear. *Supervised visits.* We asked about holidays, but they just glossed over it. Mum and Dad ... they just stood there ..." Grief's eyes narrowed. "I always think about that. Had something been done to them, or ... who knows. They were never the same after that night, and by a considerable amount. Either way, we left, and began a new life at the Rothbury Academy. One that, for me at least, wouldn't last very long."

"Why?" Robert asked.

"I shouldn't *really* have been there in the first place," Grief said, with a shrug. "I'm sure that, by now, you've figured out what kind of a facility Rothbury would be. The crazy thing was that, yes, it was slap bang in the middle of the Yorkshire countryside, but it had a village right on it's doorstep. And no-one that lived there really knew what was going on at Rothbury, which again makes me wonder if my parents had been affected in some way, because the village residents *must* have been. It wasn't even listed as Rothbury on the outside; as far as the rest of the world was concerned, the place was an army barracks. Nobody ever asked why all the transports that went in an out had no windows. They couldn't have anyone seeing that there were children inside, you see. There *were* soldiers there, certainly, but I think they were for show more than anything. The teachers—if you can call them that—didn't need the soldiers. We were terrified of the people that ran that place, and they *had* to keep us terrified. If pretty much any of the kids in Blackbird or Eagle decided to rebel, there wouldn't have been a soldier there that could have done anything about it. The teachers all had *something,* to a greater or lesser degree, but none of them had quite the talent of the kids. The teachers were the ones that found us—they had enough to do that—but *we* were the ones with the potential. Apart from the Headmaster. The tan man. I think he was their failsafe. He had *more*. But he was never needed. I certainly never saw him again, as I say. What kind of a Headmaster never deals with his own students? John saw him when it all went down, apparently, but that all happened so quickly that there wasn't much they could do anyway. Plus I think John had more than even the Headmaster."

"They were *training* the kids?" Robert asked. Grief shrugged again.

"Yes, it certainly seemed that way," he said wistfully. "Moulding us, at least, for definite. I didn't ever get to find out what the end goal was. I wasn't there very long, and the *facility* isn't there any more either. It isn't active, certainly. I have someone looking into it intermittently for me, and currently that particular site is abandoned, although there are guards on the gate for some reason. The last time anything happened there was when it was pressed into use very briefly a few years back as a temporary base of operations, during that whole business that started in Coventry and spread across the country. The walking statue thing."

Robert nodded. He remembered. Everyone in the world remembered that.

"That horrible prick that was all over the TV—Pointer—he was at the barracks briefly at the time. After the Second Arrival," said Grief. "Along with some other civilian chap. I have regular surveillance bundles sent to me, so have a lot of photos of them at the site." Robert looked at Grief quizzically, and Grief waved his hand dismissively. "I have my reasons to keep an eye on any potential activity from the Rothbury people, as you'll hear," he said. "Either way, they'd brought together, as I'm sure you've guessed, *special* children at Rothbury. You might ask how their parents allowed it, but ... there are people that operate above the law Robert, and they can be extremely persuasive. Especially with the people they had working for them. People who have a lot more than mere influence. Plus, when you looked at a lot of these kids, you can understand a lot of the parents *wanting* to send their kids to Rothbury. Either because their kids needed help that they were *never* going to get at a regular school ... or because their parents were scared."

Robert didn't say anything. It was hard enough to conceive that someone like Grief existed, but the fact that he wasn't the only one ... that he was the *least* of them ...

"Some of the teachers had to be scared too, I think," Grief said. "You've seen a taste of what I can do, but as I say, some of these kids ... they had different sections there. There was Sparrow, Blackbird, and Eagle. It wasn't anything to do with age, either. I was in Sparrow and there were kids as old as fifteen in there. John was in Eagle, of course. We boarded in our different sections, were taught there. We'd have events—mixers—very rarely, where the segments could mingle, but it was made *very* clear that no-one was to ... *do* anything, even for fun, and we'd meet the other kids. That was nice. They felt normal then. I mean, *I* felt normal in terms of what I could do—I wasn't like them—but I didn't feel normal socially. I felt like the outsider. The reverse of my old school. I was the one that couldn't do anything, and everyone knew it. No-one teased me though. That was an extremely firm rule there; bullying or even mild teasing was met with *unbelievable* punishment. In hindsight, I can see why; any kind of mental torment might, in turn, create unseen mental blocks. Might make the kids less efficient, harder to control, less capable. Rothbury walked this incredible tightrope between ruling through fear and trying to keep us happy as long as we stayed within the lines. We had games consoles, carefully selected films to view on big TVs in our dorms—movie nights—and they'd bring in things like horses and set up shooting ranges. Activities. It was as much like a summer camp as it could be, really, when not training. The training, however was *very* grueling. It was just a shame they had to keep everything under such a tight rein. That we were away from our families. It was a very strange place."

Grief rocked on his chair, lacing his fingers on his stomach.

"Even in Sparrow though, I was by far the lowest. I mean, there were children in there that showed signs of something intermittently; occasional pre-cogs that would, like once a month or so, suddenly jump in their seats like they'd seen something terrible, then look around themselves as if they had no idea what had just happened. Then they'd say, when asked, something about ... actually, I remember one example: Trevor Pontin saying something about a hanglider and another guy in class, Lenny Frame. That night a microlight crashed on the A45, causing a three car pile-up that killed Lenny's mum. They took Trevor Pontin up into Blackbird after he did that sort of thing two or three times ... but he came back in the end. Then one day he wasn't in class anymore, and we didn't see him again. They'd sit with us for hours a day, working on meditation with us, mindfulness, awareness. Trying to get us to break the ice, open our potential. To say that I am grateful today for those meditation classes would be an understatement, even when they upgraded the intensity dramatically. Meditating at a distraction, with mild pain. Solo training in the Nullification Chambers with mild pain stimuli, trying to generate an automatic defence response in us. They were extremely difficult. But the lessons learned in those endless meditation sessions serve me today the same way that breathing serves you, Robert. Did you know that they did a study on Tibetan monks in London? This wasn't a Rothbury thing, this is public knowledge. They tried it in Tibet, but the monks didn't like it; they felt that they were being treated like primitives. So the examiners soothed over the resentment, and brought the monks to London and treated them very respectfully. And they got them hooked up to monitors to measure their brain activity, these men that had mastered the art of meditation and practiced it for hours a day. They found their brains operated in ways no one had ever seen before. It performs miracles on the brain, meditation." He sighed, shrugging again. "But it can only do *so* much." He said this in such a heavy, weary manner that Robert didn't think that Grief was referring to his time at Rothbury.

"But sometimes," Grief continued, his mind back to his story once more,

"When we were in C Block, which had the higher floors, we could see the Eagle kids when they were doing outside work. Not all of them were outside; only the ones whose skills necessitated outdoor practice. But we saw them, nevertheless. We saw what kind of level they were on compared to us." Grief smiled, and Robert saw admiration in Grief's grin. *Despite everything*, Robert thought, *you wish you'd made it into Eagle.* Robert thought this so clearly that he wondered if it might not be some sort of feedback from Grief's abilities.

"I can remember one day very clearly," Grief said. "It was raining, that was what made it stand out even more. There were three kids out on the Eagle training quad, along with three examiners and the prerequisite armed soldiers. I'd hoped to see John; I only got to see him at the mixers, and he was his old self whenever I did, smiling gently and shrugging, not talking. He seemed to be doing quite well at Rothbury, better than I was certainly. I don't think he missed Mum and Dad very much. Anyway. That day we were supposed to be doing ESP drills, but I wasn't paying attention, especially when I knew the Eagle kids were doing *outdoor practice*. Don't get me wrong; there had been days when absolutely nothing of interest would happen in these sessions. One day I remember there was about fifteen boys and girls standing in a semicircle in front of about thirty of these huge black blocks laid out in the quad, the blocks having these funny antennae and ... well, I guess you could say *hooks* sticking out of them. And the kids were touching these blocks, staring at them moving them, and sometimes the blocks would vibrate a little, but other than that absolutely nothing happened. But the examiners were taking notes like their lives depended on it. I wished I knew what was going on, but that was certainly extremely boring to watch. But today was already different. Today they brought out these three cows."

Grief sat forward, hand out before him, seeing it.

"I *nearly* missed it," he said. "They lined up the children maybe twenty feet away from the cows, one each. Two boys and one girl. The girl couldn't have been older than ten, and the two boys looked about twelve. And they just all stood there for *so* long, that even myself—who was always desperate to see what the Eagle kids could do—began to give up on anything actually happening. I was about to look back at the training video on my screen when it all happened pretty much simultaneously. If I hadn't been looking I wouldn't have even noticed because it was somehow so gentle and quiet."

Grief extended one finger and held it up.

"The first cow started to moo. But it wasn't a noise that I've ever heard a cow make before. It turned its head on one side and held it there, as if it was trying to get water out of its ear, but it just kept making this ... *noise,* like a normal moo but *lower,* much lower, a real bass note. And it was making it over and over, *mmm, mmm, mmm,* perfectly repeated like the thing was keeping rhythm. Then it stopped and just stayed like that. Head on one side, not moving ... then it started to walk. It made its way over to the kid, then turned and walked straight back. Then it did it again. It kept doing it. Even when they took the kid away, it kept doing it. It was there for hours, walking back and forth across the quad, until a security crew came and shot it."

"I was so busy watching the *third* cow though—I'll come to that in a second—that I nearly missed the fact that the second cow had started to smoke. Its whole skin was starting to give off this weird white smoke, even though its skin was completely normal and the cow wasn't even making any noise. It looked quite relaxed. Even when it burst into flames it didn't make a noise, didn't even move in fact, and then its skin *was* blackening. The thing didn't make a single sound and eventually keeled over, looking like a cow-shaped block of coal. The rain had no effect on the fire either."

He sighed, and spread his hands. Like the cow, Robert didn't make a sound.

"But the third one ... even after everything I've seen and done, that was the one I will never forget. That was the girl's cow. She was Eagle standard, all right. I couldn't really figure out what I was seeing, at first; I wasn't sure if it was dust in the air, or some kind of localized heat haze, even though it wasn't hot. It just looked *weird* around the cow though, and looking at it actually started to make me feel sick, as if my eyes couldn't figure out what they were seeing and my brain was getting nauseous as a result. Eventually though, I could see the shape of it. Then it was as clear as it was unbelievable."

"It was only half-formed, but once seen the shape of the fourth cow was unmistakable. Cows are large creatures, and hard to miss, so a see-through one appearing out of thin air grabs at one's attention. It was identical to the girl's cow in every way from stance to marking, but it just wasn't ... *there* yet. The teacher or examiner or whatever the hell they were—they were wearing the baseball cap, certainly, but even the security teams wore those—passed a baton through it, and the thing actually *rippled* like water. It was solidifying though, that much was clear. At first I could make out the background behind it easily, but when I went to look at the same spot again it was harder to see. Either way, it never made it all the way home. The girl started swaying, and even from where I was sitting it was crystal clear when the blood burst from her nose and ears and eyes. It was like something had exploded inside her. The second that happened, the fourth cow vanished and both the girl and the original cow dropped down stone dead. The teachers ran over, already radioing for backup but they knew it was a lost cause. It certainly wouldn't have been the first time they'd seen something like that."

"But here's the thing, Robert. *This* was the caliber of student that John was bundled with. Children that could set things on fire if they thought about it hard enough. Children that could, given enough effort, stop your heart. Extremely dangerous individuals that had to be handled using extremely complicated and highly effective psychological techniques to keep them in line. But all of them—*all* of them—were scared of John. My brother was the most feared child at that school."

Robert found his voice.

"But *why?*" Grief smiled.

"John's gift was different to theirs, Robert. A lot different."

"But what *was* it?"

Mister Grief told him.

"That ... that's it?" Robert asked, confused. Grief smiled sadly, did that gentle shrug of his hidden bony shoulders again.

"At first, it might not seem that frightening at all. But when you think about it, what it might mean—and believe me, *all* the children loved to play the *what would you do if* game when it came to thinking about the unthinkable possibility of squaring off against one another—everyone, to one degree or another, decided that there were fates worse than death. If you take the idea to its extreme, take it to the very maximum ... I, personally, would rather die."

Robert thought about it. Put like that ... maybe he would, too.

"I, of course, was on the other end of the scale. If any kind of bullying had been tolerated in that place, I would have been the laughing stock of the school ... or perhaps not, given that everyone knew who my brother was. Apparently it wasn't uncommon for there to be several kids in each year's intake that were sent home. Kids like me, who had never actually displayed anything prior to their inclusion but whose *siblings* had, leading to kids like myself being brought in as a precaution or speculative measure. From the way my private sessions were being repeatedly cancelled, or the amount of time spent literally amusing myself, it was clear that I had been written off and that it was just a matter of time until I was sent away. That was absolutely fine by me. And then the day came that Mister Williams came back. The day he took his hat off."

***

They'd all talked about possible reasons why Mister Williams had been away from school for several months. Paul Clarkson claimed that he *knew* why; that Williams had had a minor heart attack while playing cricket. When everyone asked how Paul could possibly know this, he'd just shrugged in a knowing way and tapped the side of his nose. Everyone thought that Paul was a lying arsehole after that. Not only did everyone know what the baseball caps were for—even if they never discussed it—but what Paul was claiming was Eagle level stuff, and no one in their whole ranking, let alone their class, was capable of that. To put it into perspective, the best anyone in Mister Grief's class could do was make the lights go on and off.

They'd had a revolving door of stand-ins from the faculty, which essentially meant that there was no disruption at all in their training. The idea of having a regular tutor was purely a way of paying lip service to their previous world of education; all the teachers had the same techniques, the same teaching themselves, and there was certainly no teacher/student bond other than fear. No one had actually *cared* that much that Williams was gone. It was just a matter of childish curiosity.

Then one day, he came back.

It hadn't even been first thing, as Mister Carraway had taken the register that morning (another pointless throwback; none of them could even leave the compound, and *none* of them would even consider not turning up for class. They'd been waiting to start a double period of Focus when Williams had arrived, walking into the room to take the afternoon register as if he'd never been away.

He certainly didn't bother to explain his absence, either. Instead, he waddled into the room and simply sat at the desk without a word. He'd been overweight and middle-aged when he turned up at Mister Grief's house to take him away, and whatever had happened during his absence had clearly taken a toll on his appetite and waistline, but he still had that waddling gait, even though he looked twenty pounds lighter, and tired. Terribly, terribly tired.

The students waited patiently for him to speak, but for a moment or two Williams just looked around the room, as if seeing it for the first time. He looked dazed, almost. Then he picked up the register awkwardly, as if figuring out how his hands worked, and opened it. He looked at the words on the page in front of him, and sighed.

"Hello," he said, without looking up. His tone was that of a dead man. "McCoy?"

"Here," said a corresponding voice from the back.

"Guthrie?"

"Here," said an older voice. Age was a very loose factor in class assignment at Rothbury.

"Drake?"

"Uh huh."

Williams' eyes suddenly became sharp and looked up, Rothbury instinct kicking in.

"Here, sir," Drake added, quickly. Williams' eyes dulled again, and he went back to the register.

"Lehnsherr?"

"I am here."

Mister Williams then read out Mister Grief's name, and stopped. He looked up, and Grief wanted to back away in his seat, to avoid the man's eyes. Pain was written all over them.

"Here, sir," Grief said, as quickly as he could, in case he'd done something wrong. Williams didn't respond; instead his eyes continued to moisten.

"You were the first one I collected," he said eventually. "Did you know that?" Even without looking around, Grief knew that every pair of eyes in the room were on him now.

"No ... I didn't know that sir," said Grief, desperate for this strange diversion to end, his unusually pink skin already darkening easily to crimson. He wanted to add something else, but couldn't think of anything.

"We didn't even really *want* you," Williams said, but now he seemed to be looking through Grief and talking to himself. "But we took you anyway as a *just in case*. An off-chance. We took you away from your family on a slim possibility."

Grief—and the rest of the class—were stunned. The teachers at Rothbury were almost robotic in their daily interactions, devoid of pleasantry or human insight. And here was Williams, not only talking with this darkly whimsical tone as if he were daydreaming, but doing the unthinkable, seemingly; he sounded as if he were actually criticizing Rothbury. And at the centre of all that was Mister Grief.

Grief wished he were like Campbell over in Eagle; he wished he could make everyone think that he wasn't there. But he couldn't do that. Grief couldn't do *anything*. Williams continued to stare, blinking gently, and Grief returned the gaze. Not through confidence or defiance, but in the same way that a terrified dog sometimes will, too scared to look away even when it wants to show deference. Eventually, it was Williams that dropped his eyes. When he spoke next, it was to himself.

"This was a mistake," he muttered.

"Sir?" Grief suddenly blurted out, confused and opening his mouth like some automatic nerve reflex, his body a frozen muscle looking for release.

"Yes?" said Williams, quickly, his eyes helplessly sad.

"Uh ..." said Grief. He hadn't even meant to speak, and he certainly didn't have a sentence planned. "Are you ... alright?" There was a barely audible intake of breath from the rest of the class. Asking a Rothbury teacher if they were alright was like asking the Queen if she'd had a nice shit. Williams looked as if he were going to cry.

"Of course," he said, but then his hand went to his mouth and he turned his face away, eyes blinking rapidly. "I must admit ... I mean ..." He rubbed at his face, shaking his head slightly, and sighed. "Yes ... Madureira?..." he asked, already knowing the next name on the register without looking at it.

"Uh ... here. Sir."

Wiliams nodded and rubbed at his face again so absent-mindedly that he briefly—and crucially—lifted the brim of his baseball cap so that he could rub all the way onto the top of his head of thinning hair. Grief then felt a lead pipe smash across the back of his head, and his face flew forward onto his desk as the pipe progressed along his spine, over and over. He was dimly aware that there *was* no pipe, but that didn't matter as he just wanted to die anyway, the thought of drawing breath for even a few more seconds being utterly abhorrent.

The rest of the class looked on, surprised but not shocked; similar physical reactions were fairly common at Rothbury, but they were curious to know if Grief was going to be one of the handful of kids every year who died in class. It *was* very rare in Sparrow, but it did happen. Williams, for his part, had gone the other way to Grief, sitting bolt upright as if someone had suddenly jammed a broom handle up his ass. His misty eyes were wide now, and bulging, and his jaw was clenched so hard that his face seemed two inches wider. He'd sat up so sharply that the hat, halfway up and then released as Williams' hand opened all the way in shock, fell clean off his head.

Grief, of course, saw none of this, lost inside the steel trap of Williams' emotion. Even as his tongue lolled on the desk, foam running from his mouth and pooling against his cheek, the urge, the *need* to will his body back under his control so that he could run to the nearest window and throw himself out of it was all-consuming. A very distant, disconnected part of his mind watched all this and thought *so* that's *why I could never do anything. Even the No-Hat tests and guided explorations ... the examiners weren't feeling like* this. Of course, none of that mattered. Nothing did, under the concrete wave of Williams' despair.

The still-conscious part of Grief's mind frantically tried to make sense of it, but of course he couldn't, because there *was* no sense, no rational thought; this was raw emotion, not logic or memory. There was only lead, iron, cold, *weight,* a chasm that swallowed him whole as inside his head he screamed against the dying of the light and embraced it all at the same time. He felt blood vessels burst inside his nose, and he just had time to think *like the girl, thank God* before his world went dark.

***

"I was in a coma for six weeks," Grief said, matter-of-factly. "It was his son, you know. Williams shouldn't have been back at Rothbury at all, grieving like that—you'd wonder how they let him—but I found out how he managed it later on. Obviously, given the nature of the place, they had regular monitoring and tests for this kind of thing, especially with a teacher coming back after a bereavement. But Williams was desperate to throw himself into his work. He needed to escape. And he knew how to beat the tests, because he'd helped design most of them. Plus, he'd apparently put on a golden performance at interview. The mask only dropped when he got into class. I think he'd underestimated how hard it was going to be."

"What happened to him?" Robert asked. His shirt was completely soaked through with sweat by now, but he didn't really notice. "What happened to Williams?"

"They kicked him out, obviously," Grief said. "He came to see me a few years later, a long time after I'd gotten out of the military hospital, after I went home ... before I left again. He wanted to thank me, which was understandable. He knew I hadn't *meant* to do what I did, but he wanted to thank me anyway. I was polite to him, but nothing more. I don't think he was a bad man as such, but I don't know how many good men would ever work at Rothbury."

"When I woke from my coma, I just wanted to die," Grief continued. "Not as badly as before—that reaction was amplified by my body's unprepared response—but I couldn't handle the minutes of the day that I spent conscious. I never shut down or fitted again, not the way I did that day with Mister Williams at Rothbury. That was the shock of it happening for the first time. Who knows why it even happened that first day? Perhaps it took a grieving psi-sensitive like Williams to set me off, or maybe I had just come of able age and hadn't realized it yet. I was twelve years old, and in the very early stages of puberty. Perhaps that had something to do with it. Either way, it had happened. I had absorbed all of Williams' grief for his dead son. I had taken on his burden. Can you imagine? At twelve?"

Robert couldn't.

"As you probably know, Robert, this is what I can do for you. I can take your grief away. I can take it away, and you will still remember everything about your wife. I just take the pain. You will miss her, but I will have taken your capacity for true grief, regarding her at least. This I can do for you."

"You really can?" Robert whispered. Grief nodded. "What ... about you?" he added.

"This is why I charge a lot of money for it, Robert," Grief said. "I can handle it better than most—I've been trained in the ways of the mind better than most people on this planet, Rothbury students aside—but it's still ..." He looked down, and didn't finish his sentence. Instead, he continued his story.

"I wanted to go back into my coma. I just wanted to sleep. The Rothbury people had put two and two together and realized roughly what had happened. It wasn't hard to do so. Williams didn't have much choice but to come clean about his own mental state, and to his credit I gather that he was actually forthcoming about it. Like most of the teachers at Rothbury, Williams was, first and foremost, a scientist. He was fascinated by what had happened, wanted to share it with the researchers ... not only that, can you imagine his *relief?* They only had to take one look at the state of me, one look at the state of him, and know of the moment that had occurred between teacher and student in a place like Rothbury. It was obvious."

Grief noticed Robert's empty water bottle, and stood to get him another. Robert heard Grief's knees crack audibly as he did so.

"Naturally, for a short while, I was a subject of great interest," he continued, fetching the liquid and handing it to Robert. "It wasn't just a school for creating weapons, after all. There were obviously an endless number of possibilities and government applications for the children at Rothbury. The kids there *did* see their parents, you know. Myself included. Just not very often.

And most of the graduates apparently led civilian lives afterwards, just in regular government employ, albeit with a lot of red tape and silencing agreements. They were only truly cloak and dagger if they went into the secret service. You have to remember, by the time most of the children graduated from Rothbury, they couldn't *be* more indoctrinated. They would die for the place. The idea of blowing any whistles was laughable. Plus, they owed their future careers to the place."

"But what about the kids that died?" Robert asked, taking the bottle gratefully and already unscrewing the cap.

"There were never any complaints," Mister Grief said, solemnly. "You think the people in charge didn't have a great many ways of making sure that didn't happen? And I'm not even talking about threats or violence either."

Robert thought about this, and realized this was probably extremely likely.

"How do you know all this?" Robert asked, suddenly wondering. Grief smiled.

"Of course I have a few contacts of my own. People that know how to find things out. I did eventually go back to Rothbury for a little while, after all. As I say, I was a source of fascination. They'd had empaths before, but this was something on a whole other level. Unfortunately for them—even with their own experts and graduates working on me—I was in no state to perform."

"You recovered?"

"Yes. Quicker than most people going through the process. I would say perhaps eight months. You have to remember, there was no conscious thought with that which I'd inherited from Williams. That makes it both harder and easier to get over. Harder because there's logic to apply to the process, and easier because it's like a chemical in your bloodstream. You can, to an extent, tell yourself that there's no reason to feel like this ... but even that doesn't help too much. It's like explaining to a severely depressed person how great their life is. It doesn't matter. Logic isn't a tool you can use; it would be like trying to put out a burning building with an idea. I think because my brain knows on some level that ultimately, it isn't my own, the pain passes faster. Although, as with any grieving process, there is never *truly* an end. It will dissipate, and lessen—in some cases *nearly* completely—but it never *fully* leaves. You simply have to learn to live with that particular weight on your shoulders."

Something occurred to Robert.

"So every time you do this ... it adds ..."

"Do you remember what happened at the wake?" Grief asked, interrupting. "What I did there, at the pub?"

Robert did. His anger had been drawn out of him like snake venom sucked from a bite.

"Yes."

"Anger and grief, and to an extent, jealousy. That's what I can work with," Grief said. "They're so much more prevalent, easier. I wish I could perhaps take more positive emotions—balance myself out, as it were—but I can't. I don't think I could live with myself if I did, anyway. Even so, they're out of my reach. I can *feel* them in others sometimes, but I can't get to them. Anger is different to grief though, Robert. Anger passes, unless it's *tied* to grief. It's quicker. It's like water. It runs away and leaves a residue that evaporates quickly. That's why I could take it from you and—for want of a much better term—pass it so easily. As I have already told you, I'm very well trained, and the first thing they deal with at Rothbury is aggression, for obvious reasons. You will *never* find more calm people than Rothbury graduates. Clinically so. I didn't graduate, but even so. Grief, however ..." He paused, and searched for the words.

"Grief is like tar," he said eventually. "It's like wet concrete. It doesn't run, it *oozes.* It's glacier-like in its movement. And as it goes, it leaves a trail that sets. Managed correctly, that trail can be a mere *glaze*, but it's there nevertheless. In some, it becomes a thick layer. Either way, it stays, Robert. It stays. Anger flares, and dies. Grief is constant, and strong. It flares as well, but even its normal burning is like a quiet inferno."

Robert knew this. He knew it very well. Grief nodded, taking Robert's silence as agreement, and continued.

"After a while—once they understood my limitations—the interest in my abilities waned quite quickly. I think, perhaps, if I worked differently, that wouldn't be the case; if I could take grief and dissolve it, walking away afterwards with as little care as a tradesman going on to his next job, then things would have turned out differently. My life certainly would have different. But the people of Rothbury and their associates prize mental stability above all things. Even the minor in-field tests I was subjected to had a devastating effect on me. Even with my mental training—I was a child after all, only recently recovered from a terrible trauma—and I think eventually I was classed as too much of an operational risk. Subject to the usual disclosures—including my parents, of course, being called in for the Wise Monkeys Procedure—I was sent home. Unlike the Eagle children, who never got to go home until they were twenty-one and fully immersed in the Rothbury mentality, regardless of whether or not they graduated. Some—the volatile and dangerous ones, of which there were a few—never left the program. The Blackbird children who were sent home for whatever reason were regularly medicated—the parents were *procedured* to make sure this happened—but the medications were extremely expensive. I often wondered why they didn't just neutralize the children that were no good to them, but apparently it was written into the Rothbury 'mission statement', as it would be called these days, that Rothbury would 'Protect the Nation, and the Children Of Rothbury.' Those were the founder's words, Oliver Rothbury himself. I guess his modern-day counterparts considered the occasional deaths each year of a few children going through the process to be an unavoidable hazard ... but either way, there were never   according to my sources—any intentional hits. The romantic in me would like to think they were honoring the mission statement, but the realist in me suspects that they simply didn't like to remove *any* potential assets, damaged or untrainable or otherwise. But they monitored us. Of *course* they did. Even the Sparrow children who were sent home. Children like me. Anyone kicked out early knew they would be watched. None of us *dreamed* of blowing the lid on it. While it still existed, anyway," he added, arching an eyebrow slightly in a way that said *hence me telling you all this shit.*

"Is this why you have all the secrecy?" Robert asked, sitting up, his eyes suddenly casting the room for any potential bugs. He felt as if, were he to look out of the window, he would see a black Mercedes in the car park, two men in black suits and shades seated inside. Perhaps wearing black baseball caps too.

"Yes and no," Grief said, rolling up his thick coat sleeve slightly to reveal his skinny wrist and his watch again. He checked the time, rolled the sleeve back down. "Sort of, I suppose. Rothbury as I knew it pretty much came to an end when John came home."

"John graduated?" Robert asked. Grief threw his head back and roared with laughter, a deep, booming sound that was greatly at odds with the skinny frame Robert knew to be under the coat.

"No, no" Grief said eventually, chuckling. "John didn't *graduate.* Oh ... no, no he didn't. But he came home all the same."

"But ... he was in Eagle," Robert said, confused. "He was—no offence—but the way you talk, even when your abilities began, he was in another league to you. Why did they send *him* home?"

"They didn't," Grief said. "He left. He walked right out of the door. I know this part because I heard it directly from the horse's mouth."

"You were there when he came back ..."

"Yes. It was a few years after I left Rothbury, however. Though my parents had visited him several times, I hadn't been allowed to go. Once you left Rothbury, you didn't go back even as a visitor. So you can imagine my surprise when he walked through the front door of our house on a Saturday afternoon."

"What did your parents say?"

"They weren't there. He'd waited until they left. I'll never forget how calm he looked. He didn't even really seem in a particular hurry, which made sense I suppose. When I think about it, I assume he'd have had quite a major head start while they figured everything out. Anyway, he walked in and said hello—which in itself seemed strange, I still wasn't used to hearing him speak—and he actually gave me a hug. And he was big, Robert, really big. I'm tall, but John was tall and *dense,* a beast of a kid. He'd grown a lot since I'd last seen him. He's even bigger now. John likes to eat."

"Wait, you still see him?"

"Oh, yes. I should think I'm about the only person he likes. We don't see each other often—the nature of our lifestyles makes it difficult—but we do still get together. Most people wouldn't understand it—he's a ... how do I put it ... not a lot of people would want to spend too much time with him, I think—but I do love my brother very much. Despite his quirks."

Robert tried to picture this hulking brute that Grief was describing. John, the boy that the other kids feared who became a man.

"Quirks?" Robert asked. Grief cocked his head, trying to find the words again.

"Yes," he said, thoughtfully. "I could, even then, already see that something was different behind his eyes. He wasn't the same, certainly. The way he smiled, that's the best way I can put it. Before it had been this laid back, amiable thing. Now it was this ... *smirk.* Like everything was amusing. Like he knew better. As if he had nothing to worry about any more."

Robert paused at this. He knew what John could do. It was impressive, certainly, and he understood why the other kids were so scared of him ... but for John to have nothing to worry about? How was that possible? And then he thought about the many practical applications of John's gift, and how really— on a small scale—he guessed John really *could* do pretty much as he wished, within reason.

And what would that realization have on a teenaged boy, Robert thought.

"But what about the training, and the indoctrination?" Robert asked, his internal monologue reaching a dead end that he couldn't answer. "Wasn't all that supposed to keep him, you know ..." Robert laid his hand flat and slowly sliced it horizontally through the air in front of him.

"Oh, John wasn't *crazy,* Robert, not by a long stretch," Grief said, almost sounding offended and dismissing the very idea. "That just couldn't happen at Rothbury. I think it was precisely John's extremely easygoing nature that was the difference maker. Think about it; very early on they identify the potential powder kegs through rigorous and thorough psychological testing and what they called Insight sessions. Those children had extra sessions as well as the usual constant orientation. Over time, the 'safest' children were established and given the minimum of reinforcement, or minimum by Rothbury standards at least. John, of course, was one of those. They took his willing and relaxed nature to mean that he would never be a problem, and indeed, their tests backed this up."

"But they didn't know that—just as he did at his old school the day he realized what he could do—John would eventually quietly decide that he'd had enough now, thank you. All the reinforcement and indoctrination ... he would have gone with it, because that was John. And when tested, he would have said all the right things. Not sneakily, not planning anything bad, but just doing what he thought was expected. But none of it would have *really* gone in, because John just wasn't wired that way. So what they ended up with was, for the first time, a very powerful teenager who wasn't with the program *and they didn't know because he didn't either.* You have to remember, the trouble kids at Rothbury were always so easy to spot. John didn't even know that he was, effectively, a rebel." Grief smiled affectionately, but there was also sadness there.

"And with a casual shrug and a smile, he decided to leave," Mister Grief said. "And they would have tried to stop him. And with an equally casual shrug and a smile, John made sure they didn't. As far as he was concerned, it was only fair. He just wanted to go home, and they'd had enough of his time. He didn't kill them, after all. He didn't mean them any harm, and to him, it wasn't a big deal. He didn't understand that it *was* a big deal, of course, but he did it anyway. To him, the only thing that they would see as a really big deal was the fact that he was leaving. That's John. He won't understand *why* things upset people, but he'll understand that they do and act accordingly. He knows what people want to hear. I think that's why he's so ... detatched."

Uh huh. I don't think I ever want to meet this guy all the same, thank you, Robert thought. *Powerful people that don't understand* other *people are very dangerous indeed, and the ones that mean no harm are often the worst.*

"All the same, his experience upon leaving—what he dealt with— certainly changed him somewhat," Grief said. "Having to do it to so many of them, so many staff and guards, and having to do it to some more than to others in the chaos, no doubt. That will certainly leave its marks on an impressionable young mind. He'd grown, Robert, and not just in the physical sense. Grown under unpleasant and sudden circumstances. I wish I'd known what was going on inside his head that day he came home. On the outside, at least, we made small talk; how I'd been, how Mum and Dad were, what it was like for me being back at normal school (even though it was, of course, a different school to the one I'd attended previously.) I asked why he'd waited until Mum and Dad were gone. He'd shrugged. *Too many questions,* he'd said. *Probably not enough time to answer them. I can't stay long.* All the while we talked, that expression never left his face. Mild amusement, like I was something in a zoo that he found cute. But I knew my brother still loved me. I could tell by the way he held me when he left, after packing some supplies and disappearing. As I say, he didn't have to worry too much about being caught, or at least being unable to escape, but all the abilities in the world can't do very much after a sniper's bullet has passed through your brain. He was right to play it safe."

"My parents arrived not that long after John left, and of course were immediately terrified, as well as concerned for John. They rang Rothbury, and the line was engaged all day. I'm not surprised. The chaos must have been unbelievable. The SWAT team arrived that evening and turned our house over. My parents and I were taken away again and questioned vigorously. We told them the truth, of course, and we knew nothing anyway. We didn't know where John was. As it turned out, I didn't see him again for five years. Anyway, roughly six months after John left our house that day, I had my second incident. I was about fourteen or fifteen, just walking down the street in town with some friends. My life—my social life, at least, if not my home life, my parents by now two zombies that simply paid the bills and fed me—was relatively back to normal. The counselors at Rothbury were the absolute best in human existence, and before I'd left, when they were still trying to gauge my usefulness, it was very much in their interests to bring me back to as sound and undisturbed a state of mind as they could. It didn't really work completely, but it helped a great deal (although to their dismay their attempts to work me around to 'performing' again brought on the worst possible hysterics. The biggest nail in the coffin for my time at Rothbury.) Plus, I think the nature of my abilities, plus their constant regular training, had an unforeseen delayed or latent effect on aiding me in the recovery process, something they could not have known at the time. A year after waking from my coma wishing desperately to die, I was back to being a relatively normal boy. There was still the concrete, however. That glaze on the soul. Back then, it wasn't too thick."

"I still had my home visits from Rothbury staff, but the uniform was different. Rothbury as I knew it had ceased to exist, the site shut down after the disaster with John, but the program was still going on in one form or another. They were checking I'd kept my mouth shut, essentially, and for any developments in me. There hadn't been any, and that was the way I wanted it at the time. I know they'd have maintained other checks as well, ones we didn't really know about. But other than all that, I lived almost the same as the other boys I knew, and even though I was not one of them and never would be again, I had friends. We did the things teenage boys do. So that day, when the old woman walked past us, I'd pretty much stopped worrying about when the next hit would come. I had almost begun to believe that it never would again. And there I was, with six other boys who lost in a discussion about which girl in school they'd most like to sleep with even though none of us really knew what we were talking about, completely unaware of the old lady in the grey raincoat coming the opposite way up the street. The recent loss of her husband—I didn't know the details, but you can get some from the *feel* of it, a widow is different to a widower—poured into me as if she'd emptied a hot kettle down my throat."

The mention of it reminded Robert why he was there. He was amazed to find that, in all of the talk about John, he'd briefly forgotten.

"It's a cliché, but it really is true; it moments of great mental drama, everything slows down. It really does. I started to drop to my knees, turning as I did so, visually drawn to the source of the hit. And I *saw* the change in her, seeing her back as she continued along her way. She actually stopped. That droop in the shoulders lessened slightly, and she began to look around herself, not quite sure of what was going on. Meanwhile the weight was filling my bones and I couldn't breathe. And I just thought *no, not again, I can't do this* and somehow the reaction was instinctive. I felt something inside me *push* it away, reject it, purge it from my body and mind as if I were vomiting up some disgusting bug. My skin—I remember this very clearly—breaking out in a cold sweat with relief as her grief left me, and I watched as she lowered her head to her hand and began to slowly walk again, holding her face, perhaps feeling its resettling inside her as just another fresh wave. Grief is at its cruelest like that. Its temporary passing making you believe that things are getting better, only for it to destroy you anew when it returns, the fall harder as a result of your pleasant altitude. I became aware of the boys laughing at me, wondering why I'd fallen and mocking me as I lay on my back gasping with relief. I didn't care. I couldn't believe how lucky I was. I sat up and watched the old woman continue on her way, feeling pity and thinking that which always comes with it from the un-bereaved to the bereaved; *I feel for you, but I'm so glad that I'm* not *you."*

"That was when I realized that I could control it. I know they'd told me that at Rothbury, but even with all of their 'help' I still was having a breakdown even at the thought of engaging with someone's mind like that. Chance, however, had created a situation that showed me otherwise. And again, perhaps I wouldn't have had the ability were I a younger boy. Having a choice changes everything, Robert. Don't you think? If you are someone who is frightened of being attacked, when that attacker appears out of nowhere, unbidden, the terror is heightened. Knowing that you can *prepare* for that attack, face it upon your own terms and when at your best ... that is different."

"I'd been failing in school, Robert. Badly. The classroom environment seemed so strange to me now, and I could never relax in there. On the playground, in the street, with my friends, all of that was fine. But I couldn't engage with school anymore after Rothbury. The very early, distant stages of an idea began to form that day, but it didn't come to fruition until John called me."

"He rang you? Was it the first time he'd spoken to you after he'd left?"

"Yes. I was eighteen. I'd left school at sixteen with no qualifications of any worth and had been carrying out manual labour for a building company. Yes, I know; I'm skinny, certainly, but I'm stronger than I look. The money was lousy. As you can tell Robert, I'm nobody's fool, and eventually I think I would have found something better through hard work or gumption and worked my way up. But that all changed when John called."

"So you said. What did *he* say?"

"He told me to get out. From anyone other than John, of course, you'd think that would be a frantic, panicked call, but it wasn't. I could hear him smiling down the phone. He wanted to help me, but I think the drama amused him all the same. *They're cleaning up loose ends,* he said. *It might be different if you were still a kid, or if their little school hadn't been shut down. But Rothbury as we know it is a bust and the one's like you, the ones who weren't really useful—the ones who became adults—they're finally being seen as too much of a risk.* I asked how he knew this, and he laughed the way he does, as if everything is just silly. *I have a lot of people in the right places. I'll tell you all about them. I'll introduce you to a few. But you need to get out of there and never go back.* How long for, I asked him. *For good, to be on the safe side,* he said. *But don't worry.* He said that last part as if he were talking about a difficult job interview. *I'm going to take care of the last elements of Rothbury. Be smart, don't use your cards, stay off the system. I'll let you know when you can come up for air.* I nearly asked how he'd find me, but I realized that I already knew. I asked how long I had. *I don't know. Might be next week, might be today. But I'd leave now if I were you, to be on the safe side. Hole up somewhere. I'll come to you.* He made good on his promises. He made good on *all* of his promises." Mister Grief actually smiled, like a proud parent.

"But if he did ... then why still all this?" Robert said, gesturing at the shithole of a room all around them. "Why bother?"

"Because, quite frankly, you never know," Mister Grief said, shrugging again. "My real name is on a system somewhere. As I said to you, I don't *think* I'm in any real danger. I'm certainly not a very social person anymore, so it doesn't cause too many problems in my day to day life to be careful and live a nomadic existence. That side of it, at least, rather suits me."

"And the idea? The idea you had? This was it?"

Mister Grief nodded.

"My hand was forced. I withdrew the small amount of money I had and left immediately. I have never seen my parents since, but ... there really wasn't much point in that relationship by then anyway. They were just ... shells. My money didn't last long, and I had to take action. It was terrifying and exciting at the same time. The idea of what I would be doing to myself was almost unthinkable, but I had also been preparing for the last three or four years. Continuing my Rothbury training. I thought I could take it. And the thought of the *money* that I could make ... as I say Robert, I've only ever approached men of means such as yourself. The ones that can afford me. Grief kills some people. And the rich men it would kill are the ones I visit. I read a *lot* of obituaries. And I set myself a limit, many years ago. Ten clients. As you know, you are number nine. Ten would be three million pounds. Enough to keep myself comfortably on the move for the rest of my life."

"But why not just find one really, really rich guy who is grieving and get him to pay you three million? People with that kind of money would pay it."

"Indeed," said Mister Grief, a faint smile playing around his lips. "And tell me; how do I get near these people? These super rich, already wary of charlatans and snake-oil salesmen trying to separate them from their fortunes?"

"John!" Robert snapped, annoyed. "The people *he* knows!" Mister Grief chuckled, that smirk spreading some more, and Robert's annoyance grew. Then Grief's expression changed, and he suddenly touched Robert's hand. The anger flowed out of Robert like sand through an hourglass. That in itself was annoying, and Robert *tried* to stay angry, but it was impossible.

"Don't ... *do* ... that ..."Robert breathed. Mister Grief released Robert's hand and closed his eyes, then shuddered for a moment.

"My apologies, for annoying you and for taking that liberty. I thought it best. I didn't mean to upset you. It's just that the idea that these people would help out with these kinds of errands for me ... or even John ... no. These are the handful that Rothbury failed to keep track of. Their other mistakes. Rothbury was doomed even *before* John left. *They* found *him*. He was far too useful for them *not* to come to him, frankly. But the only intel or tasks they were interested in were dismantling Rothbury, not helping out with the business plan of a fellow former student. They achieved their goal, and disappeared for good. No, the only people I could get to were people like yourself. The low-level millionaires. And as I say ... you may even be the last. Two million seven hundred thousand is sufficient, if used correctly, and I should think that I'll be doing well to last more than another thirty years with my health issues. Those also take a large chunk of the money. Medical help off-the-grid is extremely expensive."

"Health issues?" Robert asked. Grief smiled, but kindly this time, and spread his hands. *Of course,* Robert thought. *You don't pass through the furnace of eight other people's torment and come out unscathed. It oozes. The cement sticks.*

"I *am* trained, and I *do* pass through it a lot better than a normal man," Grief said, "but I can still only take so much. Eight clients in twenty seven years. I've spread them out, obviously. I try to enjoy the time inbetween. But it's getting harder, a lot harder. Yes ... I think you'll probably be the last one."

There was a long pause that said it was time.

"So ...?" Robert asked, quietly. His heart was thrumming with excitement now. He was about to experience that which countless millions around the world yearned for; a truly supernatural, inexplicable experience, and not only that, one that would benefit him in a way that he couldn't even describe. It was about to happen *now.*

"So," Grief said. "Oh, wait. I haven't taken today's dose." He fished into his pocket, and took out a silver strip of tablets. Most of the sections were open. He gestured for Robert's water, and Robert gave it to him, done with it. Mister Grief popped four of them out of the packet and swallowed them, flushing them down with the water. "The dose is for two, and I take that for eight weeks to get them into my system. Then on the week building up to a client, I double it. Inadvisable medically perhaps, but it makes the early stages more bearable. Only a little, but it helps. Anything I can do to ease it, I do it, however little."

Robert nodded. Antidepressants.

"Will there be any ..." Robert nearly didn't ask the question as it sounded so stupid. *Fuck it,* he thought. This whole thing was insane. There *were* no stupid questions. "Will there be any side effects?"

"A few," said Mister Grief, nodding solemnly. "I was coming to those next. These are important. You *will* remember your wife, as I say, but your grief is, of

69

course, tied into your love for your wife. You will still love her, but part of removing grief is removing the dependency, and removing the dependency will diminish your love slightly. Well, not diminish ... how do I put this ... it will make it harder to access. Less immediate. Your memories be slightly less crisp, too. Still with you, I've assured you of this, but dulled a little. Grief sharpens the past, Robert. This will be better. Do you understand these things as I've told them to you?"

A distant, detatched part of Robert's mind thought *what is this, a call centre* while the rest of him thrummed like an engine at high output, and he nodded without speaking.

"Once this is done, you will leave this room and go home," Grief continued. "You will pack a bag, and you will leave the country for two months."

"Two months?" cried Robert, but Mister Grief's expression didn't change. "Okay. Two months," Robert said after a moment, acquiescing. Grief held all the cards.

"You will spend eight weeks in four countries, one country for two weeks at a time," Grief said. "You will keep moving. Use this time to readjust. Enjoy your freedom."

"Ok, ok, I will, but why?" asked Robert, desperately trying to make it clear that he wasn't disagreeing.

"I was about to tell you," Mister Grief said, slightly testily. A change seemed to have come over the man's demeanor, now that they were at the time where business was to be concluded. Antsy. Anxious. It was understandable. "The reasons are twofold. One, for the sake of your own social circle. A sudden and inexplicable change in your day to day outlook will be welcomed at first, then suspicious. People will either worry about you, or begin to suspect foul play. Your wife's death was accidental, after all."

The slick of ice cold oil ran through Robert again, as it always did at the thought, but he bristled at the very idea of an accusation being aimed at him.

Suzie had fallen. He hadn't even been there, she'd been in a whole other country for crying out loud. How could anyone even think about blaming him? He did get a life insurance payout, certainly, but—

Where were you, Robert? Why didn't you save her?

The partner of grief, guilt, spat its venom at him as usual, and Robert was suddenly deeply, deeply glad that he had gone to see Mister Grief. He couldn't take any more.

Coward. Coward. Coward.

Maybe. But people didn't see out the unending torment of their grief by *choice.* They didn't have one. He did. And he was fucking well taking it.

"A long break gives you at least some excuse," Grief was saying, jolting Robert out of his internal debate. "You've started the process of moving on after some time away, able to face your former family home with some resolve and begin the climb back up. That is what they will think. That's reason number one." Grief drew in a deep breath and rolled his neck, not looking at Robert as he continued to speak. This was the last mental preparation, it seemed, the final touches before the descent. "The second reason is me. I could give it *back* to you. You are the only person who I could offload it onto. And after the first few days, when I can't take any more, I will be desperate to do so. I have money of my own, as you know, and resources. You need to be moving. If I can't find you, I can't return it. If I know you're moving, that will make me think twice in my madness. After roughly the first month, I *can't* give it back. I don't know why. Something must seal over in the mind, perhaps, or enough of a change in the original host for their brain to no longer be a possible vessel again for their own grief. Believe me. Once, I *did* give it back. That was obviously highly unprofessional, and problematic for the client. I don't count him as one of my eight times as I didn't complete the process. I then found out the hard way the next two times I tried that the cutoff was roughly a month, as I say. I'm embarrassed in a way to admit that, but you know all too well the desperation that comes with grief."

"How do you do it?" Robert suddenly whispered. "How do you *keep* doing this? To know what you're going to be taking ..." Robert looked down at his own chest, gesturing towards it with a clawed hand as he tried to find the words to express what he meant. "I know, you've been trained, but even so ..."

"I've always told myself what any grieving person tells themselves, Robert," Mister Grief said, smiling sadly ... but his eyes were distant, and scared. Terrified. "That continuing will all be worth it. I will have freedom for the rest of my life. And I'm a greedy man, Robert," Grief said with a bitter chuckle. "I don't think I told you that. I made a decision as a young man, and once I started on that road—after the first two clients, when I nearly gave up—I decided that if I was going to have gone through that, it was going to be worth it. I decided that the *second* half of my life was when I was going to live, Robert. And live well."

"And now you're nearly done," Robert said, softly. "You'll soon have your grand total. The goal. Do you think it was worth it?" Grief's expression was blank.

"I will return to collect the payment in two months' time, when you have returned home" Grief said, continuing as if Robert hadn't asked the question. "You will have it in cash by then. I do hate to add this, but you don't want to default on your payment. I apologize for adding that, but I just need to know that I made that clear." Grief's face was suddenly so serious, his stare so intense, that Robert not only found himself drawing back slightly, but realizing that bearing the grief of eight other people would not only leave cement on the soul, but on the mind. For that moment, Mister Grief looked insane.

"Of course," Robert said, hurriedly. "I understand." Grief nodded, and the moment passed. In front of Robert sat, once more, a tall, gangly, pink-faced man with an oversized coat and a deeply sad expression on his face. Mister Grief rubbed his hands over his face suddenly, breathed out with a slight moan, and then held out one skinny hand.

"Remember, you will have to let yourself out," he said, almost inaudibly quiet. "This is why we don't do this at your home. I will be here for a while afterwards."

"Now?" Robert said, suddenly feeling panicked. "As in right now? Now?"

Grief didn't speak, and instead simply furrowed his brow and nodded impatiently, his eyes closed. Robert looked at Mister Grief's outstretched hand, offering him that which he'd come for.

Do you want this? Do you really want this?

Of course he did. He'd gone over the edge once. His grief wasn't serving him; it had become a weighted noose around his neck, dragging him to the bottom of an endless black sea. Robert took a deep breath, and thrust his hand into Mister Grief's. At first, nothing happened. Robert had expected some sort of electric connecting, or at least a sense of being drained, but all he could feel was the surprisingly cold hand of Mister Grief gripping his own. Then Mister Grief let out a sigh, and gripped tighter, and the process started.

It was slow at first, beginning with Robert's arm slowly becoming more and more dead. He could *feel* his arm going to sleep, and yet his heartbeat picked up slightly as he became aware of his shoulders softening, his neck feeling lighter and more loose. It was like he'd been injected with some kind of muscle relaxant. Grief gripped Robert's hand more tightly, but Robert could barely feel it; his hand was so relaxed that, temporarily, his nerve endings weren't receiving as they should. Mister Grief let out a low, animalistic moan, and his head dropped into his trembling free hand, but Robert continued to feel lighter and lighter. His lower back suddenly and noticeably softened, and Robert felt like he could float away.

Think of her. Think of your wife.

He did, and the stab was still there, and for a moment Robert was confused; it wasn't working? Then what was happening here? But then he realized how the stab was less, how it didn't bring with it the automatic thought of the days ahead stretching before him like a road laid with razor blades, and he knew that everything was changing.

Picture her. See her.

He could. Almost as clearly as before. He remembered their wedding day, remembered her laughing uncontrollably as they cut the cake, delirious with the reality of it all, and the stab came again, but even less now, the ache minor and brief. Then it went altogether.

It's working. It's working.

He tentatively felt for the memory, the one that he'd been thinking about as he'd taken the knife to his own wrists, the one he was terrified to return to. Her in the early years, lying in bed beside him wearing both his t-shirt and the contented sweaty after glow of good sex, stroking his face and saying *I'm always gonna look after you.* It was that touch more distant now ... *but ....*

It was nice. It was a happy memory. Without the pain, it was good to think about.

Robert opened his eyes wide in disbelief, not knowing whether to laugh or cry with delight. And he saw the freshly broken mess before him.

Mister Grief was hunched into a ball, clear liquid dripping through the splayed fingers of the hand that covered his eyes. His shoulders, covered by the enormous coat and balled around his ears, seemed to have swallowed his pink head, swollen as it was now with the veins that stood out in clear relief against his skin. His entire body shook, and another ruined moan escaped from his lips, flecks of spit bursting forth as he did so. Robert released Mister Grief's hand like he'd been burnt. Like Mister Grief was contagious. They were done. Robert could feel it. He could see it in everything, in the shitty carpet, in the shitty décor, in the shitty lighting. Grief is a filter, and we place it into the molecules of everything that we see without our knowledge. Now, for Robert, it was gone, and he was seeing the world in a way that he didn't even realize he'd stopped seeing it.

"Are you ..." Robert began to ask, not knowing what else to say but, despite himself, not really caring. It was an unbelievably stupid question, and besides, he just wanted to be out of there, *away*, wanted to just go *crazy* with relief. And those who have known grief—if they are honest, and know the depths of their hearts—fear the grieving. They fear its return, and Robert was no different.

Grief put his other hand to his face, said something unintelligible, and tumbled off the chair to the floor, curling into a ball and beginning to rock back and forth.

You will have to let yourself out, he'd said.

Robert watched for a few moments, fascinated and torn, observing something that once was so familiar and seeing it now like a interested patron of a museum.

You can't help him. You know you can't. There's nothing you can do. Let's go.

"I'll have the money ready for you," Robert said, awkwardly, as he moved towards the door, feeling like a terrible human being and reminding himself that Grief had come to him, not the other way round, that this had been *his* idea and that he knew what he was doing. Even so, leaving someone like this ...

There is nothing *you can do.*

"Thank you," he added. "Thank you so much. *So much.*"

Then he turned and left, leaving Mister Grief on the floor of his room in the Formula One.

***

Jerry hadn't said a word as Robert told him of everything that had happened in Mister Grief's hotel room. He'd simply sat on the sofa nursing his drink with his expression completely blank. Now that Robert was finished, he was realizing that he had no idea if Jerry thought that he was completely crazy, or if his friend believed him.

"Obviously, I did as he said," Robert continued, watching Jerry's face now and beginning to feel a little foolish. He'd been so lost in his recollection that he hadn't even stopped to consider if Jerry had been on board with the whole thing once it got *really* crazy. "I didn't do four countries in eight weeks—I thought that was a bit much, that Mister Grief had forgotten how normal people live their lives—but I made sure I went a *long* way away. Australia for four weeks, New Zealand for four weeks. I didn't see hide nor hair of Mister Grief, which is understandable really."

Jerry said something so quietly that Robert couldn't hear it.

"Sorry?" he asked, thinking *I guess this is where I find out if you're calling the loony bin or not.*

"I said ... how did it feel afterwards?" Jerry asked, his face suddenly so full of yearning that Robert immediately forgot his relief as soon as it came. Robert smiled gently, and considered the question. How could he describe it?

"It was ..." he started, trying to find words other than those Mister Grief had used and struggling to do so. "It was *warm,* Jerry, and I don't mean the weather. When the memories remain and the grief is gone ... to be able to think of her and not feel that *ache* ... it felt warm. A sadness that she was gone, but a sadness like ... like the way you feel when a good party is over. The memories became a comfort. That's the best way I can put it. And the *change* ... to not wake up every day dreading the time between now and sleeping again. To not feel like every step meant pulling your feet out of mud, to not struggle to breathe ... to get up and think *Ok, breakfast at a café, read the paper, then maybe go and see an early movie.* The difference, Jerry. It's a cliché, but it was like being born again. It really was."

Jerry nodded slowly in response, and Robert could see that he still hadn't done it justice. How could he? How could express the inconceivable relief?

"Ok," Jerry said, and Robert saw that his eyes were beginning to water, his nose wrinkling as he held it back. Robert had offered his friend, a man who was not only dying of thirst but who had given up on the very concept of water, a drink. "I want to do it. I want ... I want that."

"You believe me?" Robert said, needing him to say it. Jerry nodded quickly, wiped at his face, straightened up.

"Yes. Yes, of course I do. Robert, *look at you.*" Jerry gestured up and down Robert's proud form, standing on the opposite side of the room. "Now look at me. This is where you were. *Look* where you were. Even if the man was simply insane or a liar and a very, *very* good hypnotist ... it worked on you ... I want that." He drained his drink in one go with a shaking hand, and set the glass down. "He said he had one more in him, didn't he? That he needed one more? And it can't have been long enough for him to have recovered and taken on another client yet," Jerry continued rapidly, already hungrily moving on the practical side of things. He became animated, his eyes shining. It was a different Jerry to the quiet, reserved man Robert usually knew. "So I can be next. How can you contact him? Oh wait, he was coming to collect, wasn't he? Has he already been?"

To Jerry's surprise, Robert looked confused for a second; then Jerry saw comprehension dawn on Robert's tanned face. Robert closed his eyes briefly, waved a hand, deadly serious.

"No, sorry," he said. "I hadn't finished. I've not explained this very well. Sorry, shit, I'm an idiot. I didn't mean that."

"What? What *did* you mean?"

"Mister Grief ... he can't help you, Jerry."

"Why not?" Jerry looked angry, his face flushed, like a child hearing a broken promise. The anger of the desperate man.

"Because Mister Grief is dead," Robert said, gently.

The room fell silent. Robert looked sad himself ... guilty. Jerry's face went from red to white, stunned by the news. The open cell door had just slammed shut in his face.

"But you said!" Jerry cried, confused and dismayed. "*He can help you,* you said that!

"I did," Robert said, his tone still calm and measured. "But I didn't mean Mister Grief. He's not who's going to help you."

***

FIVE DAYS EARLIER

Robert's doorbell rang. Since he'd gotten back from his trip, he'd found himself happy to stay in—unlike before, when he'd been constantly torn between curling up into a ball on the bedroom floor and desperate to be out in the open air, in the car, driving insanely fast to escape the weight on his back—but after his time away, and his release from the prison that had become his life, being home was *nice.* Having guests again and being *happy* to have them there was just wonderful, even if he had to put on a bit of a show now and then to stop people thinking that he'd lost it and was in a world of his own where he'd never been married, or on drugs.

But he always flinched at the sound of someone on the doorstep.

He didn't think Mister Grief would be coming to collect for some time, but even so, he had no desire to see him. It wasn't just concern that Grief may arrive and announce that he'd changed his mind. The thirty day returns period had already been over for a whole month. No, Robert simply did not *want* to see him. Robert respected Mister Grief—pitied him even, felt for the man—but Grief now embodied everything about Robert's life before what he would refer to, in his own head, as *the treatment.* He didn't want it coming back into his life in any way, the way an alcoholic doesn't want to sign for a booze delivery for someone else.

But despite all that, he'd been hoping that Mister Grief would come soon, because he had to. He needed him to talk to him about Jerry. He needed to be able to contact him in case Jerry didn't get better.

It was around eight in the evening, and therefore Robert looked through the front door's spyhole before opening it, performing that curious quirk of human nature wherein we assume that the only people that would come to our homes to do us harm would do so after dark. A very large man stood on the doorstep, and although he wasn't immediately concerned, Robert's eyes flicked to the door's chain out of habit. It was on. The man was standing slightly off to the side, so Robert couldn't make out any features, but the breadth and height of the shoulders that he *could* see told him that his evening visitor was somewhat of a unit.

"Hello?" Robert asked, speaking through the door without opening it. Men this large didn't just turn up after eight at night, and he had no deliveries due. "Can I help you?"

"Good evening, Mister Terence. Yes, I believe you can help me," a deep voice said from Robert's front porch, speaking with an amused tone. Robert didn't like it. He immediately felt uneasy. "I gather you have a balance to settle, and I'm here to speak to you about that."

Robert felt very cold all of a sudden, a blend of guilt and fear, caught out and exposed. This person knew about what had happened with Mister Grief, and this was *not* Mister Grief. He had no problem paying Grief for the service he had rendered, and had fully intended to pay and had been ready to do so. But here was a third party, someone who not only knew what had happened, but had turned up to collect Grief's money. This was not good. This was supposed to be *secret,* and for a reason.

The Rothbury people. The last remnants of the organization. Oh, shit.

Then:

Calm down. He could just be someone Grief sent to collect the money from you?

Robert began to panic. He didn't know what to do. Feign ignorance? Admit it?

At least talk to the fucker before you start singing like a canary or lying your ass off.

"I've not received any collection letters," Robert said, trying to sound confident and pulling out the first thing he could think of as his pulse raced.

"And I don't like people turning up at night, either." The last part was an attempt at bravado, but it sounded exactly how Robert felt. Terrified.

"No, no, I understand," said the man, his deep voice resonating through door's wood. He sounded as if he was grinning. "Not ideal, I agree, but I'm not here for very long and this is the earliest I could arrive. I much prefer to take care of business as soon as possible. As for letters, you wouldn't have received one. Our mutual acquaintance was hardly one for paperwork, as you know."

Was?

Robert pushed his eye to the spyhole again, dimly aware of a sensation in his head. It was as if there were pins and needles inside his mind. In his brain.

Spiders. Like spiders trying to get into the cracks in my mind.

His strength faded a little, and he struggled to focus his gaze through the small fish-eye lens. He noticed the type of jacket the stranger was wearing. A donkey jacket.

"Yes. I have the right house, I see," the voice said, and it sounded satisfied, that amused tone ever present. "Why don't you let me in?"

"*Rothbury* ..." Robert murmured, and his voice was slurred. Then the spiders were gone and the world was in focus again, as his ears took a moment to realize that the gargling sound coming from the other side of the door was laughter.

"Oh, no," the voice croaked, coming out as a hiss through its guffaws, "hardly. I could show you, but you wouldn't want that, so you're just going to have to *trust* me." A chuckle again. "Mister Terence, my brother is dead. I believe you knew him as Mister Grief, and that he performed an extremely valuable service for you. My name is John, and I'm here to collect the fee for that service; I know you have it ready, in cash, under the bed upstairs. I know I don't *need* to threaten you; you're a man who intends to pay his debts. This is better for us both. You don't need to open the door for me to make sure I get my money, so why don't you open up and we can both have a drink to my brother before I'm on my way?"

John? Grief is dead?

'*My brother was the most feared child at that school.*'

John didn't need to threaten, as he said, nor was he making any threats. Yet at the same time, he clearly was. Unsure of what he was doing, Robert opened the door with a hand that was shaking so much it could barely undo the chain.

***

"I like your house," John finally said, after taking in the living room without speaking for nearly five minutes. Robert had just stood there dumbly, too scared to speak or to ask any questions. As he'd looked around, picking up pictures and replacing them with a nod of agreement to an unseen party, the smile had never left the big man's face, turning to Robert every now and again and flashing the grin his way, enjoying the awkwardness.

And he *was* big, huge in his jacket—almost identical to his brother's—but stocky where Grief had been skinny, and taller too, surely pushing 6'6". He seemed to fill even Robert's large living room, and it wasn't just his size. The man had a magnetism, an aura. Robert kept expecting to notice steam rising from John, whatever was in him being given physical presence. But there was no steam, just John's ever present grin shining from the ghostly-pale skin of his face. Where Grief had seemed almost frail, John was thunderously robust, a blonde crew-cut topping his fleshy block of a head. He seemed slightly older than Robert, but only older in the way a piece of wood can harden with time.

The grin wasn't malicious. But it was expressing an amusement that, Robert felt, came from seeing the affairs and concerns of ordinary people as just that: amusing. To see that in someone on John's alleged level of ability was a terrifying thought.

"I think we should toast him, don't you?" John said, his deep voice seeming to boom off the walls of the previously silent room. "You and I are strangers, and my brother was far more to me than he would ever be to you, but I haven't yet been in the company of anyone who knew him. I don't socialize." *I bet,* Robert thought, but didn't respond. John's grin spread a little wider, and he pointed to Robert's liquor cabinet. "Shall I?" Robert simply nodded, wanting to ask so many questions but frightened to say a word. John plucked a bottle of tequila from the cabinet—a highly unusual choice for a neat toast, and yet Robert somehow wasn't surprised—and took two glasses from the top shelf, placing them on Robert's coffee table.

"A toast, and I shall be on my way," John said airily, bending to pour a generous measure. "After collecting my brother's fee, of course. He would want me to have it. I'm sure you agree."

Anything you want. Just get out of my house.

"How ..." Robert said, and froze when John looked up, sharply. When John cocked his head to the side, raising an eyebrow, Robert shivered, but took the cue. "How did he die?" John chuckled ... but there was a twitch at his left eye.

'I should think I'm about the only person he likes,' Robert thought, hearing Grief's voice again. It was apparently true.

"Guess," John said, and Robert suddenly knew, nearly wetting himself at the realization.

"Suicide," he whispered, and John's smile turned into a closed-lipped smirk as he nodded slowly.

I'm responsible. I was the one that tipped him over the edge, a job too far. He couldn't take it, the last layer of concrete set too thick, was too much. And now his brother is here.

John saw the terror in Robert's face, and laughed out loud.

"Don't worry, Mister Terence," he said, finishing the drinks and closing off the bottle once more. "You were a client, and he knew the risks. I think he overestimated his own durability, or rather underestimated the cumulative damage he was doing to himself. I did tell him, but he knew best. Little brothers, what can I say?" He straightened, handed Robert a glass and held one himself. "He was found hanged six days ago. He'd left a note, and what it says is my business only as it was addressed to me. Don't ask how I know, and I think you can guess anyway. I have my people. I already knew about you, of course. My brother and I always knew of each other's clients."

Robert didn't know what to say, and couldn't meet John's gaze. He felt relief ... but there was still the news that, client or not, he was at least part of the reason that a man had taken his own life.

It was his choice. He knew what he was doing.

The thought didn't make much difference.

"I shall miss him," John said, still with that ridiculous grin at total juxtaposition to his words. "I should really toast him at his burial, but even with my reach I'm not sure that will be possible. The body is in Australia and getting it transported without causing too many ripples—or the body being intercepted for research—will be difficult." John's smiling gaze bored into Robert's eyes as he flinched slightly at John's words.

Australia.

Robert's guilt turned back into a selfish, terrified relief. He'd had a very, very near miss.

"Here," John said, lifting his glass and—when Robert didn't respond, standing instead in a stunned daze—gripping Robert's wrist with a catcher's mitt of a hand and lifting Robert's glass for a forced toast. "There we go," John said. "To my brother. Drink." The last part wasn't an invitation. It was a command. Robert snapped out of his funk and drained the tequila, coughing furiously after he did so. He noticed even John stifle a slight cough, but the smile never left his face. "Thankyou, Mister Terence, I'm sure that my brother would have appreciated that. And now, if you can fetch the fee for me, then I shall be on my way."

Robert couldn't get up the stairs to fetch the briefcase fast enough.

He carried it back down into the living room and handed it over to John's huge, waiting hand. The big man took it without opening it to count it. He knew it would be correct.

"Thank you Mister Terence. You won't see me again. I'll be seeing a client in town this evening and then I won't return."

"A client?" Robert asked without thinking, regretting the words as soon as they'd left his mouth.

He was going to leave, why are you keeping him talking?!

"Yes," said John, managing to look more amused than ever by the question. "Unlike my brother, I have no, shall we say, after effects from the work I do, even though I work with people with similar or identical ailments to yours. And unlike him, I don't worry about pursuit any where near as much, although I do take *some* precautions. And my work, to me, is *fascinating*," he said, and his eyes narrowed. He meant it. "He told you what my gift is?"

Robert nodded. John chuckled.

"He told you that they were all afraid of me, then," John said. "Doesn't sound frightening, does it? At first thought? When compared to children that can kill you with their minds? But there are other ways of dying."

Robert didn't say anything.

"But yes, the same gift can be used in other ways," John said. "I could have helped you myself, if you'd come to me ... but most would prefer my brother's way, that's for certain. Grief doesn't give you people a lot of choice though, does it? You'll take any way out, if it was an option. Psychologists will tell you that grief is your friend, but that's because it's an unavoidable process with a goal at the end. If my brother's way had been available to all, they'd say otherwise. I've been doing it for a very long time, since my teens even. Well, not like *now*; at the very start, it was all accidental, but I was still *doing* it." John chuckled gently to himself, almost purring.

One half of Robert's brain was busy registering *you people* while the other was registering what John was actually saying.

'People with similar or identical ailments to yours.'

Jerry.

"John," Robert said, trying to keep the tremor from his voice and hardly believing he was even saying the words, "I might need to be able to ... contact you. I know someone that might need your help."

***

Robert told Jerry how it would work. Jerry immediately scorned it, angry that the better way had been an inadvertent tease and nearly devastated by its loss. Robert pointed to his own wrist, to the thin but pink scar not covered by a watch.

"If I pulled back *your* shirt sleeves, Jerry," Robert said as gently as he could, paraphrasing Mister Grief himself, "what would I see?"

That was a part of the story that Robert had left out. The part about Mister Grief leaving something in Robert, a very faint echo of himself, a layer of his own. That Robert could walk into a crowd and *know*, the individuals standing out to him as if they were wearing coats made of dull light. Even those laughing with friends, putting on a near superhuman effort to hide the truth. It *was* only an intuition ... but too deep to be described as such. Jerry cried out to Robert from the other side of the room without even knowing that he did so.

"That's too much," Jerry said, absent mindedly rubbing at his wrists. "It isn't worth it."

But he didn't look at Robert when he said it, and Robert saw the cogs turning.

***

Jerry blinked, and the first thing he noticed was his bedroom door closing as someone left, pulling the door behind them. Then he noticed that he was in his own bedroom, seated on the edge of the bed itself, fully clothed. He had no idea how he got there.

Wait, where was I this morning?

He didn't remember ... did he? He remembered having breakfast. He'd seen Robert last night ...

In the left hand corner of the room, his video camera was set up on its seldom-used tripod. The lens cap was on the floor, and the camera lens was turned to the wall as if someone had wanted to get a close up of the wallpaper. *No,* to expose the mini-HDMI socket in the back of the camera, where a cable was attached that led to the flat screen TV—

The TV was on, and a video was playing. Whoever had just left must have set it in motion just before they did. A man's face was on the screen. A man with a blonde crew cut and a thick, solid-looking head. The face was incredibly pale, and the man was smiling.

"Hello, Mister Palmer," the man onscreen said. His voice was deep and commanding, but sounded as if he was remembering something funny. "Do not be alarmed. You may or may not remember our meeting, and if you don't then you soon will. This isn't an exact science, I'm afraid, and sometimes other unintended elements get involved, but those often come back by themselves. I always leave an orientation video to ensure a smooth transition, if only to get you through the first few days."

Jerry felt like he should be scared, or at least *alarmed* as the man onscreen had said—Jerry had no idea who this man was, or what he was talking about—but something at the back of his mind told him that all was well. The man was telling the truth, and he knew that somehow this was all part of a plan. He listened. A thud came from downstairs as someone closed the front door behind them.

"In a nutshell, you need to know this; you were married to Mandy Palmer for twenty years. You had two children, Lisa and Karen, who you will remember. Again, if you don't right now, that will come back very quickly."

Jerry raised his eyebrows lazily. Yep, Lisa and Karen. Of course he remembered his girls. They were coming back from their auntie's today, a much needed break for the pair of them.

Much needed why?

He couldn't remember.

"She died, I'm afraid, and you couldn't go on living as a result. And so, introduced by a friend, you came to me."

That one came straight away. *Robert.* Robert had helped him.

"I agreed to help you for a fee of five thousand pounds that you will notice is missing from your account."

Something flashed across Jerry's mind at the mention of money, a discussion that had taken place. The memory wasn't of price though, it was of something said *during* that discussion.

Let me explain it this way, Mister Palmer. My brother dealt in feelings. I do not. Say you were a great lover of jazz. And you went to the greatest jazz concert of all time, performed by Charlie Parker himself, and you were so moved by the performance that not only would you never forget it, you were in floods of tears. That is how much you loved the experience.

I do not love jazz. And so I would remember the concert, and if I happened to know anything of jazz myself I would perhaps notice the standard of the performance. But I would not be moved to floods of tears. I would simply see the concert.

"To your left you will see a large envelope."

Jerry looked to his left. There, on the bed, lay a manila envelope that said MANDY PALMER: A LIFE in handwriting that he didn't recognize.

"That is a dossier that you compiled with my help in order to function within the realms of your family, friends, and financial matters," the man onscreen continued. "Any inaccuracies contained therein are entirely your own, and I take no responsibility for anything that you may have left out. I strongly suggest that you memorise it immediately."

Jerry found himself nodding. Of course. It was only reasonable to say so. Dimly, he tried to get his head around the fact that he'd been *married* ... he remembered the girls being born. And holidays. And birthdays. He felt like being told of a wife he didn't remember should mean the loss of twenty years of memories, but that wasn't the case at all. He remembered the last twenty years; it was like being asked *do you remember where you live.* Of course he did. Yet in all of his memories ... there was a just a slightly *missing* part, a greyness that caused intrigue, but no fear. No confusion. It somehow made sense.

The man onscreen stopped speaking, and then disappeared as the camera turned to reveal Jerry himself, wearing the same clothes that he was wearing now. He looked uncertain, terrified, very much at odds with the way Jerry currently felt.

"Now?" onscreen Jerry asked to someone off camera, presumably the previous man. "Uh ... this is, uh, to say that, uh, you agreed to this and that this is what you want." Onscreen Jerry paused in his script, and then spoke from the heart, eyes flooding. "I'm sorry, man. I couldn't ... I just couldn't ..." He paused again, then continued with a voice that was oozing sorrow. "She was beautiful. She was just ... amazing. You'll see the photos and you'll think she was beautiful, but believe me, that won't do her the justice she ..." Onscreen Jerry stopped again. "I'm sorry," he repeated, and then he was waving the camera away wordlessly. The other man then came back onscreen, still grinning.

"Please erase this tape, " he said happily. "As previously agreed."

Something pinged into Jerry's mind. A warning.

You know what I can do. There are other ways to die.

Then Robert's words, strangely:

He could take everything. *The memory of how to walk. Or of who you were, along with the ability to read, or understand any language, or what people were. Imagine having an adult brain but experiencing the world with as much knowledge of it as a baby. You wouldn't know what your own fingers were, how to eat ...*

He would erase the tape, for certain.

"Good luck, Mister Palmer," the man said. "You'll be fine." The tape ended.

He heard the front door move again downstairs, and this time it was someone coming in; six pairs of feet, Mandy's sister Pauline and the two girls. He heard them laughing, and he knew that was good.

Jerry looked down at the dossier to his left, and picked it up. It was sealed, and heavy. He would read it straightaway. The calmness in his head was both strange and blissful, and he didn't know that it was because it had been the very opposite for quite some time. Part of him had died, he knew, just like his apparent wife; yet he wasn't concerned. It was the *darndest* feeling.

You owe Robert a drink, he thought, and knew this was true, if not how much.

He knew for certain that he was hungry, though. That needed to be taken care of straightaway. He tucked the dossier under his arm, and began to make his way downstairs. He'd start reading over a sandwich, holed up in the study with a beer. He'd say hello to the girls and Pauline first, see how they were doing. It'd be good to see them.

Halfway down the stairs, without realizing he was doing it, he began to whistle.

2. The Crash

Stress, and the distraction of a phone call (plus, of course, many other processes that Sarah couldn't possibly know about) all led to the crash. Sarah simply thought it was because she wasn't paying attention, which she wasn't.

"Danny, I'm heading home now," she spoke into the air inside her BMW Mini, the dashboard's Bluetooth setup and mini microphone picking up her words. "I'm literally going to grab the fabric and shoot straight out again. Don't panic, we're still going to have a lot of time."

"Those *wankers*," Danny's frantic voice said over the Mini's speakers. "They had one job to do. Fucking *puce*. Who has *puce* in 2015? When have you *ever* ordered *puce*?"

"I know, and I'm getting a *major* discount next time, but listen: it's sorted now," she soothed, trying desperately to reassure. If Danny got stressed out, his fragile artistic temperament went to hell. They didn't have time for the tears and tantrums that happened the *last* time an order went wrong. "The delivery guy dropped the replacements off half an hour ago, as promised. The *tables* are all dressed, at least?" Danny's responding scoff was as clear as a bell, even over the slightly unreliable mobile signal Danny was having to use at the country estate.

"Yes, of *course*, Sare," he said, sounding exasperated. "Just grab the stuff and get here as soon as you can, and this just might possibly, maybe, *somehow* avoid being a total and unmitigated *disaster*. Why, *why* does this always happen to *me?*"

Us, dickhead, Sarah thought but didn't say. *Why does this always happen to us.* She loved Danny like a brother, but as far as business partners went, his rampant and frequent drama queening could be a real pain in the backside. She was stressed out to all hell herself, and the last thing she needed was to be managing Danny's fragile state of mind. They could fix it. The wrong order had arrived and arrived late, sure—their usual suppliers being uncharacteristically slack—but they could fix it now the supplier had made good, sending out the correct order via same day courier. They could go through the night if they had to, she told herself, even though it would make the next day tough to say the least.

Are you cut out to run a business?

It wasn't the first time the voice in her head had spoken up to ask that question, and she knew that it wouldn't be the last.

Something small jumped inside a bush when it wasn't supposed to, or perhaps it jumped too early or late. Either way, a pigeon that was supposed to be sitting on top of the bush for another three minutes and forty four seconds took to the air in a panic, shooting forwards at windscreen height.

Of course you are, these things happen to every startup—

The pigeon flashed across Sarah's windscreen and startled her into yanking the steering wheel sideways in an instinctive effort to avoid a collision with anything. Unfortunately, this had the opposite result to that which was intended, and Sarah's Mini crashed into the door of a Mercedes Benz parked nearby.

She'd only been doing just under 25mph--it was a residential area, after all--but that was still enough to cave in the Merc's driver side door. She'd tried to brake in time, but had failed dramatically, and now her Mini had come to a stop resting up against the Merc. Its alarm started to sound, a squalling repetitive shriek that pounded against Sarah's shell shocked brain.

Normally, Sarah would have been thinking *Oh my god, I just hit another car, is there anyone inside it,* or perhaps *Oh my god, that could have been a child,* or *Oh my god, that bloody pigeon.* But today, as she blinked stupidly in the shocked aftermath of a low-speed car crash, all her brain could latch onto was the mental image of the flash she'd seen.

Blue. It had been blue.

It had. The second the Mini's front bumper had crumpled the Merc's door, even in the blind, in-the-moment panic that came with all crashes, the thing that had stood out the most had been the blue flash that had filled Sarah's vision for a nanosecond. She'd had flashes before that had been similar; the time she'd fallen from her horse in her twenties (when she still had Buttercup) and banged her head.

Poof, white flash. And then there hadn't really been another one until she'd reached her third decade a few years ago, that time she'd slipped on some ice while Christmas shopping and landed on her chin. Bang, white flash.

But this had been different. This had been just that fraction of a second longer, long enough to freak her out. Her entire field of vision, filled with blue, the street and the cars and the houses and the sky all disappearing for a moment; and hadn't there been a sound as well?

Not a different sound. A longer *sound. The noise of the crash seemed to ... lock. Like a stuck CD. Not 'bang', and over, but bannnnnnng, for as long as the blue was there. And then it had ended.*

It had to be whiplash, and shock. Shock could affect anything.

Can you get whiplash at twenty five miles an hour? You hardly even moved in your seat. That was a collision, but it wasn't what you could call a crash.

She was pretty sure you could. She was pretty sure it was one of those things that could happen in any situation, like dying by falling out of bed.

But your head didn't jerk. Did it?

It must have done. Why would there have been a flash like that otherwise?

"Sarah? What the hell was that? What happened? I heard a bang."

Danny's voice. In the panic of the crash, she'd forgotten that he was still on the phone.

"*Fuck!*" Sarah gasped. It wasn't said in anger, more in dismay. "Yes! Yes I bloody have, there was this pigeon--"

"Are you alright?"

She checked her neck. There was no ache there, but she was pretty sure that whiplash didn't hurt straightaway.

"I think so," she said, trying to breathe slowly to get her heartbeat to slow down. "Hold on a second."

Still slightly stunned, thoughts of the room dressing forgotten for a moment, she got out of the car and moved around to the front of it to look at the damage to both the Merc and the Mini. The blatting of the Merc's alarm was even louder now that she was out of the protective bubble of her own vehicle. The enormous dent in the Mercedes Benz' door looked even worse from out here ... but her front bumper, miraculously, seemed only to be slightly cracked.

That's gonna be ... expensive.

She was insured, of course, but the household budget was maxed out as it was since she'd started the business. This was going to put the premium up, plus she hadn't gone with an insurer who would protect her no-claims bonus because her current one had offered a cheaper overall price. The premium would go up even more. Dave had been incredibly understanding about them having to tighten their belts while she chased a dream, but even so...

"Sarah? Sarah?" said Danny's voice over the car's speaker. She'd left the door open, and Danny's questions were just audible over the sound of the Merc's alarm. Sarah didn't move. After a moment, her head turned, and looked both ways up and down the street. It was a quiet street as it was, and today there was no one around.

Yet.

"Sarah? What's happened? Can you still get here?"

The room dressing. Time was tight as it was. She still had to pick up the fabric and get back over to Danny, and despite what she'd said to him—and to herself—she really wasn't sure if they *could* get everything ready in time, at least if she wanted it to be to the standard the client wanted. And Sarah's darker instincts whispered the poisonous, selfish words into her mind that so many people contemplating the same action say to themselves:

Look at what they're driving. They can afford to get this fixed. It'll be nothing to them, but disastrous *to me.*

She made her decision.

Sarah almost ran back around to the driver's side of the Mini in her haste, heart beating hard all over again. This was the first criminal thing she'd ever done in her entire life. After all, she'd always been the good girl, the one that played by the rules, chasing life's house points. She told herself that she was doing it for Dave, to not put any more financial stress onto already stressed shoulders, but every instinct in her told her that was just bullshit. It was wrong, and she knew it. She'd made a mistake, and was making someone else pay for it, and probably making them pay out a lot.

They can afford it. They can afford it.

She jumped back into the driver's seat and slammed the door shut, the Merc's alarm mercifully quieting down a fraction once the door was closed. It still didn't quiet the alarm going of inside her guilty head.

"Don't worry, Danny, there's no harm done here," she said in a trembling voice, feeling a little sick as she said it. She reversed the Mini, wincing as the dustbin lid-sized dent in the Merc's door was revealed in its entirety. "I'm on my way to the house. I'm literally gonna run in, grab the boxes, and run out." She thanked God that Dave was off today. It had saved valuable time that she hadn't had to sit in to receive the delivery, and as she thought this she realized that she was already starting to forget that which she'd *just* done to a stranger's car. Was it that easy? She felt even more sick and anxious. Danny's voice on the phone sounded shocked.

"Have you just done a *runner?*" he asked in an almost comical playground whisper.

"No, of course not," she snapped, flushing bright red even though she was alone. "I told you, there's no damage, I was lucky. Look, I'll call you again when I'm on my way." She ended the call without waiting for a response, and two minutes later she was pulling up outside her house.

She'd forgotten her house key.

"*Fuck!*" Sarah said again, this time definitely in anger. She taken the spare car key that morning in her haste, not wanting to waste time finding her usual bunch, but forgetting that the spare set had no front door key on it. As her hands clenched on the wheel and her mind raced, the answer already came to her.

Dave's off for the day, you idiot.

Relief washed over her. Of course. That was a bloody narrow escape. She snatched her phone out of its dashboard holder and dialed Dave's number. He'd in bed right now, sleeping off the previous night's late shift, and thanks to the earplugs he wore in bed he never heard the front door. Her number was stored in his iPhone's Do Not Disturb feature, however, and he kept it by his pillow so she could get in touch in an emergency. She felt bad ringing it—this technically wasn't an emergency—but she desperately needed his help all the same.

What if he's not in?

No. Dave never went anywhere on his days off. The phone began to ring, and Sarah used this time to close her eyes and breathe, to slow down the blood pulsing in her temples.

You can do it. It's going to be okay.

Then she saw the crash again, and her stomach turned over. She could always go back tomorrow, leave a note—

You know you're not gonna do that.

"Hello?" said Dave's voice in her ear. He sounded sleepy.

"Baby, are you in?" Sarah said quickly, wanting to verbally kick him into high gear but trying to keep it together. "Are you in bed?"

"Yeah," he yawned. "Fancied a nap. Everything ok?"

"Afraid I need you to let me in," Sarah said, opening the door and getting out of the car. "Left my key. In a *real* hurry. Where are the boxes?"

"In the hallway," Dave sighed, obviously not too keen on getting out of bed. "Let me know when you're five minutes away and I'll get up and keep an eye out."

"No, I'm already *here*," Sarah said testily, but trying not to snap. It wasn't Dave's fault that she'd been stupid enough to leave her key, even if he wasn't being helpful. "I need to get in *now*, baby. I'm sorry. You can just open the door and go straight back to bed."

"*Unnnnnn*," Dave said, but she heard sheets being flung back as he sulked his way out of bed. "Okay, okay. Coming down."

"Thanks. Sorry," Sarah said, and hung up as she crossed the street. What they called their 'house' wasn't really a house at all; it was a large flat that was located above a plumber's office, but because the entrance to the flat was at street level on the side of the building that actually faced the street, being all brick with one doorway to access the stairs—the glass frontage of the plumbers office being at a right angle to the street itself—it always *felt* like they could call it their house. They didn't own it, but they were saving for a place. *Saving slowly,* she thought as she flicked through the recent calls section of her phone to find Danny's number. In her state of high anxiety, she was suddenly wondering about the centerpieces; they were supposed to be laid out in pairs. Had she told Danny that? She was so wired that she was doubting everything.

Was there any CCTV near that Mercedes?

She didn't think so, and couldn't worry about that now. She began to hop gently from foot to foot on the doorstep.

"Hello?"

"Danny, what did I tell you about the centerpieces?"

"What do you mean?"

"You know they have to be in pairs, right?"

"What do you mean?"

As she drew in a deep breath to keep calm, it occurred to Sarah that Dave should have come downstairs by now. She peered through the frosted glass panel in the front door to try and see some movement, and saw none.

Has he ... has he gone back to fucking sleep?

Anger immediately exploded in her head like a spouting geyser. Now she had an excuse to vent, whether she realized that was the reason why she was about to lose it or not.

"Hang on Danny," she said, an uncharacteristic snarl in her voice, and put him on hold as she re-dialled Dave's number. He picked up after two rings.

"This better be *really* good, as I've just laid down again."

"You haven't opened the fucking door!"

"Of course I have."

"Dave. Don't be a dick right now. It's the last thing I need."

"Sarah, don't *you* be a dick. Don't blame me because you forgot your fucking key. The door's open, I unlocked it, get in and get your stuff, don't wake me up again please."

"You haven't even come downstairs, I've stood here the entire time!"

There was a sigh down the line.

"Baby, I know you're stressed, but there's a *very* simple way of ending this bullshit. Turn the door handle, and open the door. Sleeping now, bye."

He hung up. Sarah was too angry to even move for a second, exacerbated by her confusion. Dave had sounded genuine. But he hadn't even come down the *stairs*, so he couldn't have opened the door. She'd been standing there the entire time. Knowing that it wasn't going to work, she tried the handle. It was the kind that wouldn't turn if the door was locked, and of course, it didn't move as much as a millimeter.

"Sarah?"

It was Danny, off hold and back on the line now that the other call had ended. Too angry now to even respond, Sarah simply dialed Dave straight back, finger shaking as she dialed.

That fucking arsehole. That arsehole! *He thinks* now *is a good time to do this. This is* not *funny, he knows what a big deal today is—*

Dave picked up.

"Bloody hell, I was just about to put it on airplane mode so this really better be very good indeed--"

"*Open the fucking door!*" Sarah hissed, wanting to scream but not wanting anyone in the houses on the opposite side of the street to hear her. "*I can't believe you're doing this!*" She felt tears of frustration and hurt start to bubble up, shocked at what Dave was doing. He was so understanding, always, but sometimes these misplaced attempts at humor were very ill-timed; this, however, was just so *mean*, given the circumstances, given how much he knew this event meant to her.

"What the hell are you talking about?" Dave snapped, angry and shocked now himself. Sarah *never* spoke to him like that. "I've *opened the door*. The door is *open, open* the door *is*. Stop taking your stress out on me, get a grip, open the door--"

"It's *locked!*" Sarah barked, interrupting. "You've, you've, you've gone back to sleep and just, just, *dreamed* you unlocked it or something because you were thinking about doing it *but please just actually come downstairs and open the fucking door!*"

"I've *done*—fine. *Fine,*" Dave barked, and the only sound coming over the phone's earpiece was the sound of the bedroom door being flung open and Dave muttering to himself. She waited on the doorstep, breathing heavily, more wound up than ever. They *never* argued.

Then she heard a door opening on the other end of the line.

... what?

Dave spoke.

"Are you winding *me* up or something?" He didn't sound angry now. He sounded confused.

"What do ... what do you mean?"

"You're not even here!"

"What do you *mean?*" Panic had started to creep into her voice. Dave wasn't joking. She could hear that he wasn't joking.

"Sarah, I mean I'm standing here with the door open and *you aren't here.* I can't let you *in* if you're not here."

"I *am!*" she shrieked. She suddenly wondered if perhaps *she* was the one dreaming. "Dave, *stop* it." A sob came into her voice, and Dave heard it.

"Baby ... baby," he said, but she could hear the confusion in his voice, and her anxiety shot up even further. What the fuck was going *on?* "I'm ... look, I need you to calm down, ok?"

"I'm *here,* I'm right *here,* what do you *see?*"

"Baby, look, I'm standing right on the doorstep and I can see the pub across the street, the neighbor's houses, and a couple of cars, and you aren't here. I need you to calm down, and breathe, and tell me what's happened."

"*Nothing's happened!*" she yelled, and began to yank on the unmoving door handle feverishly. "*I'm right here!*"

"How can ..." Dave paused, searching for some kind of logical approach. "Where are you parked?"

"I'm parked directly across from the house!" she cried. "The Mini is *bright red* for crying out loud, how can you miss it?"

"It's not there, baby," Dave said, his voice quiet and low now. She could hear the worry in his voice and it made her feel crazy. He thought something had happened and she'd gone nuts, she could tell. Cracking under the stress of her first major booking. "Look, uh ... where's Danny?" he continued. "Can I talk to Danny?"

"Don't fucking *do* that Dave," Sarah said, openly crying now, the stress and confusion and anger and dismay all piling up. She felt like she was going to faint. "I know my own goddamn doorstep. I know where I *live*. *I'm here*."

"Wait, I can see you," he said, suddenly, brightness coming into his voice.

Sarah looked at the closed door in front of her.

"Where are you?" she asked, bewildered.

"I can see you right now," he said, ignoring her. "Was this some sort of joke? Look ... whatever, look, screw it, just park the car and I'll bring the boxes out, I'm up now. I want to check that you're ok."

Park the car?

"What do you mean, park the car? I already parked! I parked across the street!"

"Sarah ..." Dave began to say, and then he stopped. There was silence down the line for a second.

"Dave?" she asked, her voice weak.

"I've ... I've got another call ..."

"What? Don't you answer it!"

"It's you ..."

WHAT?

"You're calling me ... your call is ... waiting ..."

Fear turned to total panic. This was a nightmare. It had to be. She needed to wake up.

"*Don't answer that!*"

"I ... wait there," he said, and the line went dead as he switched to the other call and put *her* on hold. Sarah stared at the phone in silence as Danny's call became the active connection, and Dave's name was faded out to show that he was on the other line.

"Sarah?" Danny said again, his voice tinny, coming from a foot away as Sarah gawped at her phone in silence. Numb, with a shaking hand, she put the phone to her ear.

"Hello ..." she whispered.

"What's going on? Have you got the stuff? I'm hands free here but I need to concentrate."

Sarah didn't answer, her eyes scanning up and down the street for another red Mini that may be approaching, anything that may explain *anything*.

"Danny ... I don't know what's ..."

Her eyes fell upon something very small a few feet away, and her heart froze.

It was a small leaf, perhaps detached from one of the neighbors hedges, almost entirely missable if not for the fact of its greenery against the concrete of the pavement. That, and the fact that it hung in the air half a foot above the ground, unmoving.

Sarah's hand fell away from her ear, her hand still maintaining a grip on the phone as her subconscious remembered that she was waiting for Dave to call back. On shaky legs she crossed the few feet before her to where the leaf was suspended. She started to crouch to get a better look, but her left leg just buckled, and she had to halt her downward momentum by putting out her empty right hand in time, bringing her almost into a runner's starting position with her face conveniently close to the impossible leaf. She didn't notice the pain in her knees as they ground into the hard pavement. How could she, when looking at the utterly impossible?

The leaf was blurred. It had been caught mid-motion, and as incredible as the fact of its suspension was—as if it were held in a block of invisible ice—the faint trail it left in the air behind it was even more so. *Trail* wasn't the right word; it looked somewhere between being stretched, and copied and repasted over and over again, a fraction of a millimeter further forward each time.

And Dave had been saying she wasn't there.

"Danny ... Danny ..." She looked at her phone. Danny had hung up.

She stood, slowly, and looked up and down the street. She noticed for the first time just how silent the street was; she hadn't been thinking of anything other than getting the boxes, of talking to Dave to get him to open the door, of what needed to be done next and next and next. But now she heard the eerie stillness, and realized that not one car had been past in all the time that she had been there. She looked back at the leaf, caught in the action of being blown gently up the street to wherever its final destination would be.

To her right was a lamppost. She reached out a hand and touched it; it was solid, real. She rapped it gently with her knuckles. There was no sound. And when she thought about it, hadn't there been a complete absence of noise when she'd been tugging on the door handle?

Her phone vibrated in her hand, showing that Dave was trying to reconnect, and she lifted it up with whiplike speed.

"*Hello?*" she said, the word crumbling halfway through as she started to cry. "Dave, please don't hang up, I'm so scared--"

"Sarah?" he asked, and he sounded almost as scared as she was.

"Yes, yes, this is me, baby, baby, I don't know what to *do,*" she sobbed, falling back against the lamppost. When she heard Dave talking next, terribly, it was away from the phone, addressing someone else. "She's on the line now, talk to her. You ... you have to hear this," he was saying, his voice flat and stunned. Then someone else came on the phone.

"Hello?" Sarah heard her own voice asking, crisp and clear and terrifying through the phone's sophisticated speaker. Sarah couldn't speak. "Hello?" the voice said again. It sounded impatient.

"Who are you?" Sarah whispered, already knowing the answer but not allowing herself to think it.

"Who are *you?*" the voice asked, a tone of stressed annoyance thick in her voice. Sarah understood why. The woman on the other end of the phone had enough on their plate without some lunatic playing games down the phone. Having to pick up the fabric was taking up time they couldn't afford as it was without having to deal with *this* crap. "Do you think this is funny?"

"Did you hit the Mercedes?" Sarah asked, not knowing that she was going to ask it. There was no immediate answer from the other end of the line, but Sarah did hear a slight intake of breath. Again, she understood why. The other Sarah had heard the voice, recognized it, and Sarah knew that, to the other Sarah, she was sounding like an outside manifestation of her own guilty conscience.

"How do you know about that?" the other Sarah asked, but she didn't sound as sure now, didn't sound quite as angry. "How do you sound like me?"

"How do you sound like *me?*" Sarah whined, and began to lose it. "*Get out of my house, get the fuck out of my house, let me in, let me in--*" She ran back to the front door and began banging on the handle, aware now of the complete lack of any sound of impact. She flicked off her shoe and began to smash its kitten heel against the door's frosted glass panel, but the effect was the same. An impact, yes, but no sound. She may as well have been hitting a mountain.

"Don't ... don't call this number again," the other Sarah said, sounding openly scared and Sarah screamed as she heard Dave in the background barking *no, don't hang up* and then the line went dead. Sarah stood on the doorstep in the silent street and made frantic whining noises and she tried to dial Dave's number over and over again, the phone trying to ring but never connecting, not even starting to ring or tell her the call failed. Crazily, she had five bars of signal.

How do I have signal, she thought, even as terror filled her skin. *This place isn't alive anymore.*

The phone buzzed in her hand, and she nearly screamed again with surprise, but it wasn't Dave. It was Danny, calling in even if she couldn't call out. She pressed answer.

"Danny!"

"Hey Sare, listen, the caterer has been on the phone--"

"Danny! Wait, wait, something's happened, something really, oh *fuck*, uh, uh, can you, can you ..." What could he do? How could he help? "Could you come and get me?" The request was ridiculous, impossible, she knew. She was beyond help. She'd somehow—

The crash. The place you hit the car. The blue flash. That sound. There must *be something there. You still have a chance.*

"Oh, for crying out loud, are you kidding? I won't have time to--"

"Doesn't matter, doesn't matter, just keep talking, I need you to keep talking ok?" Sarah babbled as she half sprinted, half hobbled across the street—she only had one shoe on now--to the car, and jabbed the keys into the lock. A fist twisted in her gut when she now found that they wouldn't turn.

It's being here. The car's been here too long already.

Fuck it, then. She would run. It was only a few minutes away.

"Keep talking? Are you ok?"

"No, I'm not," she gasped, kicking off her other shoe and beginning to run up the street. "I just need, *fuck*, I just need you to stay there or I think I'm going to go crazy, ok? Just ... keep ... talking."

"Well what the fuck has haaaaaaaaaaaaaaaaaaaaaaaaaaaaaaaaaaaaaaaaaa," Danny said, and Sarah screeched to a halt.

"Danny? *Danny?*" she shrieked.

"aaaaaaaaaaaaaaaaaaaaaaaaaaaaaaaaaaaaaa," was all Danny continued to say, his voice locked into the endless repetition, a damning, teeny foghorn from the depths of some particularly perverse hell.

"*Danny!*"

The phone has been here too long too. Run!

She did, but stopped once more, almost immediately. The street before her, the houses, the bushes, the parked cars, were now tinted blue.

"Danny ..."

It thickened, and spread, but it wasn't coming forward; she saw now that it was already around her. The concrete upon which she stood, her clothes, her skin, the phone in her hand, all covered in a bluish tint.

She couldn't speak. She could only watch as the blue continued to thicken, becoming flat, solid. It filled the world, filled her eyes.

"aaaaaaaaaaaaaaaaaaaaaaaaaaaaaaaa--"

She tried to look at the phone, crazily wondering about signal, but she couldn't see it. All was blue.

Dave oh my god Dave where are you

Then—although there was no one there to see it—the street, the sky, everything, even the blue itself, was gone. All was as it should be. The only ones who would even vaguely know any different were Dave and his wife Sarah, who stood arguing in their hallway as Sarah scooped up boxes containing fabric that, unbeknownst to her, was colored Puce yet again.

3. Hold On Until Your Fingers Break

The sky lit up as if it were daytime—so quickly that it could be dismissed as perhaps a trick of the eye, a streetlight or car headlamp refracted through the blurry tears of a blink—and then the air seemed to thicken. There was a sudden increase in pressure that settled over the whole town, turning it into a miles-wide steam room. Then the alien atmosphere passed as quickly as it came, disappearing into a cool, crisp autumn breeze. It was 5:30am, and nobody noticed any of this. They never did.

*

Tom woke up and, for a moment, had no idea where he was. This was not the normal early morning confusion of the hungover man; this was something far more deep and profound. His eyes didn't recognize the bedroom that he was lying in. His fingers didn't recognize the feel of the toweling bedsheets. Panic began to flutter in his chest, even through the fog of the recently woken mind, and would have dug its claws in deep had not the simple sight of the *Anchorman* Blu-Ray box lying on the floor sent up a signal flare from the depths of his memory:

This is your room.

Everything clicked. Of course it was his room. All the posters and photos were his, the pile of unwashed laundry in the corner was his, the plate with the half-eaten pizza slice gathering mould on his desk was his, the man bag, the open laptop on the floor, all his. His mum refused to clean up after him anymore. *The door stays shut when you're at Uni,* she'd said, *so I don't see it. I'm done with it. Maybe the second or third time you come back to a festering crack den will make you think about cleaning it up before you go. Miracles happen.*

It was a plan that was clearly starting to work. Tom took in the familiar sight around him and, for once, felt his skin crawl. He had to admit, it was a pigsty.

Don't let her get into your head, man. You'll be Mr Middle Class Suburbia 2015 before you know it.

He swung his legs out of bed, realizing that he was still fully dressed from the night before. He didn't remember picking that particular outfit. He rubbed his head as a throbbing began to commence its beat in his temples. He needed some water, and badly. His skin felt bone dry. As he got to his feet, he wondered what the hell they'd done last night. This felt like a hangover, that was certain, but he hadn't had a night that he couldn't remember at all since his first year at Nottingham. Plus, he didn't like to *really* get hammered during the holidays, due to having to stagger home to his mum's place. She *worried* so, and with Dad no longer with them, he wanted her as happy as possible for as much of the time as possible. She deserved it.

Did Terry come round? Terry came round and we ... uh ...

Nope. It wasn't coming yet. Too early. He decided not to worry about it, as thinking only seemed to be making what was clearly the beginning of a monster headache worse. It'd come to him, and he'd no doubt see Terry later to piece their stories together.

If he remembers any more than you, which is highly doubtful.

Terry was a bigger drinker than Tom, certainly. It was one of many facts about his best friend that was lifted straight from their encyclopedic shared knowledge of one another. After all, they'd been friends since primary school; two six–year-olds in the same class that found out that one was called Terry and the other Tom? They were always going to make *sure* that they were best friends. They'd even gone away to the same university. Nottingham was—

Tom stopped dead in front of the mirror, horrified. He looked deathly ill.

He let out a little gasp as he saw just how dehydrated he was; his skin was so dry that the lines in his face stood out further and made him look as if he'd aged ten years. There were dark circles under his eyes—although he hadn't been sleeping that much recently, he had to admit—and his hair was flattened on his head from the night sweats, appearing thin. He was paler, too. He looked back at the mattress he'd just vacated, visible due to the duvet being flung back. There was the faint outline of a drying damp patch, roughly the length of his body.

Jesus. How much did you drink? You sweated it out in your sleep; you're lucky your body didn't just purge and make you throw up. While unconscious too, and you know what happens then.

His eyes were slightly bloodshot too.

Water. Get some water in you before your mum sees you like this.

It was a plan. He headed into the hallway, listening out for the telltale signs from downstairs. He could faintly hear a radio, and the sound of movement coming from the kitchen. Satisfied that the coast was clear, Tom darted into the bathroom and stuck his head under the cold tap, drinking greedily as the surprisingly cold water brought him further back to consciousness.

Idiot. You shouldn't be getting that hammered at home. You shouldn't have listened to Terry.

Because it would have been Terry who was the driving force behind whatever escapade they'd undertaken last night. It always was. It was why Tom both loved him and was constantly exasperated with the guy. Tom could never say no to his best friend.

Can you imagine what it's gonna be like when we go out for your twenty-first?

He shuddered at the thought as he dried the spray off his face with a towel, and that was when the doorbell rang. Tom moved to the balcony, taking mild care to stay out of sight, and peered over it into the downstairs hallway to see who was at the door. His mother came into view, resplendent in pink marigolds freshly adorned for some unspecified job in the garden. She was a lousy gardener—everything died apart from the grass—but she'd never lost her enthusiasm for it.

Tom saw her peer through the spyglass, then begin to unlatch the door.

"Tom!" she called, without looking up. "Out of your pit, it's for you!"

He smiled gently, and watched the door open. Though the face of the visitor on the doorstep was obscured by the visor of a baseball cap, Tom recognized the clothes immediately. Orange hoody, T-shirt and blue jeans. It was Terry.

"Hi, Gina," said Terry, his voice sounding as delicate as Tom felt. Terry had been allowed to call Tom's mum by her first name since he was twelve. In fact, Terry was such a part of the furniture that he called all of Tom's neighbours by their first names, apart from Mr Church next door. At that thought, Tom glanced to his left, looking out of the upstairs window; there, of course, was Mr Church, as Tom had known he would be, shuffling around in his far superior backyard carrying out gardening errands of his own. Terry and Tom would still call Mr Church *Mr Church* if they were in their sixties; neither of their grandparents still lived, and the kind old man had practically been a surrogate grandfather to them both, and a replacement father to Tom ... which made it even more unusual that calling him anything other than *Mister* felt strange. Tom's mum was never quite able to make use of the horticultural advice the old man regularly gave, however.

"Go bounce him out," said Gina to Terry, a wry tone in her voice. "Lazy sod's still in bed. I'm assuming you two stayed out late last night? Honestly, where is there to even *go* in Coventry on a Wednesday?"

Wednesday? Tom tried to think back over the last few days, struggling to do so through the buzz in his head.

"Ah, we always know the best places to go on any given day," said Terry, and Tom could hear the grin in his voice even if it was visually hidden by the peak of the cap. His mum sighed, smiling and shaking her head, and gestured up the stairs as she began to turn away. As Terry began to climb them, Gina called after him.

"Ah. Wait. Hat indoors. Off," she said curtly, but still with a smile. Terry hesitated, clearly unsure if Gina was joking. "Come on," she insisted, holding out a hand now to take it. "Old fashioned, but it was always Mark's rule. Give give give."

Terry hesitated again, and then removed the hat. The smile disappeared from Gina's face, and even Tom put his hand to his mouth. Terry looked just as dehydrated as Tom did.

"*Terry,*" said Gina, moving forward automatically with a mother's instinct and putting one hand on the boy's forehead. "You look *shattered!* What on earth did you boys do? You look ... I'm sorry, you look terrible!"

"Food poisoning," said Terry with an embarrassed shrug. "We had a few pints and late curry, but it must have been dodgy as hell as I've been throwing up for most of the night. I was just coming to see how Tom's been, to be honest, as we ate the same thing."

Tom didn't need the lack of the familiar next-day curry aftertaste at the back of his throat—he always had them hot, and was always aware of that in at least one of his two ends the next morning—to know when his friend was lying. An uneasy feeling stirred in his stomach, and Tom didn't think it was from last night's curry. Why would he lie?

Nothing to worry about though, surely. He knows you don't like Mum to worry. He doesn't want her to know that we got so hammered we look like zombies the next morning. Better mild, overnight food poisoning than knowing you were out binge drinking.

So why did he suddenly feel so

afraid

nervous? Either way, Gina didn't know Terry the way Tom did; she bought it.

"Oh, bloody hell," she said, guilt in her tone as she already began to make her way up the stairs. "I didn't hear him moving around in the night, I was out like a light ... "

Thinking quickly, Tom quietly nipped into the bathroom and silently locked the door. He heard two sets of footsteps on the stairs as he moved to the back of the bathroom.

"Tom?" came the sound of his mum's voice from the other end of the hallway. "You awake, love?"

"Yeah," called Tom, sitting on the closed toilet, not needing to put any false weakness in his voice. He felt lousy. "Just on the loo. Bit of a rough night's sleep last night. Think I had a bad curry. Feeling better now though, think it's … uh … you know. All out."

Might as well go with Tom's story. If you need a reason for looking like this, it'll do.

"Oh; how are you feeling now? Do you need anything?"

"Yeah, much better thanks."

"Terry's here, I'll stick him in your room if you're up to a social call?"

"Yeah, cool."

If Terry had answers, Tom wanted to hear them.

***

But Terry knew nothing either.

"I have absolutely no idea," said Terry, his face blank and worried. "Seriously. I was going to ask you the same thing. You seriously don't know? I can't even remember the start of the night. I mean, *nothing.*"

The boys stared at each other, gravity lowering onto them and whispering wickedly of news that could be far worse than they feared. Tom realized that he was missing exactly the same information too; he recalled nothing about the start of the night. He couldn't even remember the rest of the afternoon before then.

"Wait … are you serious?"

"I'm serious."

Silence in the room. Frightened eyes widened and held each other, saying everything.

Drinking wouldn't do this. Not just booze. Or even drugs. Not a whole day. Would it?

This was crazy. The previously impending monster headache had now arrived, and it was knuckling its way through his temples and spreading across his skull.

"Did you get hold of anything? Before, I mean?" asked Terry, seeming to read Tom's mind. "Any pills or anything?" Tom started to say *no* and immediately stopped. He had no idea. He tried to think of the last time he'd even seen Clint's mate Neil, who usually sorted them out if they wanted anything. He'd surely remember that; dealing with Neil was always so unpleasant that it made Tom feel dirty afterwards, like he needed to wash the experience of the man off his skin.

He couldn't remember. Had it been that long ago?

It could *have been yesterday. You just don't remember.*

The dazed, ill feeling seemed to become thicker, making it harder to think. That was the problem, wasn't it? Getting his thoughts straight. He rubbed at his eyes, and Terry did the same, both of their brains throbbing. Tom swigged from the glass of water he'd found on his desk, passed it to Terry.

"We need more of this," he said, tapping the glass. "Sugar, too. Let's ... let's not get wound up. We're physically fucked. We need sorting out." Terry nodded eagerly in response, seeing something to cling to. Terry's usual big mouth was absent; the swagger had evaporated. Terry was scared, and seeing that made Tom's stomach roll. Terry was *never* scared. "The doctor's," Tom continued. "I'll get an appointment. I can usually get in same day."

"I'm not registered there."

"Doesn't matter. I'll share whatever shit they give me with you." He didn't say what he really thought, what they both thought; tablets wouldn't fix this. Memory loss, nausea. That equaled head trauma, and they both knew it. The headache screamed its confirmation.

But your head isn't painful to the touch right now, is it? There would be a point of impact.

They looked at each other again, breathing steadily. Scared little boys, no matter how they saw themselves.

"Don't worry," Tom said, nodding, his face blank and completely failing to look reassuring in any way. "I'll give them a call. We'll get this sorted out."

***

On the other side of the Atlantic, plans were being made. Suspicions had been confirmed, options had been presented, and a Hail Mary solution had been chosen. It was audacious, inspired, and despite its risky nature, those in charge not only thought that it was the best way to go, but secretly knew that it was the only option. No one said what they were thinking; that it was too late, that even if the theory was perfect, the physical preparations were woefully behind schedule. Even if the whole world came together to help, nothing could be completed in time, with the pinpoint calculations required.

They were right. Project Omega Supreme was destined to fail utterly, and all was already lost.

***

The incident with Mr Church was made even worse by the fact that so many people were there to see it.

Earlsdon High Street was usually, even on quiet days, relatively busy. Today was no different, even for midweek, and the people milling on the path between the One Stop and the City Arms were a major hassle for the two aching, shuffling young men who had to wind their way between them, living a hungover real-life version of Frogger.

They'd been lucky; told by the receptionist on the phone that if they came down immediately that they could be seen straight away, but they'd have to be there within ten minutes. That was normally easy, the clinic being located just off the high street and easily within walking distance of Tom's house on Palmerston Road, but today the light hurt the boys' eyes. Each step rolled Tom's stomach over like a barrel of piss. They walked in silence, breathing heavily as they went, and only spoke up once Mr Church started screaming.

They'd spotted him in the distance long before he saw them. He'd been making his way from the off-licence to the Moor Street side of the road, where the pavement became clearer of people. He was wearing his trademark grey raincoat—it wasn't raining—and the bald head on his tall frame stood out amongst the majority of the crowd. He moved with the stiffness of an elderly man, but always maintained an air of dignity, as if his thoughts put him on a plane slightly higher than those around him. They probably did; Mr Church was a very clever man, well read and happy to hold forth on a variety of subjects. This made it all the more disturbing when this demeanour broke entirely at the sight of Terry and Tom walking down the street.

It was a double take in its purest form. Church looked one way to check the traffic before crossing the street, then as he looked back the other way his gaze crossed over the two boys. For a brief second he started to make his way over the road, then stopped dead as his brain caught up with his eyes. Church straightened up and stared back at the boys, wide eyed, colour draining from his face. He squinted slightly, as if wanting to clarify what he was seeing, and then his face went slack. As did his hand; his fingers released the handle of the plastic bag that they'd been gripping, letting go as if the handle were suddenly too heavy for them to retain. The bottle inside shattered audibly as it struck the concrete through the bag's thin surface.

People around Mr Church turned sharply at the sound, eyes falling upon him in time to see one shaking hand fly to his mouth, the other coming up and out before him, fingers spread, as if to hold the boys back from coming any closer. A moan slipped from his lips, before his hand mashed against his mouth, cutting it off.

The boys stared back in stunned and horrified silence, an unshakeable part of both of their lives transforming sickeningly before them. The day had been hazy and unreal enough already; Mister Church? Gibbering like a lunatic in the street?

"Wha ..." said Tom idiotically, unable to say anything else. He flashed a glance at Terry, who was staring at Mister Church as if he were from outer space.

"*No,*" barked Mr Church suddenly, snapping Tom's attention his way once more. The man's voice, always so low and smooth and completely at odds with his lanky body, was high and strained, madness twisting it into something barely there. The hand that was held forward clenched at nothing and turned into a fist, one that shook spastically and impotently before him, and Mister Church's wide eyes glistened and shone. "No, *naaaaaaargh, nah, naaaaaaargggggh—*" Both hands flew to his cheeks and clawed at the thin flesh, and the bottom lip crumpled inwards as the head shook. People around stared and moved their children behind them, one or two following Church's horrified gaze and glaring accusatorially at the boys as they stood gently swaying on their feet. They were rooted to the spot, useless in the face of madness.

Then Church was running—*running,* at his age—away up Moor Street, even managing to push a younger, burly man aside in his haste to be away. Everyone on Earlsdon High Street watched him go, a fleeing bald scarecrow in a grey raincoat that flapped as he ran.

Then the shocked faces turned to one another—*did you see that? What was that all about*—or to the boys, even as the small amount of human traffic around them began to make its way on to wherever its destination had been. This was modern, new-money village life in England; nothing was too much of a commotion to not be quickly swept under the carpet once it had passed. No one dared ask the boys any questions, or said anything to them, but their eyes revealed their thoughts. Perhaps one look at the state of the pair made them think better of it.

The two boys remained standing there as bodies filed past, statues in a trickle of humanity.

"What ... the *fuck* ..." said Tom, eventually. Terry didn't say anything, staring as he was at the spot that Church had just vacated. He looked even more pale than he had earlier, and Tom knew why. This had just become a lot bigger.

That isn't a coincidence. No way Mister Church freaks out in a way completely alien to the rest of his life, and at the sight of you, after a day you can't remember. This is ...

A flighty, electric feeling began to fill Tom's limbs, and he cleared his mind as quickly as he could. Freaking out wouldn't help anyone.

The doctor's. Just get to the doctor's. You obviously need to talk to Mister Church, but you can't fucking handle that now. A stiff breeze is gonna blow you over right now. If Church has bad news, it'll finish you off.

"Come on," said Tom, slapping at Terry's arm gently. There was nothing else they could do. To discuss further would be to court madness. "Let's ... let's just get to the doc's. Come on."

"I think I'm gonna be sick," said Terry, so quietly that Tom could barely hear him. It was like something out of *Invasion of the Body Snatchers*. First Church, now Terry, both acting utterly out of character. Tom understood why in this instance; it was like the flight simulator thing he'd read about in an online article about video games.

It had been about some people getting motion sickness whilst playing first person shooter games. A similar phenomena was the nausea experienced by around half the number of people that used static flight simulators. The principle was apparently to do with the disconnect between the motion that the eye was seeing and the physical sensation of stillness that the body was experiencing. The brain's confusion would manifest itself as nausea, and the end result for a small portion of gamers was a need for a lie down.

This was a similar effect. The world around them was utterly mundane and normal, and yet there was a rapidly growing fear and unreality that just kept trying to break through and take centre stage in their minds. It couldn't, not yet; the normality was smothering everything too much, and the result was a swaying mental displacement that left only the option of pure function.

They needed the doctor before anything else.

"Don't think about it," said Tom. "Let's just go."

"I'm not coming," said Terry. "I need to lie down. See what he says. Give me whatever he gives you. I just need … I have to lie down."

"Really?"

"Yeah. I don't *need* to go, do I? Do you … do you want me to come?"

"No, you don't have to. I'll let you know what he says."

Terry hesitated, eyes drifting back to where Church had been standing.

"*What did we do, man?*" he said, quietly. Tom didn't answer, and Terry nodded to himself gently and turned away, beginning to make his way back up the street. Tom sighed, and began to make his way across the road towards the clinic, coincidentally following the path that Church had just taken.

Doctor's first. One step at a time. Check up on Church when you get home.

***

Tom saw the note on his bedroom floor, lying almost out of sight under the edge of the bed. Amongst all the other clutter in the room he might have missed it, if not for the thick, black, jagged marker pen handwriting standing out against the stark white paper.

He'd just arrived from the surgery of an unimpressed-looking Dr Garala, who, while telling Tom that he'd send him for a blood test to be on the safe side (but that Tom was merely experiencing symptoms of nothing but a particularly nasty hangover) had used a tone that made it fairly clear what he thought of people taking up his time when they'd clearly just been out on the sauce. Tom hadn't been relieved by this news. Garala had taken one look at him and wanted him out of the door without really giving it much thought. Tom had known something was going on, and it wasn't just his physical condition that had been making him feel sick. But he had just been so *tired* ...

He'd almost been in mid-collapse onto the bed when the note had caught his eye, stopping him gently in his tracks. He hadn't recognised it at all. As he looked at it now, some of the writing was hard to see at this angle, and messy too. Even in his current condition, even amongst the madness, Tom still felt the flicker of excitement dash across his queasy stomach. He was a young man, after all.

Someone's phone number? Who did we meet?

It was written on a folded flyer for a weekly student night at the local club, Kasbah (which would, for everyone young enough to remember sneaking in, always be referred to as the Colly.)

Kasbah? Something happened at Kasbah? We went there then?

It wasn't a phone number. It was a warning in black and white, and both the nature and dim familiarity of it made him want to vomit. The messy, hurried handwriting read:

dONT TRUST HiM

The pounding in Tom's ears merged with the pounding that suddenly came from the front door downstairs; his mum was out, and Tom suddenly wondered, dreamlike, where she actually was. The thought was blasted aside by the lunatic realisation that he recognised the handwriting on the hastily written note.

It was his own.

He stared at it in sudden mental silence for a moment, struck dumb. He knew it meant something.

You got drunk. You wrote yourself a note for some reason. That's all it is. You probably had an argument with Terry and wrote this while you were drunkenly sulking.

The creeping flesh on his arms told him otherwise. He swayed on his feet—

The already-forgotten banging on the front door came again, jolting Tom to alertness. On instinct, he began to head towards the front door like a man sleepwalking, dimly happy to be doing something that made logical sense, a process that he understood. *Knock at the door, answer the door. Then get some coursework done, yeah? Good to get ahead. Good to not have to worry about cramming everything in at the last minute again before term starts. You could—*

He stopped on the upstairs landing as a thought came through the fog. Going with it, he scurried to the upstairs window and peered out of it to see who was at the door. His heart skipped again as his suspicion was confirmed; the grey suit and bald head were clearly visible. It was Mr Church. Tom looked at the note in his shaking hand once more:

dONT TRUST HiM

Only when the banging on the door came for a third time did Tom begin to descend the stairs, the hallway spinning around him.

***

Church actually smiled when Tom opened the door. The smile didn't reach the eyes, however; along with the shaking body and beads of sweat on his forehead, the forced, trying-to-look-casual grin that was plastered onto Church's ash-grey skin made him look like a corpse. He looked alien, frightening. The man that Tom had always loved—if he'd never truly known it—was nowhere to be seen. This absence was, strangely, the biggest punch to the mental gut of the entire day so far. It was horrible.

"Thomas," Church said, trying to sound cheery but with a shake in his voice. He always used Thomas, never Tom. He was the only person Tom didn't mind doing it. "I apologise on two fronts; one for repeatedly knocking on your door like this, but also ..." the smile faltered and Church looked down for a moment. When he looked up, the corpse-smile was gone, and his eyes were

118

almost pleading. "Also for the very embarrassing display earlier. I was ..." He shrugged, lost for words. "It was a shock, to say the least. I think that may have been a panic attack. I haven't felt like that before. On another day ... I have would been fascinated rather than terrified, I think." This last part was a flicker of the real man, but it soon vanished as Church looked worriedly around himself and leaned forward conspiratorially. He looked like a hungry bug. Tom found himself taking a slight step backward.

"Thomas ... I think ..." Church said, his breath shallow and rapid. His breath stunk. *Where did you go, Mr Church?* "There is a small chance that I'm wrong. Very small. But I see the differences ... the ones that even your mother wouldn't see. I thought I'd see them one day soon ... but by God ... *not already.* Anyone else would just think that perhaps you were unwell. And I'm sure that you *are* nauseous. But I think my suspicions are correct. Since I saw you I've been trying to tell myself otherwise but ... I think I'm correct. Am I?"

Tom swallowed, realising how dry his throat was, and found his voice.

"Mister Church ..." Tom began, wondering how to respond. He had reached a point of mild despair after an extremely difficult day, and Church's appearance, vagueness, and fucking *breath* made him talk to his neighbour in a way he never had in his entire life. "Please. What ... what the fuck are you talking about?" He leaned on the door frame and put a hand to his aching forehead, waiting for a response and just wanting the day to be over. Church actually looked mildly startled by the language, but Tom, who normally would have been horrified to speak like that in front of the old man—let alone *to* him—didn't care.

"Is it happening? Are they right?" Church asked quietly. His eyes were all noise, however; desperate. "Is that why you're here?"

"Mister Church. I went out on the piss last night. I last saw you, what, a few days ago? As far as I know, nothing of any relevance has happened in between those two events. *I have no idea what you're talking about.*" If it wasn't for everything else, Tom would be worried that Church was having a mental breakdown … if not for the fact that he somehow *knew* that Church was right to be scared. Church's brow became even more wrinkled than it already was, and his mouth worked silently as he tried to understand Tom's words. Then his eyes lit up.

"Amnesia. Of course. He expected that as a possibility … oh my God." Church's hand went to his mouth, and his eyes became watery. "I'm right then. You did it. You *both* did it."

Terry?

"You mean me and Terry? Mister Church … Arthur …" Tom used the man's first name, breaking the unwritten rule. "What did we do? What's happened?"

"You don't remember. Of course you don't remember," said Church, his voice cracking as his eyes continued to fill with tears. "So I've got to … I've got to … *oh God …*" Church's hands flew to his eyes and he began to sob, stunning Tom with a sight that he would have considered impossible before today. To his own surprise, Tom darted forward and put his arms around his neighbour, surprised at how thin and fragile the old man felt in his embrace. He felt like a trembling bird. After a moment, Church threw his arms around Tom as well, and the two men, one at the end of his life and one at the beginning, stood on Tom's doorstep in a mess of wide-eyed confusion and sorrow. All Tom could do was watch the trails left by a passenger jet, making its way slowly across the blue sky above them. White trails against blue, a contrast that brought to mind a memory of black against red glossy paper, and as Tom held his crying, elderly neighbour he saw the flyer/note he'd found in his bedroom. After a while, Church pulled slowly away, composed and embarrassed. He put his hand on Tom's shoulder and nodded, looking at the floor as if steeling himself.

"I need to show you. And I need to show you both, together. Can you get Terry?"

"Yeah, he's in bed—"

"Get him. Get him and bring him to my house. How soon can you get him?"

"Half an hour maybe? Mr Church—"

"I don't mean to be deliberately obscure, Thomas," Church said, pulling out a handkerchief from his pocket and rubbing his eyes and nose. His words came through heavy breaths. "And I'm sorry. But you won't believe me unless I show you, and you both need to hear this together. I ..." He didn't know what else to say, and looked blankly at Tom. "Half an hour then. Yes?"

No. Half an hour my ass. He's giving you some*thing* now.

"No," Tom said. "No, you don't need to give me a full rundown, you don't need to go into all the details, but you can tell me *some*thing. *What's going on?*"

"You wouldn't believe me—"

"Bollocks, I'll decide that. Tell me—"

"Everyone is going to die, Tom. Everyone," said Church, his eyes hollows in his head. "There's nothing anyone can do to stop it. And you, Terry, and myself are going to be the only ones who live." He waited for a response, but all Tom had was a little sound in his head going *eeeeeeeeeeeeeeeeeeeeeeee.*

"Half an hour. Let yourselves in. I'll be in the basement."

Church turned and walked back along the high hedgerow that divided the two houses, never looking over his shoulder. As he disappeared from view, rounding the shrubbery and making his way up the path to his house, a visual broke through the noise in Tom's mind:

dONT TRUST HiM

***

Of course, the thought on repeat in Tom's head for the next half an hour was *Church is crazy. Obviously he's crazy. Church is crazy.* It was the correct thought, the normal thought ... if not for the note in his pocket that felt like it was a lead weight, and the sick feeling in his gut that said even louder *Church is sane.* There was no way he wasn't going to do as Church had asked.

He hadn't bothered getting into the debate of it with Terry either. He'd simply gone to Terry's house and dragged him, mumbling and complaining, from his bed, telling him that Church wanted to see them. While that had made some sort of logical sense to Terry's half-asleep and queasy brain, as they'd walked the short journey back to Church's, Terry had started to come to and ask more and more questions. Tom had kept telling him that Church had come to see him, that he'd wanted to see them both, and that was all he knew.

"Is he gonna scream at us again?" Terry scowled, some of his old swagger and passions coming through the fog of sickness. "I just can't *wait*. He obviously knows something about yesterday, that's why. He's done something. *Man ...*" Terry sighed, slapping at his thighs in frustration. "What's the old fucker *done?*" Tom knew his friend, and knew that this was all just defence. Terry wanted answers as badly as Tom did. But Terry was equally scared.

"Don't call him that," said Tom, but none of the vicious defence that would have normally come with such a rebuke was there this time. They'd reached Tom's driveway, next door to Church's, but Tom didn't continue past. Instead he turned and headed towards his own house.

"What are you doing?" asked Terry.

"Wait here," Tom said, opening the front door. He disappeared inside the house for some time, and Terry waited, breathing slowly with his eyes shut. The body-sickness had abated some, but not much, and he desperately wanted to be lying down in his bed. *Another five minutes and I'm just gonna go home no matter what. This is baaaad and it can wait one more day. I can't take much more. I don't care if—*

Terry's eyes opened as he felt something being thrust into his hand. He felt the dull, solid handle of a large kitchen knife now sitting in his unprotesting grip. His head jerked up, suddenly sobered, and saw Tom's flat, unwavering gaze. Tom was putting a kitchen knife of his own into his jacket pocket.

"What ... the fuck ..." Terry stammered.

Church was an old man, but now Tom thought that maybe taking Church at appearance level would be foolish indeed. There was indeed no way Tom wasn't going to do as Church had asked ... but that didn't mean he was going unprepared. The note had been a warning.

***

Church opened his front door and took in the two boys in front of him. His eyes wavered on Terry for a moment, searching his face, and nodded solemnly as if to say *you too.*

"Come in, boys," he said, stepping back and gesturing into the kitchen behind him. Tom knew the sight well, normally one of warmth and welcome, but now he was very aware of the weight of the knife tucked into his jacket pocket. Nobody said anything as the pair trudged into Church's dated kitchen. The styling of it was like stepping into a time warp, always had been. It had always fascinated Tom how Church's house had the same layout as his mother's, but still looked like something from the set of a 70s' TV show. Church was already heading into the depths of the house without a word or a look behind him; Terry looked at Tom nervously for confirmation, and Tom nodded. *Go on.* Terry went first. He had always been the braver of the two of them.

They rounded the hallway door to see Church moving a large decorative vase. It had guarded the corner of Church's floral-wallpapered hallway for as long as Tom could remember, and yet Tom was surprised to notice that there wasn't much of a track left by the vase's base in the shag pile carpet. The vase had been there so long that Tom would have expected a near-permanent groove to be left in the fibres beneath it. There was none.

He moves it a lot. It never sits there long. You just thought *that he never moves it.*

The immediate following question of *why* was answered straight away. Church bent and began to pull at the corner of the carpet. It came away easily to reveal a clumsily cut trapdoor in the floorboards.

A basement? But our house doesn't have a—

Church lifted the trapdoor's lid; it opened smoothly, and as it did the dark hole beneath lit up from within to reveal a ladder leading down. Church had obviously rigged the basement to light up as soon as the trapdoor moved. The man in question straightened up and turned to face them. He looked distant, like his anxiety had reached so much of a fever pitch that his emotions had just flattened out.

"This way. Don't worry. It perhaps won't come as too much of a surprise to you to hear that you've both been in there before. It's quite safe."

He turned without a word and began to gingerly descend the ladder. Tom found himself moving forward as if in a dream, stunned into dull automatic action. *Church has a secret basement in his hallway. You've been in it before and you don't remember why.* The thoughts passed through his head and shut down any sense of reality as they did so. He gripped the wooden struts of the ladder—it looked as if it had been there for some time, made of cheap wood— and began to descend, looking down to see his feet moving closer to a rough, uneven concrete floor beneath. He heard Terry urgently hissing something but Tom ignored him, moving in a daze and knowing that nothing was going to stop him from seeing what Church had down there.

He reached the bottom and took in his surroundings. He'd expected more. The room—if it could be described as such—was as basic as it could possibly be. *Bunker* would have been the more appropriate description, albeit a very small one. The whole thing was probably only six feet by six feet square. Modern bulbs sat in decades-old light fittings that had been roughly wired into the walls and onto the wooden support pillars. The walls were made of stacked and mortared breeze blocks, and had a few power and phone cables running down them.

Did he dig this himself or something? He must have done this decades ago.

Against one wall stood an old trestle table, upon which were three computer monitors; two quite modern, and one very old. They were all

124

switched off. Next to them was a blocky device about the size of a printer that Tom couldn't identify. To the right of this setup was what looked like a large bank of data processing units, standing at roughly the same size and width as a fridge. What caught Tom's eye were three small devices lying at the front edge of the trestle table, sitting there like three bloated and exotic bugs made of metal.

It was clear that these were evolutions of the same concept. The device on the left was the largest of the three, about the size of a 1980s' mobile phone. It was roughly the same shape too, except with what looked like a trigger or switch covered by a plastic guard on a hinge. It looked homemade. The device to the right of it was a similar shape but slightly smaller, this time with the covered trigger on the back; it looked slightly more slickly made than the previous unit. The third was about half the size of the other two, and made of very smooth-looking plastic. Tom then realised that his first instinct about the printer-looking thing on the table had been correct; it was a 3D printer. They hadn't been in the mainstream long enough for Tom to recognise one straightaway, but looking at the third—and clearly most recently made— device, Church had 3D printed the plastic casing. It looked, upon closer inspection, as if the top half of the device was actually a lid. Tom guessed that this unit's trigger was hidden underneath. Behind all three of them sat a smooth metal box about the same size as the average modem, perfectly rectangular with a single red LED in the centre of it to let an observer know that it was switched on. It was of a similar build style and quality to the largest of the three devices, and Tom guessed that the two of them had been built at roughly the same time. Church was standing by the table with his hands behind his back, looking at nothing as he waited for Terry to join them.

Tom heard Terry reach the bottom of the ladder, breathing heavily, but didn't turn around. Church spoke.

"The handsets are used in conjunction with the central unit, and the central unit has to be attached to the core processor here," he said, gesturing to the fridge-sized bank behind him. Tom found himself thinking not about the madness of the knife in his pocket or Church's secret bunker, but about how amazed he was that Church had anything to do with technology at all. He'd never seen Church use or even discuss a PC, and as far as he was aware the man had never owned one. He only mentioned current affairs or philosophical topics like the genial old gent that he'd always been. Core processors? Tom would have been stunned if he'd seen Church with a smartphone. Again, the poisoned sucker punch—of seeing a loved one peel away that character like a snake shedding its skin—left Tom reeling. Church continued, sounding as dazed as Tom felt. "The secondary field generated by the central unit could potentially be quite devastating, on a small scale level; that's why I had the reinforced walls added in here. When these houses were built—I bought it 'off plan' as I believe they say—I had the basement added. I wish I'd had it made larger, but money was tight and I didn't think I'd need much room ..." Church paused, his gaze glazing as he was carried away by a memory. His eyes then came back, blinked, reset, and he resumed speaking. "Of course, I feel strange telling you this. You must already know, on some level. Obviously, I have never had confirmation that the entire system worked. Until today." He looked at the boys. "I turned the central unit on for the first time very early this morning."

"Not last night?" asked Tom suddenly, surprising himself.

"No," said Church, looking confused.

"Why?" asked Tom, surprised that his question wasn't *what does it do*, but then he realised that surely the *why* would provide the *what* ... and he wanted to know the answer to both.

"The same reason that even my brother never turned it on before he died," said Church, grey as a storm cloud. "To actually trigger the handsets would be a gamble of potentially catastrophic proportions, but we always thought that the central unit *should* be safe as long as it wasn't actually engaged ... but we didn't know for *certain*. Ninety-nine percent isn't enough certainty when weighed against the existence of humanity. You have to remember, it was only *built* as a failsafe for escape. For all of his genius, my brother was ... troubled. It was only ever to be switched on in the face of a *potential* ... well, there isn't another word for it. A potential apocalypse. And only to actually be *used* once that apocalypse was certain."

dONT TRUST HiM flashed before Tom's eyes, but all he heard was the truth. He knew it.

"The fact that you two are here ... as you are ..." said Church, raising his hands as if to say *what can I do,* "tells me that I was right to turn it on."

"But what does it ..." muttered Tom, but the word *apocalypse* kept snagging at his mind. "Apocalypse? You mean like, as in, like, like the end of the world? I mean ... *what?* How could—"

"It's an asteroid," said Terry's voice from behind Tom, flat and heavy and very, very sad. "Extinction class. The kind that killed the dinosaurs. They had a plan to stop it, and it didn't work."

Tom slowly turned in a circle, watching Church from the corner of his eye as the older man nodded solemnly, gently placing a hand over his mouth. His wide eyes took in Terry, standing with his shoulders slumped and his head turned away.

"Terry. Terry ... what ..."

Terry sighed and closed his eyes.

"You were right to turn it on, Mister Church," said Terry. "They told you this morning. That's why you armed the central unit." Church didn't answer, instead walking to the wall and leaning against it, his own eyes closed now. Tom stared at Terry, another terrible snake, shedding comfort. "They tried the Don Quixote technique. It took too long to prepare. They knew it was already too late, but they tried anyway. It failed and that was it. Everything was ... ." Terry opened his eyes and looked at Tom. There was no guilt there, no anger, just the same old familiarity ... but *different.*

"*Terry?*"

"They launched the orbiter, Sancho," said Terry to Tom, with a weary,

127

exasperated tone, but his eyes never left Tom's. "The concept was simple; Sancho orbits the asteroid, constantly relaying data, acting as a precision guide for Hidalgo, the impact craft. The coincidence was staggering. They'd only started work on it as a preventative measure a year before, once congress had approved a ten-year development plan. NASA can only detect ninety-five percent of large, near-earth asteroids. They spotted the rock that would end the world too late; it was less than a year away. The technology wasn't ready, the *crafts* weren't ready. Every available genius on the fucking planet jumping on board wasn't enough to shave off nine years of research and development. Hell, even the research didn't matter. Even when the calculations are perfect, the research sound, *they spotted it too late.* Long story short; it failed, miserably."

Tom couldn't take any more. He dropped to his knees and threw up, but Terry didn't stop talking, his voice like a lead metronome ticking in Tom's head. *He knew that all of this was true.* He could see the looped TV broadcasts in his head, the government messages interspersed with paid-for texts from people who wanted to send some last words to the rest of the nation, to loved ones that they couldn't get hold of. He remembered the day that even those stopped. The simple, emergency broadcast text filling the screen. *He remembered pulling the trigger ...*

"The rushed alternatives failed miserably ..." Terry was saying. "By then, the window of prevention was closed. That was when we decided that there was no choice." Terry nodded at Church, still leaning on the wall. "The three of us. We decided to use the device. There was nothing to lose."

They had. Tom knew it, could remember the feel of the smooth plastic of the most modern of the three handsets nestling in his grip. He looked at it where it lay on the table. Untouched yet, the plastic guard still covering the trigger.

"I'm sorry, Terry," said Church, his voice barely audible. "I feel that I should be the one to divulge all of this, but you'll have to understand, this is somewhat of a terrible ..." He trailed off, wiped at his face. "I was half expecting this, yet I never believed that I could actually be *correct*." He sniffed heavily, curled his hand in the air while he pulled a handkerchief from his pocket. "Would you mind? I don't feel ... that I can continue. And by the sounds of it, the amnesia has only affected Tom, here."

"It does, sometimes," said Terry, sighing. "Not always. It's only ever got me once or twice." He walked over to where Tom still knelt on the floor, choking. Terry squatted down and looked at his friend; again, there was no compassion on Terry's face, just a strange weariness. He looked like a mechanic tasked with fixing the same fault on the same car, *again.* "Anything?" Terry said. His tone was almost pleading. "It comes back quick sometimes. You *know* all this, mate. The basic stuff ... you always remember *that.* Come on. Save me a job." He sighed. "I wanted to avoid all ..." Terry cut himself off, about to say something that he shouldn't, and Tom was about to ask what he meant when a psychic boot lodged itself in his brain.

"It's a time machine. The central unit is a time machine."

"Not quite," sighed Terry, sitting fully on the floor. "Think. What is it?"

Who built it? Church's brother. Church's brother built it, designed it. Church's real surname is Galiaskarov. Not Arthur, Alyosha. His brother, Piotr. His brother that had died of a brain haemorrhage before Tom was born. Before Tom's family had even moved into the street. The Americans got them out of Soviet Russia in return for Piotr working for their military R and D. They needed Church as his handler, even though Piotr was older. Piotr was indeed disturbed, and only lasted five years before being laid off and committed to an asylum. Medication got him under control and he was released into Church's care, where he developed blueprints for a superior propulsion unit—

The memories were a rush, an attack.

"NASA? You ... you went back to the US government after they had your brother committed?" Tom mumbled, looking at Church. Despite everything else, Tom had to ask. He was delirious. Terry smiled slightly and nodded. It was coming back to his friend. He wouldn't have to go through it all again.

"No," said Church. "We sold them the design in return for a small financial settlement and help with getting UK citizenship. The accent was the only thing they couldn't help with. I fixed that myself. We wanted no more government work, and the time in the asylum actually helped my brother tremendously. For a while. The people there were very good, and the medication helped calm him down. It was only as he got older when his paranoia started to return." He held up his hands and looked at them. "Piotr was the genius. I was a carpenter. I could only help him so much."

You know this, just like you already know the rest. Church already told you, before.

"What was he paranoid ab—"

He was paranoid about the world ending. It was Piotr that made Church have this basement excavated before the house was built. Piotr had been the key to not one, but two new lives; how could Church refuse him, how could he not allow his brother everything that Church could grant? The central unit became Piotr's life's work. Church took a job, supported them both, never married, while Piotr did his research. Church left him to it; Piotr would keep him updated constantly—incessantly, whether Church liked it or not—until the day he made his breakthrough. The theory of the Overlay.

"The Overlay Device is that which will save us ..."

The Overlay Device was his failsafe. Once the blueprint was complete, Piotr became so much more calm. Once he finished building the central unit, he became calmer still. Once he completed the first trigger, Piotr became ... well, normal. Almost.

Tom's wavering gaze fell upon the triggers once more, terribly familiar and silently ominous.

He spent a year or two building the second handset, almost casually, like a hobby, but still with a purpose. One would save Piotr alone. Another would save his brother as well. The third device ... the third device ...

He couldn't get it. Tom shakily raised an arm, pointed to the plastic, most modern version on the table. Church followed the gesture, saw where it led.

"I had it made a year ago," he said. "Partially to see if Piotr's designs could be reproduced, and—I have to admit—partially because when you spend so long around such mania, the intent can be contagious. Did my brother, with his uniquely wired mind, have some insight that the rest of us did not? I could dismiss it after all this time, of course. But as an old man begins to fear his approaching death, he begins to think of the sneaky, cheating ways that it may come early. How did I know that Piotr's previous models had not corrupted somehow over time? *And what would it hurt me to pay a small fee to have them built?* To have an insurance policy? I have plenty of money. I own this house. Though the designs raised a few confused questions, there was not enough in the nature of the handsets alone to cause any real outside curiosity. The nature of the device, after all, is based on radio frequencies, believe it or not. That was what Piotr said, anyway. Radio frequencies that the central unit ... makes use of."

"To ... to ... travel through time," Tom whispered. He heard Terry shift his body, getting comfortable.

"*No*," Terry sighed, sounding exasperated. "*Think.* Why were they scared of the device? Why didn't they turn it on? Why didn't they ever tell anyone about it?"

Tom twitched, neurons firing in his brain, shock rippling through his body.

Because that was the one thing that Piotr was unsure about. His calculations made the theory irrefutable—at least to his hair-trigger mind—but there was one element that was 90/10. But ninety percent still wasn't sure enough.

"It *is* a time machine—"

But also something else. It sends you back ... and sideways.

"It's a backwards side step ..."

Piotr realised that chaos theory proved that time travel is impossible without creating a paradox. Therefore the very concept of time travel itself—in the way humans had always imagined it—was also impossible. So he found another way.

Tom's eyes grew wide and bulging as he remembered, seeing anew the unimaginable and unfathomable genius of the man that had worked in this very basement, a man who, if he had not been cast aside and left to his madness, could have changed the world. A technological Jesus, applying his endless skill into his basement-built scheme of lunacy. Lunacy that had saved Tom's life.

You can't travel backwards in your own reality. So you hop into another and travel backwards in that.

No. That wasn't quite right either. That wasn't *big* enough, *vast* enough.

The Overlay Device ... it copies your reality.

The fridge-like machine, standing like a sentry in that basement, guarding Tom from—ironically—escaping the awful reality of the situation. He hazily remembered that he'd been thinking about the new university term only the night before ... hadn't he?

The device creates a duplicate reality. Then it takes you to that reality's past.

"What Piotr was scared of ... what he didn't know ..."

Was how *the duplication worked. It shouldn't actually fully happen until the triggers were pulled. And he was, as Church had said, ninety percent certain that turning the device on—*

"—creating the copy point, the point in time that you can travel back to—
"

—wouldn't cause any duplication at all ... but ninety-nine percent is indeed still too much margin for error with the world at stake. If the duplication was, as suspected, a copy-and-paste procedure, then there was nothing to worry about.

"But if ... if Piotr was wrong ..."

It could work the other way. It could be an overwrite rather than an overlay. Cut *and paste.*

Tom goggled at Church, unbelieving.

"And you … you turned it on? You didn't pull the triggers but … you turned it on?"

Church nodded.

"If Piotr was wrong," he said, strength returning in his defiance, "I would have been erased—replaced by an exact, to-the-nanosecond copy of myself, along with the entire world—before I had a chance to pull those triggers." He held Tom's gaze, daring him. "I risked myself as much as everyone else. But I had been told that it was guaranteed to be too late."

As much as everyone else? thought Tom, wildly. *As in the entire world?* His mind went blank in the face of such scale.

"The world at large doesn't know about the asteroid yet," said Church, as Terry let out an actual moan of frustration and lay back on the floor. He began to kick his heels together, slowly, aggressively, banging out a steady beat as Church spoke. "I do. I received a phone call this morning from someone at the space agency. Someone that had worked closely with my brother during his time there, someone who Piotr had talked of his fears and plans with even then. Someone who knew of the true, sheer scale of my brother's genius in a way that even those in charge did not."

Memory's leather hand slapped Tom once more.

Michael Wicker. The contact's name is Michael Wicker. He wanted to come here—

"He told me about the asteroid. Not in a direct way, of course—my brother always referred to any potential apocalypse as *Blippo* for some reason, and hearing that word for the first time in nearly two decades nearly made me faint—but gave me a secure number to contact him on. He told me what no one at the agency or the government would admit. It was too late. He did have faith in my brother. He wanted to know if Piotr had ever completed that which he had always talked about. I said that he did. I was asked if, in return for the warning, that I would contact him again should I decide to use the device. God help me, I said that I would. But he isn't with you, is he?" Church said, closing his eyes again.

No. He isn't. You found out why some time ago; Michael Wicker is already dead. He is shot shortly after receiving Church's call on the "secure" line. Secure enough that they never find Church ... not secure enough for Wicker.

"Nope," said Terry, grimly. "Afraid not. Not for lack of trying, either."

Trying? Trying, plural?

Tom froze. Terry noticed.

"Anything?" he said. "You remember now, don't you?"

You had *tried to save Michael Wicker. Amongst other things. Other people.*

Terry leaned forward.

"The amnesia, the nausea this morning ... that happens sometimes. That's relatively normal. But that's not why you look so bad today, Tom. You remember why, yes?"

You've told the people in charge to try something else because Don Quixote doesn't work. They have. They didn't work either. The Overlay point, early this morning, it's already too late for anything else to be ready in time. You've wanted to take others with you but the Overlay can only take three.

"You aren't sick, and you aren't dehydrated. This isn't our first trip. Or our tenth."

We've tried everything. *The world, every one you create, is doomed. Now it's about self-preservation.*

And then something happened on the last trip.

"Tom ... you look that way because you're not twenty years old anymore. You're thirty-one. We've been running away from the end of the world for the last eleven years."

Everything in the basement went grey, and Tom remembered.

***

After a while, they had it down to a fine art. The first negotiation, the explanation. It worked great *then*. *Now*, however, they both knew that it wouldn't work any more; it's a trick they could no longer pull off. The thing they couldn't decide on was what to do *next*.

The initial conversation was always like a script with minor variations. Even the first time it was surprisingly easy on a practical level—even when Tom had no idea what he was going to say—but he came to realise that the outcome would pretty much be the same no matter what they did. On an emotional level, however, things were very different.

Talking to yourself was easy—especially when you're the version of you with all the answers—in the sense that you know your own mind, and communication was therefore simple on a level beyond anything Tom had ever experienced when talking to another person. But even so, persuading yourself when you're someone that second-guesses themselves ... that created a few roadblocks. The pain of the second guess. That's what made everything go wrong *last* time.

And no matter how many times they travelled, Tom never got over seeing the look in his own eyes when he woke himself up.

The first time was the worst ...

***

The trigger clicked, and the basement blurred; then it bent, and froze, like an old VHS temporarily paused, before settling back in exactly the same way. It was so identical, in fact, that Tom believed instantly that it hadn't worked at all, despite his pounding heart and a fresh metallic taste in his mouth that simply hadn't been there before. The fear before pulling the trigger had been indescribable, and yet with an edge of hope. It was the hope of a desperate young man; the news had been relayed to the world that morning that Don Quixote had failed. After he'd finished holding his mother and crying—she eventually fainting in his arms—he'd laid her down on the sofa, and then the doorbell had rang. A red-eyed Mister Church had been standing there, telling him that he had something to show them both. He and Terry. That had been how it started. Church had told them a lot. Who else would he tell? He didn't know many people, and Tom and Terry were the closest thing to sons he'd ever had. They were the only people he would be expected to tell.

Tom swayed on the spot, standing on wobbly legs on the basement's uneven surface, but didn't have time to deal with it as immediately he could hear Church gasping. Then there was a thud as Church collapsed to the floor.

His heart. He'd suspected it was likely even before he used the Overlay—his heart was weak and he didn't know how it would handle the shock—and every Church since knew that it was going to happen, because the boys told him. Church never survived the trip.

Yet he always came. He knew he was doomed, but he wasn't going to die without solving the greatest puzzle of his life. The boys could say nothing to prevent him doing so, and they weren't even sure that they should, given his argument. Even when they showed that reality's Church his own body, covered by a blanket at the back of the basement. He still came. So they'd tried CPR lessons, even trying to travel with defibrillators handy … they didn't work. Technology rarely survived the trip either, only the triggers. And they had to be passed on. The ones they brought with them, anyway.

The heart attack was quick, and quiet. The two boys wept and moaned in the basement, hands stuffed into their mouths to prevent waking the sleeping Church of this reality, slumbering as he was upstairs. A Church that had taken an extremely strong sleeping tablet in order to get back to sleep after the phone call that had rocked his world. The phone call that had made him turn the Overlay machine on, setting the save point. They silently mourned both the loss of a childhood friend but mainly the loss of everything. This was real. It was all real. A *half-eaten tuna sandwich that hadn't been on the dusty counter before—hadn't been there when they'd pulled the triggers in a reality that was months ahead in another future—was the harbinger of the end of the world.*

They didn't speak, found the blanket rolled up at the back of the room that would become all too familiar. They wrapped Church's still-warm body in it and ascended the old ladder, limbs trembling. Church's trigger now weighed on Tom's pocket like an unbearable, accusatory burden. They were younger then, and at least the nausea of the leap had passed almost instantly. When they were older, it would feel worse each time.

They had the plan in place, and moved silently through the night to carry it out. Tom would be first. Then the three of them would go to see Terry.

To see yourself sleeping is exactly as uncanny as you imagine it would be. It's even worse when it is the rubber stamp on the fact of the death of everything.

They'd brought the gag and rope with them. One time, another time, they'd forgotten it entirely; that had been very tough. Tom's doppelganger finally managed to bite him as he subdued himself. Terry was on gagging duty, Tom's job was to pin his own arms and get them tied. Once or twice it had gone so wrong— that reality's Tom escaping to his mother's room, where he had barricaded the door and called the police—that the boys had abandoned that trip entirely and pulled the trigger again. No point in trying to fix that *mess.*

It is, Tom often thought, very easy to convince yourself that madness is real when it's an impossible copy of you saying it, even after being woken and subdued in the night. Tom regularly felt a strange sense of pride in how quickly his other self adapted to the knowledge, even though it was understandably hard to take. Crying and vomiting were at a minimum. They were always able to loosen his bonds before heading to Terry's.

They also never told the other Tom why they'd come, or what they wanted them to do, until Tom and Terry were together. It'll be easier to explain it to you both together, *they said. It had worked on Tom when Church had said the same thing to him, and Tom rightly guessed it would work just as well coming from*

137

himself. After all, who would know better?

As much pride as Tom felt seeing himself rally magnificently, he felt the same amount of embarrassment on Terry's behalf as his friend's doppelganger reacted hysterically. With all the noise, it was of immense good fortune that Terry's parents were away that night and wouldn't be back until the morning; sipping wine with friends in Leicester and blissfully unaware of the huge rock of oblivion that was hurtling through space, heading towards them to obliterate all that they knew in just a few short months. Already past the point of no return.

Tom—the original, Tom One—never looked at Terry One after that very first trip. Seeing the ashen look on his friend's face as he watched his doppelganger cry and soil himself in bed was something that Tom never wanted to see again.

Eventually, they were able to talk. They all sat at various points of the room, sipping expensive whisky to calm their nerves that Tom's Terry had fetched from his parents' liquor cabinet. They'd turned the lights on; two boys looking sick with shock, two looking even sicker. As the years passed and the trips began to add up, the difference between the two sets—the "originals" and the fresh versions of themselves—became clearer and clearer. That was the problem. That was what led to the bad thing.

"And there's nuh-nothing that we can duh-do," said Terry Two, his voice shaking as if he was freezing. "Nuh-nothing at all."

"It's already too late," said Tom One that first time. He did most of the talking the first time, with Terry One only speaking when Tom One needed backing up. As the years passed, Terry One would talk more and more during this exchange, becoming angrier and less patient. Disgusted with his own weakness. "They try the best possible plan, and it's too late even for that. It was their only shot, and it doesn't work. Church only turned the machine on when he was warned, and when he was warned it was already too late. They saw it too late. There isn't time. We can't warn them. They already know."

This exchange then was repeated in various ways with slightly different words, with the answer always being the same.

"So what do you want to do?" Tom Two said, quietly.

Tom and Terry One looked at each other. Then Tom slowly raised his trigger, resting it flat on the palm of his hand. Offering it.

Tom Two managed to turn even paler, and Terry began to cry again.

"It's okay," Tom One said, trying to keep his voice even. "It's simple. You do the exact same thing. Exactly the same as we did. You've seen that it works. You know now that you listen to us. And then you have this exact same conversation with yourselves. And you switch places."

That was the plan, and it would work for years. There couldn't be four of them, after all, not if Tom and Terry One wanted to live as themselves. Inhabit their old lives, stealing a little extra time each time. Then running again. The way they saw it—and their duplicates extremely grudgingly agreed, for they were the same people—they were saving their duplicates' lives. Warning them. And the duplicates would be doing the same as the originals were doing, after all.

"The world is exactly the same when you jump as it is for you here," Tom One said, and paused, hearing himself as if someone else was speaking. He realised that he didn't even know if what he'd just said was true. They'd only seen the inside of Church's basement and the inside of their respective bedrooms, after all. Later, he would discover that it was actually true. "We're saving your lives. You owe us this." He didn't mention the baseball bats that they had tied around their necks, hanging down the back of their shirts. There was a slight delay on the triggers, after all, and they took the person holding it with them.

Whether they were conscious or not.

The thought of sending themselves back and sideways without knowing why, however, was too much to bear, although Terry would eventually suggest it many times over the years. There were more tears, and more protestations, but they were doomed from the start. It made sense, and everybody got what they wanted; after all, once they knew what fate was waiting for them, their duplicates wanted to jump as much as the originals did. What were they going to do, refuse to go and then die along with the rest of the world? Of course not. They wanted out, even if they didn't want to go right there and then ... but that was the condition of their being able to go. That was the deal.

"What about other people?" Tom Two asked. "Are there any more of those ..." He pointed weakly at the trigger.

"No," said Terry, one of the few things he said during the first version of that first conversation. "Church said ..." He paused, and Tom didn't know if he was trying to remember the facts of what Church had said, or was just caught by the razor sharp edge of the man's death. "It can only take a maximum of three. Ever. It's like ..." He paused again, and this time Tom knew that Terry was trying to remember how Church had said it worked; how he'd taken them to his basement the very first time, and gone through the whole sorry mess while wearing the expression of a department store mannequin. "You can only ever jump a maximum six people from one reality. That's why Piotr and Church only ever built three triggers; any more would mean temptation to use more." The duplicates sat in silence, waiting for more. Terry continued. "I mean, the reality you jump from can only be copied twice, and you can't take more than three people in one jump either. Any more people than that—and any more Overlays than that—and the Overlays you create would be ..." he waved a hand weakly in the air and rubbed his thumb and forefinger together. "Thin. Weak. They wouldn't hold. And even with the strong copies, placing three people that shouldn't be there into an Overlay is pushing it. Taking any more than three into one copied reality ..." Characteristically, showing a flash of his old self, now changed forever, Terry used his hands once more to explain. He bunched up his fists and then burst his fingers open, trickling them down through the air as if representing dust. Everyone watched them move in silence, and Terry realised just how brutally he had made his point. He put his hands under his armpits, placing them in detention for their crime.

"We go see Church now," said Tom, taking over. "Together. It'll make it easier for him to believe us, though I think us just knowing what we know would *cut it. He explains things properly to you. You take his triggers, and then you go."*

The duplicates' eyes widened. Tom took a deep breath and played the trump card, even though his voice sounded as weak as a glass of water.

"We ... we brought weapons. We can *do it the hard way, but that's just pointless. You don't have to say good-bye to anybody, as you'll be seeing them again when you wake up tomorrow, just like normal. And look, it just makes* sense. *We're here. We're you. We're giving you a chance to live by warning you, and all you have to do is jump and take the* exact same *life you have now. You owe us, and the alternative is we either fight and end up with one lot killing the other, or we stick around with you here and everything is just a mess. You will have* months *with your families before you have to Overlay again, and a lot of that will be happy months where they will be blissfully unaware of what is coming. Normal months. With us here ... with duplicates of you hanging around ... well. They won't be normal ... and none of us want that. You know this makes* sense."

The conversation continues for a long time. It's madness. After a while, incredibly, the solution seems like the easiest way. To resist is to bring the madness to the people they love, one way or another, and for Tom especially this is an unbearable thought. For his mother to deal with this *... he can't conceive of it. To comply is for everything to be—for a few months at least, before another Overlay—as it should be. Precious.*

"Mum," says Tom Two to himself, both noticing that he doesn't use the word "My" beforehand, or "Our." "Can I give her a trigger?" This was the same question that Tom had asked Church, and the feeling when delivering the answer is somehow the same as hearing it.

"Women can't Overlay," *Tom said.* "Even Piotr couldn't make the maths work. Something to do with the chromosomes ... Church could tell you. But these, at least," *holding up his trigger,* "certainly can't take her. Maybe with time, if we can get the data to people ... let them work on it, then add it to what we have now each time ... they can do it. Because we'll have a spare spot on our leap, maybe ..."

Tom and Terry One try it, over time. It doesn't even come close to making any difference. It's beyond the living minds and technology of that point in human history, and the human race ends that year.

They go and see Church a few hours later, as dawn is breaking. They reveal their dual natures to him very slowly, already having seen him die of a heart attack once that night. By the time he has calmed down, it is lunchtime. By the time he has explained everything properly to the duplicates, it is well into the afternoon, and their elderly host makes them food with shaking hands. He doesn't eat. Learning of one's impending death, one way or the other—even knowing that one chooses to make the leap that will both define his life and end it—tends to deaden the appetite. Tom and Terry One eat, the bodies desperate for sustenance. Tom and Terry Two try, but can't.

The Ones are there when the Twos Overlay. There is a horrible, horrible moment, just as the Twos pull the triggers, when Tom realises that they still don't know if their reality was overlaid or overwritten; they may be about to be erased from existence. He opens his mouth to scream wait *but he already hears the click of the triggers, sees Church's sad eyes and realises that* Church *didn't forget,* Church *knows what might happen, even though it was unlikely, knew and didn't remind them, and Tom thinks* you son of a bitch *... and then they are gone. Tom and Terry One remain in the basement.*

Staying with the duplicates and seeing them off is a long process that, after a few years, Tom and Terry One abandon altogether. They don't need to be there for their counterparts to leave, after all. They tried not doing it once—turning up on the doorstep with the duplicates long enough to help the process along, and then leaving them to it—they'd waited nervously until the nighttime, and then knocked on Church's door once more. There had been no answer. After breaking in to check, they found the secret basement was empty. The triggers were gone. After that, they always did it that way.

The first time through—and the first year or two of Overlays after that—had been surprisingly pleasant. At first, it had given them a sense of peace. Being able to tell their loved ones how they felt in normal circumstances, without the screaming and rioting and fires in the street in the face of doomsday, as the world went mad at the news of its own end. It was false, of course; they suppressed the pain of knowing that these same people were already dead. Of living in a dream that had already died. They told themselves they were making peace, that they were lucky to have this time. For a while, they believed that they believed it.

They'd made a pact. Even in the years before they accepted what they already knew—that struggle was fruitless—when they were still desperately compiling research, trip after trip, equations for the experts, people who would see their own work that they had never actually carried out presented to them, complete with notes to themselves explaining how to pick up from where they left off, suggesting desperate things that they might try to fix an unfixable problem (as well as personal notes advising them to say loving or forgiving words to such and such and so and so) the pact stayed in place.

They would not tell their family and friends what was coming. Seeing them go through it the first time was enough. Never again.

At first, they would try to take someone else with them, using the dead Church's spare trigger. Choosing one from their small group of friends was agonising. The first they decided to ask was Martin. Of course, he didn't believe them, knowing Terry's penchant for a wind-up ... but the boys realised that they only had to wait until the NASA announcement. They made sure that it was only them and Martin in their group the day the announcement came, sitting in a bar near Millennium Place. They sure as hell weren't going to be in their family homes to see all that *again.*

Martin's hysterical reaction to the news report had been the same as nearly everyone else's in the bar that day. He went straight to his phone, just like everyone else, or at least those who could get through the sudden and immediate mobile network logjam. They let him, and waited, shaking. He came back, ashen-faced, but they hadn't expected his response.

"I'm staying with Elizabeth," he said. Elizabeth had only been his girlfriend

for a year by then, but he had already proposed. He was a few years older than them, but he would never get the chance to be older still. The boys had been stunned. Over the years they would comfort themselves in their own choice by saying well, for Martin, that's different. That's his fiancée. *He's not going to leave a* fiancée.

The hardest part was that the only way to get anyone to believe them was to have to wait until the announcement. They didn't want to do that. After they'd taken David—who'd gone insane almost immediately after the jump, who'd taken himself off to the bathroom and was found there sitting on the floor, hanged by his own belt tied to the towel rail—they took Shaun.

For some reason, Shaun simply didn't appear on the other side, but his trigger did.

After that, they stopped trying to take someone with them. They said it was because they didn't know what they might be doing to their passenger if that happened again, and that was true.

But mainly because they just didn't know if next time, Shaun might arrive instead and one of them might not. They started to leave the week before the announcement. While everything was still good. After a few years, however, the wall of belief that they'd built for themselves started to crumble. It wasn't making peace.

It was torture.

Tom would start crying in the middle of meals, and his mother would ask him what was wrong and he would lie and say he was just tired, or stressed, and she'd leave her seat and hold him to her the way she'd done when he was a child, the way mothers only do to their fully grown sons when they truly need them. That would make things worse, and he would force himself to laugh it off and suggest they watch a movie or similar, much to the delighted surprise of a mother used to her son being desperate to get out of the house and away from her most of the time.

Tom and Terry began to secretly worry about each other. They spent less and less time together, although occasionally they would have days where it all became too much and they would blow off steam in spectacular fashion, laughing and drinking and either feeling as if nothing had changed or managing to think fuck it *and just enjoy the time they had.*

Those times punctuated things enough to keep them going. To keep their bond.

The amnesia happened a few times, and always returned their minds to the day before the jump. Tom always figured that was the point Church turned the Overlay machine on, the middle of the night reset point that occurred when they'd been sleeping. It created a save point for the world and everything in it. The boys too. Their minds.

Their long-term memory always came back by itself eventually, the knowledge of how and why. The short-term memory was a lot harder, but fortunately, one was always able to jog the memory of the other, and it all came back quite quickly, easily. They both talked about what might happen if it happened to them both at once; they always hoped that it would manage to come back by itself. Maybe it just might take longer if one wasn't being helped by the other.

Remembering was always hell. Learning the truth all over again.

Over time, they'd noticed people looking at them strangely, asking if they were well. Terry's hair had started to thin badly once he'd reached his mid-twenties, and Tom's eyes became more and more sunken. Once the reactions got constant and too much to deal with, the bubble of reality that was their home over and over became something else. Changes had to be made to keep things the way they wanted them. Cosmetic surgery helped, but even that wasn't enough to keep them looking exactly the way people had seen them looking the day before. Seeing someone age over five years wouldn't be noticeable. Seeing it happen overnight, even when patched up with cosmetic work, stood out. Eleven years overnight was even worse. They began to tell people that they were sick, hungover. Again, it worked, but only just. They knew their time reliving their own lives was coming to an end, was almost up. Neither of them had ever said anything about it to the other. Not yet. The thought was unthinkable.

Then the day came that Tom went crazy.

"Tom, can you give me a hand with the—" his mother stopped talking as she gasped and dropped her glass of water. Tom caught it. He'd always done so, ever since the look on her face started to change; the very first time he came downstairs in the morning after the Overlay, there had been no difference at all. He was the same Tom. As the years passed, so did that first look, that first morning expression. It became curious, her brain registering something wrong but not enough to create a conscious thought. That became a mild, voiced concern. That became open worry. Until the first time she gasped and dropped her glass. Now she dropped it every time, and he always caught it. He didn't remember much about the repeated months, but he always remembered that moment.

His brain normally went into automatic pilot for this part of the conversation, but today would be different. Something, stress, time ... today, something was ready to break.

"It's all right, Mum—"

"Oh my God, what did you do last night?"

"We just had a drink—"

Aren't you sick of this?

It wasn't the first time he'd thought it, but today it was louder.

Why are you still running?

"Tom, that's ridiculous, look at the state of you—"

This is not a life. It's a lie. This isn't even a conversation now. It's a script.

"Mum ..."

"You don't need to drink that much. Why do you need to drink that much? Your father never did, it's just stupid—"

"Mum ..."

"Is this what you get like at university? Is this normal? Think about your insides, *Tom, think what you're doing to them."*

"We weren't drinking."

The words were out before he knew that he was going to say them. And just like that, Tom knew that he was going to tell her. All the old reasons why—you can't save her, you can only scare her, she won't believe you, this will go very badly for both of you—*were still rattling around in his head, but somehow today they had become very small indeed, as if they were merely echoes of someone else's thoughts that he'd long dismissed some time ago. The thought came with a large amount of relief, and the guilt and doubt that began to scream at him were, for once, quietly locked in a box where they could rage and rattle until he was done.*

"*Drugs? You were doing drugs?" Gina's face bleached. She was never one for melodramatics, but she had always had a lifelong fear of drugs since the neighbour's kid overdosed on his nineteenth birthday. He'd lived with no ill effects, but Tom had been there. For his mother, that was the equivalent of a near-miss.*

"*No. No drugs," Tom said and quietly drew his mother in for a hug. Confused, she let him. He held her quietly, standing in the hallway. Though he told his Mother every day of each Overlay that he loved her, and often, the urge to hug her was one that he had to repress all the time—Normal Tom wouldn't hug her constantly, and being Normal Tom was the absolute focus of his strange existence—but he knew today was different. He breathed in slowly, heavily, as tears threatened to spill forth like a second confession. He held them, and her.*

"*Tom?" said Gina, confused, her voice muffled against his chest. This was different and she knew it. "What's happened?" He stepped back, his hands on her shoulders at arm's length.*

"I need to tell you something. I really need to tell you something."

"*Oh God," she said, her hands going to her mouth as her imagination picked out the absolute worst it could. Whatever she imagined, it wasn't as bad as the truth, however. The box burst open, as Tom put his arm around his mother and* led her into the living room.

What the hell are you doing? What are you possibly going to get out of this?

I'll just tell her the time travel part, *he thought giddily, convincing himself it made sense.*

You sent her son away!

I'll tell her the original is coming back when I go. That's what I'll say. *Madness, Tom knew, was an excellent way to convince oneself that what they want to do is right in any circumstances, but he didn't care. His only thought in that moment was the reality of the situation that he found himself in; how to convince her? Having a challenge to overcome suddenly made everything else go away, and Tom had the delirious sensation of being in a movie.*

As a child, he'd often watched 80s' and 90s' movies where the hero has some kind of fantastical secret. He has superpowers, can read minds, can't tell lies ... can travel through time. Horror films where people are being haunted by something unimaginable and have to explain their imminent danger to their loved ones and/or the police. In ninety-five percent of these situations, Tom would routinely sit at home and gasp at the sheer incompetence of the people onscreen. They'd just come out with it; I'm being pursued by a dead man with a hook hand and a load of bees because I said his name five times in front of a mirror. Ha ha, yeah, okay kid, nice try, maybe next time you'll WHAT THE HELL IS THAT?! *They made no attempt to ease the listener in, or establish their sober credentials, or explain that they would never make a joke so sick—*

What the hell are you doing, this isn't a fucking movie novelty, or a fun challenge, *you are going to scare her to death—*

—and he always thought how he'd do it differently, present in a plausible way that would at least give the character some *chance of success. He'd always thought how he'd start with some physical evidence—*

You don't HAVE any—

—but maybe he could think up some anecdotal evidence. In fact, of course

he could; that would be even better, and hell, he was thinking on his feet, but even if he fucked it up he could get it right next *time—*

Next time? Why would you want to do it next time, or this time at all—

He sat her on the sofa, sitting down next to her with her hand held in both of his. He was smiling, almost happy, but his entire body was trembling. She was waiting for him to speak, staring at him with wide eyes as if opening her mouth would confirm her worst fears.

Tom opened his mouth, and nothing came out. All those years of Groundhog Months, and it turned out that you didn't just remember every little thing around you after a while. He'd realised some time ago that the opposite was true; you shut it out. When everything is the same, you stop paying attention. He and Terry would even sometimes forget the results of the few football games that they watched. Plus, Bill Murray had only one day to deal with and presumably decades to learn it. Tom had months, and only eleven years to absorb them.

Good. Stop this. You have nothing. You have no evidence.

I can remember something. I can remember something.

"Tom?"

He'd been sitting in silence for a good few minutes, mouth working soundlessly without him realising.

The phone rang, and it was a blessing from the heavens. Of course.

"Mum, I know who that is. It's Terry's mum. It's Becky," he said, breathing a sigh of desperate relief. "She's ringing to ask if I've told you anything about what me and Terry did last night, because he looks terrible and is telling her that nothing happened."

His mum looked even more confused, but stood and moved to the phone on autopilot, darting glances at Tom all the way. She answered, heard who it was, and her expression grew even more perplexed. Another few seconds passed, and then she stared at Tom as if she didn't recognise him.

"Hang up," Tom said, heart pounding in his chest nearly loud enough to drown out the screaming protests in his head.

"*Becky? Sorry, I'll have to call you back, I'm just talking to Tom about something,*" *said his mother. Whatever else could be said about Tom's mother, she always had an excellent telephone manner. She sounded utterly calm, even if her skin was the colour of paper.*

"Sit down, Mum," *Tom said gently. She did. It wasn't much, but it was a seed. It was something. He could tell her the truth now, and even if she didn't fully believe him, he could make some predictions of things he* did *remember for the next few weeks and eventually—*

What the FUCK are you doing? You're going to drag this out that long—

He didn't know what he was doing, not in the slightest, but his brain was working away and finding whatever solutions it could. And now he remembered the first part, the part he'd always almost screamed at the TV and movie theatre screens. Establishing things that they both already knew.

"Okay. Now you're wondering how I knew who that was, and how I knew what they were going to say, right?" *His voice trembled as he spoke.*

"Yes. How ... did you know that, Tom?" *his mother asked, but as she spoke the protective buffer of reality automatically dropped into her brain and her face briefly lit up.* "Wait ..." *A smile threatened to appear on her face, but her lips merely twitched. She was going to say* is this a joke, are you playing a trick *but her brain had already done the detective work in nanoseconds. The appearance of her son. Her knowledge of Terry's oh-so-upright mother. Her son's nature. She knew all of these things, and her brain had already run the numbers. All of the things that Tom was counting on, all of the things that movie characters somehow conveniently forgot. Tom shook his head.*

"I know, and it's not a joke. Look at me. I look very different, don't I? More than just sick?"

She nodded, silent.

"And if I was going to play a joke on you, do you think I could get Terry's mother to help?"

She shook her head.

"And of all the years that I've been your son, did you ever know me to play an elaborate practical joke on you? Or anything even approaching one that would involve me looking so different that I scare you? Or one that would scare you at all?"

She shook her head again, and now tears were in her *eyes. She was afraid.*

DO YOU SEE WHAT THE FUCK YOU'RE DOING—

Tom did, and just as he calmly realised that he was going to continue, he realised that the last eleven years of living an awful lie—one that was always doomed to come to an end—had made him just crazy enough to do so.

"So you know … that if the reason that I know what I know about that phone call was pretty incredible … that I'm telling you the truth? That I swear to you that this is not a joke?"

She nodded, lots of times, quickly. He could see her pulse pounding in her neck.

"Tom, you're scaring me."

He knew he was. He couldn't help himself. He needed *this, needed to unload this burden just once and now he had started he* could not help himself.

"It's all right. It's all right. I just need to … I need to tell you …"

The scars. I have the scars! I forgot about the *scars!*

The facelift scars. Only a year old, and the facelift had been minor, but they were there. Paid for by another version of the woman in front of him, even if she didn't know it, after Tom had cleared thousands from her bank account and disappeared to London with Terry, going for a "weekend festival" so that he could use his real ID without any questions from the police.

"Look behind my ears," Tom said, leaning forward and dropping his head. His mother peered where he pointed, and gasped.

"What are those? When did you do that?"

"That's from when I had a facelift, Mum." Through all the confusion, she still jumped liked she'd been slapped.

"A facelift? *Are you crazy? When? Why the hell would you—"*

"Mum!" *he shouted, and she stopped cold. He was panting, shocked at himself, as his cry had come from nowhere, but he couldn't let her derail him. Not now.* "I had it because I had to look younger. I had to look twenty and I didn't anymore. Because I'm a lot older than twenty."

Wait, I've lost it. This is too much now. I was doing too well and now I'm giving her too much—

She simply stayed sitting here, jaw hanging open. His mind went blank, panicked, this wasn't going right when it was going so well, the scars were a terrible idea, he should have planned this, he could have brought newspapers back with him, but he didn't know that he was going to do this—

The trigger. She wouldn't know what it was, but it was more evidence. And wasn't that how you built a case? And then I could take her to Church's—

He'd deny everything.

Okay, maybe not Church, but the trigger itself was something. It counted. It would help.

"Wait here," *he said, standing without another word and dashing upstairs, to where the trigger was hidden on the top shelf of his cupboard, under a pile of old magazines. Where he always kept it. He dashed back to the living room, holding it before him like proof of God. She looked so small sitting on the sofa, staring quizzically at the item he held. He nodded, and sat back down, placing the trigger in his lap.*

"I'm going to tell you the absolutely crazy part, and you have to believe me, okay?" *he said, taking her hand again and staring two holes through her head. He took one of his hands away from hers as he held up the trigger, turning its dull surface pointlessly in the light.* "You don't recognise this, and that's because it's one of only three in existence. This is an extremely special invention, Mum. It's what allowed me to come here." *The words sounded more certain than he felt, and now it had come to the crux of it, the next wouldn't come at all. The words felt like a block of lead ten times too large to fit through the hole that was his mouth. He pushed. He* pushed. "I'm from the future, Mum." *It sounded just as ridiculous as he thought it might. Bad sci-fi. Saturday night shit. But there was no other way to say the ridiculous truth.* "I'm your son, but I'm your son eleven years older than when you saw me yesterday. Terry's the same."

It sounded terrible, even as he said it. The people in the movies had been right. It hadn't just been that way for the sake of pace after all. His mother started to cry as the adrenalin in his body surged, hoping that it had worked but knowing that it hadn't, because he'd done such an utterly shit job.

"Oh ... oh God, Tom ..." *said Gina, tears turning into a flood.* "What did you take? What the hell did you take?"

"No, no, Mum, I'm not on drugs, I don't do that, I promise, this is the truth ..."

"Oh, Tom, oh, Tom ..." *she was pawing at his hand and shaking her head, tragic pity and anger battling in her head for dominance. This was her son, but how could he have been such a fucking idiot ...* "What ... what did you ..."

"Mum, I haven't done anything," *said Tom, his frustration spiking in his desperation to get her to understand.* "Listen to me. Listen to me. Okay? It's the truth."

"Jesus, Tom, you idiot!" *she wailed, dropping his hand and putting her face in hers.* "You don't even ..." *She stopped talking for a moment, sobbed, caught her breath, and sat up, looking at him and biting her lip. She steadied herself and spoke with hitching breaths.* "O-okay," *she said, her jaw set.* "I hear you. I'm listening. We nuh-need ... need to talk about this some more. I ... I believe you. All right? I believe you." *She hesitated and took his hand. Her grip was limp, but she forced a tight hold for a moment, relaxed it hurriedly, and looked away.* "I just need a moment. I need a moment. I need to ... uh ... I need to ..." *She was threatening to start crying again, but she held it. Just.* "It's, ah, it's ... it's a lot to take in. A lot to take in. I don't know how this has happened, what's ... I probably need a drink. I need to get a drink. I'll get us both one."

"Mum ..." *He felt strange. Disconnected by her words.*

"I'm all right. I'm all right. I need to get us a drink." *She stood quickly and*

153

headed for the kitchen. He didn't know what to do or say, but he knew that, of course, she didn't believe him at all.

I'll try again. Do I have bus tickets? A receipt in my wallet with a date on?

STOP THIS NOW WHAT THE FUCK ARE YOU DOING—

A horrible thought crossed his mind, and Tom suddenly snatched up the trigger and bolted out of the room, propelled by instinct but still moving as quietly as he could.

The kitchen door was closed.

He sidled up to it silently, hearing nothing at first but still knowing there would be something. The kitchen door was never *closed. He pressed his ear to it.*

"—taken something, Arthur, you've got to get someone round here because I don't know what to do ... no, he hasn't done ... what? No, I don't think so but I just don't know—"

Afterwards, Tom could never honestly say that there was any conscious thought about what happened next. It was as if he were a passenger in his body. All he remembers is the anger, and the absolute and total knowledge that he had to get her off that phone. He burst in the door.

*"MUM!" he yelled, and he would never forget seeing the shock and terror in his mother's face, hearing her say into the phone—to someone else, some outside aid—*he's gone crazy, he's in here now, Tom, stop—*as he barged in, her fear making everything worse, what the hell did she think he was going to do, he just wanted her to listen, for crying out loud! He charged over to her, all breath and heat and noise, and slammed the trigger down on the counter. He snatched the phone out of her unprotesting hand and threw it across the kitchen, and then turned to her. He took her shoulders in what he thought was a gentle grip.*

"Mum! It's all right, it's all right, I'm sorry, I'm sorry, just listen, *I'm not crazy, I just need you to listen," he babbled, spit flying from his lips. Her hands were up and her eyes were closed tight as she babbled back.*

"Okay, Tom, okay, I'm listening, I'm listening, I promise I'm listening—"

WHY IS SHE DOING THAT I'M NOT CRAZY

"No, *you don't understand, it's true—*"

"*Tom, I'm scared, I'm really scared, please—*"

And he was about to let go, because it was those words that didn't quite calm him but finally penetrated the veil of madness, that and seeing his own mother cower and realising that he really, really didn't want that, as Terry burst into the kitchen and fell upon Tom before he had time to move. Terry caught him around the throat with his forearm and fell backwards, pulling Tom away from his mother. She half gasped, half moaned in relief and surprise, and fell back against the counter as her legs threatened to give out.

"*Get out of the house!*" *shouted Terry from behind Tom's ear. Tom wildly wondered how the hell this had gone so wrong.* "*Go to my mum's!*" *Gina hesitated, torn between maternal instinct and urgent advice, but Terry screamed at her.* "*He's taken some really bad shit! I've got him, go!*"

"*I haven't!*" *screamed Tom, but his mum was already running out of the door, slamming it behind her.* "*You cunt!*" *he screamed at Terry, who was now beneath Tom's back on the floor, wrapping his arms tighter around Tom's head and throat and his legs around Tom's waist.* "*You fucking cunt! Why did you tell her that?! Now she thinks I'm on drugs!*"

"*What the hell is wrong with you, you asshole?*" *hissed Terry, in his ear.* "*What are you trying to do? What are you actually trying to do?*"

"*Fuck you!*" *shouted Tom. He didn't have an answer, but his rage told him he was right.*

"*We can't stay here! You're not staying here! You've screwed this one* right up*!*"

"*Fuck you! Fuck you! I'm* staying*! I've had enough! I'm staying! I don't want this anymore! I don't care what happens!*" *Tom was finding it hard to get his breath, but even with the greying edges of his vision he realised that he meant it. He didn't want it anymore. He* did *want to stay. Terry's grip was tight on Tom's throat, but Terry's voice was silent. Tom's words had hit him like a volley of bullets.*

"We're leaving," *hissed Terry through gritted teeth, holding on for dear life. He was trying to put Tom out but had no idea if his sleeper hold would actually work. He'd never tried it before, but he didn't know what else to do. He had no idea that this had been going on in his friend's head, not this much.*

But you don't talk anymore, do you, really—

Tom bucked in Terry's arms, and Terry tightened down with everything that he had left. Tom began to cough and make choking sounds, flailing more and more desperately and clawing deep welts in Terry's forearms. Terry held on despite the ragged, burning pain, and as the sweat continued to run through his hair and into his eyes, he felt Tom's struggles begin to slow. Only once Tom had gone completely limp in his arms did Terry relax, dropping his head back onto the floor and gasping in lungfuls of air. If his own mother hadn't been so surprised by Tom's mum cutting her off on the phone ("Just so unlike her,") if he hadn't asked what she said ... if he hadn't popped round to check, to be sure ...

He pushed Tom's dead weight off him with some effort and pulled himself to his feet using the kitchen unit nearby. He reached into his pocket. His trigger was still in there; normally they both protected theirs like the lifelines that they were. If the triggers were ever damaged ... Church had assured them that the triggers were built to be extremely durable, but even so, they rarely took risks with them. As Terry had the smallest, most modern trigger, it fit into his jeans pocket; he never kept it in there, but more often than not these days, after they first arrived, he would fall asleep with it in there and hide it the next day. He knew by now that his mother never came and picked up his laundry on that first morning. Terry had done his own laundry since he was fourteen years old. He knew he'd seen Tom's trigger flash by as he'd dived onto his friend, but where ... there. He quickly crossed the kitchen to the counter where Tom's older, larger trigger lay.

Fitting Tom's unconscious hand into the trigger was relatively easy. Pulling them simultaneously didn't matter; they were designed to work in sync. Church had told them that a second Overlay wouldn't be created as long as they were pulled within eight minutes and forty-three seconds of each other. Even so, they always tried to pull them at the exact same time, just in case, but they'd still managed to screw it up a few times over the years, occasionally dropping them at the key moment due to an outside distraction or a slip. Seeing the other disappear while you were left behind, however briefly, was terrifying. But it always turned out okay. So Terry knew that he could send Tom on ahead, even if he was off by a nanosecond or ten. Terry gripped his own trigger tightly, finger inside the trigger guard.

Kneeling down, Terry squeezed Tom's finger on his trigger, taking care to not let his fingertips touch the actual trigger itself ... that was key to the collection process, apparently ... and pulled that hand back like he'd been burnt, pulling his trigger with his opposite hand. There was a split second delay, and then everything was dark. And cold.

Church's basement.

Terry breathed a weary sigh, and waited for Tom to wake up.

**

Tom woke to a bright light and the sound of a door closing, and a feeling of being dragged.

"... thefug ..."

"Shit," a voice said. Tom felt himself laid down. Footsteps moved around his body. "I thought you were out for good when you went under." Terry's fuzzy shape moved into Tom's blurry vision. A messy blob moved before Tom's eyes. "How many fingers?"

"Fuzzle."

"Yeah, you're not gonna be remembering much of this. Which, thank God, is the best possible thing."

The footsteps moved away again, and the dragging resumed. Tom let it, lost in a cloud of nausea and uncatchable thoughts.

"Getting you into bed. It's just possible that all of this could work out for the best," Terry's voice gasped. He sounded exhausted. "I don't know what the fuck all that was about but ... why am I talking to you? I'm wasting my breath."

Tom felt arms under his armpits, the edge of the bed against his back. His body was dragged slowly upward, and he could hear Terry holding his breath with the effort.

"Stayig ..." he muttered.

That was something he wanted, wasn't it? Something he wanted to do?

"Staying?" grunted Terry, as he dropped Tom back onto the bed. "You don't want that, dickhead. You don't know what you're saying. Don't talk like that. You've had a bad day, that's all." Terry's voice sounded far from certain.

"Staying."

"Yeah, yeah, shut up, you idiot. Fortunately, it's all gonna be ..." he dragged Tom's sheets over him, "... gone. It's been a while since either of us had a nausea episode, but the timing ... aah ... couldn't be better," he gasped, as he stood up straight. "The long-term will be back in forty-eight hours, but if you think I'm helping you coax back the last few days ... or a memory of that performance ..." Tom heard Terry sigh heavily, and the room was quiet for a few moments. When Terry spoke again, his voice was right by Tom's head, and it was kinder, softer.

"Look. Don't fight it, man. Just relax. Trust me. It's gonna be better this way, and you don't want to remember what happened with your mum. The way you've been talking ... best to forget it. Trust me. Okay? Trust me. Sleep. Let it go."

Tom only came back from consciousness at the sound of the door closing as Terry left. His first instinct, blindly, was panic; he'd nearly gone under. He'd nearly forgotten everything. One thought was clear above all others.

Staying.

Like a man in the middle of a three-day booze binge, it took everything he had to flail and drag his body close enough to the side of the bed to feel for, and grab, a pen from the bedside table. Whenever he started to drift off again, fear took hold and gave him energy, and he heard Terry's voice saying trust me, trust me. His clawing fist found the old Kasbah flyer lying discarded on the laminate *wooden surface.*

He wouldn't forget.

trust me

He wouldn't ... what shouldn't he do ... something Terry said ...

trust me

With his brain and body's last available conscious thought and effort, Tom had time to write, with shaking hand:

dONT TRUST HiM

Then he passed out, and forgot the last eleven years.

***

After all of Tom's wailing had stopped—after Terry had left the basement, gone for a walk, leaving Church to stand in glum-faced silence—Tom eventually took the glass that Terry offered with a shaking hand. The whiskey was strong, very strong, and as Tom felt it slide down his throat he felt a little steadier ... or as much as an utterly shell-shocked man could be. The hit of old memories was like an iron fist, but they *were* old memories after all. Devastating, yes, but also with that feeling of *oh, of course.*

"I didn't know we were going to see him," said Terry, gesturing towards Church. "We don't normally bother going to the doctor's, but today ..." He shrugged. "Normally we go straight to him. We go upstairs and wake him up, remember? So we never know where the hell he would go for the day normally. I was thinking on my feet. I knew eventually all the long-term memories would come back, but usually we have to coax the really recent stuff out when the other forgets. You know how it is now, right? You remember that?"

Tom nodded, took another sip. It was soothing.

"And I guess ... I guess I was planning on never reminding you of last night," Terry added. "If I could. I didn't have time to think, I was exhausted after the Overlay myself, and after half-lugging you into your bedroom I could barely stand. I staggered home, passed out, woke up, came straight round here after talking to my mum—she caught me on the way out—and you were just peppering me with questions. I hadn't yet worked out how I was gonna play it, and you never gave me a chance ... I didn't really know what to do. I kept thinking, you know, maybe this is the time that his memories *never* come back ... well ..." He looked away, at the ceiling, finding the words. "I was hoping that, I think. The way you were talking, Tom. Talking about ... staying. Hell, I've thought about it myself enough times. And I've wished sometimes that my memory would never come back too. That I could have a reset. That maybe I wouldn't feel so tired of it."

"It was clear to me, of course," sighed Church. "Having only turned the machine on that morning, and knowing that I would only ever take you two ... when I saw you, I knew. You were clearly a lot older, and overnight at that. The answer was immediate. And there was only one reason why you would have come back."

He sighed, and covered his face again, rubbing it.

"Tom ... what was I supposed to do?" said Terry, his voice pleading. "When you'd freaked out like that, when you were *talking* like that? If it was that bad ... why didn't you tell me ... I mean, I just didn't know what the hell to do. I was stalling. When you went off to the doctor's, I went home to think and I just didn't get *anywhere.* I thought about maybe Overlaying again, tricking you into it somehow, before your memory came back and that maybe that would, I dunno, wipe that stuff out for good ... but I couldn't. I couldn't make that choice for you."

Tom raised his eyes to Terry's, shrugged, nodded, sipped from the glass again.

"Then you came and dragged me round here. I didn't think Church would come to you first. Once you told me he had ..." Now it was Terry's turn to shrug. "I just went along with it. I came here. I'd let him tell you. What else could I do?"

"We're done," said Tom, staring at the glass.

"What?" asked Terry, straightening up with a start.

"This run. Doing this. We're done. You know that, don't you?" Tom said, with his hand. "We can't play the trick any more. They're starting to notice too much."

"Oh," said Terry, relaxing slightly. "I thought you meant—"

"And I can't see that look in her eyes any more," continued Tom, staring back at the glass and speaking as if Terry hadn't, "when she sees me in the morning. Because every time I just want to scream the truth at her, Ter. I want to grab her and tell her and hold her and I can't because *I always knew what would happen.* I just ..." He paused, and looked at his friend once more. "Thank you, by the way. You did the right thing."

"Oh. Well ... you're welcome. You know," Terry said, awkwardly, but relief was on his face.

"I just ... I snapped. I just lost it. That was ... *uhhhh* ... I can't even ..." He rubbed his face, sighing heavily. "But I came to a decision in that moment that I've been thinking about for a very long time now. I don't *want* to do this anymore, Terry. I can't. I'm just ... I'm sick. I'm sick inside."

"Tom," said Terry, getting to his feet and coming over, urgent and immediately scared. "You're emotional. You're still fucked up. I know what you mean, I've thought it too, but you're not thinking straight."

"Everyone on this planet dies, Terry. Everyone. Everything. You realise that the only remnants of the human race that will ever exist, forever, endlessly, are copies of you and me? Duplicating themselves for the rest of time?"

This wasn't news to Terry in any way at all, but he knew that he still had to tread carefully.

"That's right, Tom. Of course it is. I know," said Terry slowly, gripping Tom's arm. His hand was shaking. "We've always known that, haven't we? And the simple truth is that we're the lucky ones. The luckiest. You're gonna ... you're gonna throw that away?"

"We haven't been living, man," said Tom. "We've been dreaming."

"Tom ... Tom ..." said Terry, fear locking his thoughts into a repetitive loop, "we don't have to keep doing this. We don't have to Overlay and come back to *this*. We can leave. We can take my car and go wherever, we have *months* every time, remember?"

Tom didn't say anything. The hidden bunker was silent.

"Mr Church?" Tom said eventually, breaking the silence. "I assume that you still want to Overlay? You normally do, even knowing ... you know."

Church stood up straight, mildly startled by being addressed.

"Yes," he said, quietly, "of course. I am old, and this is the single greatest mystery of my life. My brother's life. If all is lost anyway, I wouldn't pass up solving it for the sake of a few more months. I can't really think ..." He waved his hand to finish the sentence.

Tom nodded. He turned to Terry.

"I'm going home, mate. I'm going to sleep." He stood, zombielike, his face blank. Terry didn't respond for a moment.

"Tom," he said carefully. "Your mum."

"I'm not going to say anything," he said. "I'm going to sleep." He turned to the old man. "Are you all right, Mr Church?"

"Are you?"

Tom didn't reply. Church smiled sadly.

"There we are then, I think," he said.

Tom nodded in solemn agreement and walked across the floor of the bunker, towards the ladder. Terry watched him go, mouth open and trying to find reassuring, *convincing* words that wouldn't come.

"Tom ... *mate* ..."

"I'm sorry, Terry," Tom said, without turning around. "I can't talk about this now. I'll talk to you in the morning. I'm sorry. I need to sleep."

He grasped the aging ladder. It felt as faded and brittle as he did.

***

But his mother was awake when he arrived home.

"Tom! Where have you been, your phone's been—"

"Been at Terry's, felt too rough on the way home to make it all the way here. Phone died. Should've used the landline, but I fell asleep. Doc says it's probably food poisoning," said Tom, the old lie coming as automatically as breathing now. "Just got to go to bed."

Gina sighed, her fear-powered anger dissipating with it. She crossed the hallway and put her hand on her son's forehead. He placed his hand on hers, trembling and fighting the screaming impulse to tell her everything, even then. But he'd seen the results. He wouldn't make that mistake again. Not even in the face of Armageddon.

"You poor thing," she cooed, her brow furrowed. "And you normally have such an iron constitution," she added, smiling, then sighed. "Your dad was the same. Get yourself to bed and I'll bring you some water."

Tom opened his eyes and looked at his mother. His expression was inscrutable.

"Do you miss him?" Tom said. His mother blinked.

"Of course," she said after a moment. "You never really talk about him much, Tom. I don't like to bring him up to you, I always thought …" She smiled, sadly, and placed her hands on Tom's shoulders. "I miss him every day. Most of the time now it's just a little, but sometimes I can't breathe. You manage." She read her son's face for a moment, checking that it was okay to go on. "You okay with me talking about this?"

"Yes." He really meant it. She cocked her head and nodded in a *fair enough* gesture.

"You know, I always remind myself that we had a lot of very good years together," she said. "And he gave me a beautiful son. No matter what … I consider myself very lucky." She smiled fully now, put her hand on his face. He was blinking a lot, and squinting at her, as if something was going on behind his eyes.

"It's a cliché, you know," she said, tenderly, "but you look like him so much. Everyone always said it." Her eyes travelled away for a moment, lost somewhere that was unreachable across the gap of years. When she came back, she looked briefly surprised to see Tom standing there. "You can always talk to me about him. Anytime. It's all right. I won't be sad. It'd be good for me, I think. And you."

"Can we talk about him now? Before I go to bed?" asked Tom. Gina blinked a few times in surprise.

"Well ... yes," she said. "But don't you want to rest?"

"It can wait," he said. "I'd really like to talk to you for a bit. Then I'll sleep."

They sat. They talked until his mother needed to sleep herself. And after she kissed him on the cheek and ruffled his hair, Tom hugged her painfully tight. He hoped that she thought the shaking in his arms was due to him being sick and weak. Then he stood and left the room, and Tom was reminded of the nightmares he had when he was very young. The ones where his mother was on top of a very large hill, very far away, and moving farther away from him no matter how much he screamed her name or how fast he ran.

This time he didn't run. He waited until he heard her bedroom door shut, and then moved around the rest of the house silently until the sun started to rise; travelling from room to room and gently touching each object as if to confirm their existence.

"I consider myself lucky," he said to himself, quietly.

By the time the sun was fully up, he'd left.

***

"You sure we shouldn't leave *something*. They're going to worry," said Terry. Tom shook his head.

"I know," he said. "Plus, police. Make things harder if there's a missing persons report. But unless you want to leave a note and keep Overlaying every week, or having to keep e-mailing, or texting, or calling ... we can't do that. I can't do that."

Terry became even more pale, but nodded. He opened the car door, and Tom moved round to the passenger side. The sun was up now, but it was still very early, and everyone inside Terry's house was asleep. The backseat was full of bedding, as well as their bags. They had no plans, after all—talking about even the idea of leaving had been hard enough, even without discussing a destination—and they wanted to be as prepared as they could for any eventuality, even with the brief packing window that they had. Tom was very, very glad that the arrival time of each Overlay would be at night. They could always be packed and gone before anyone awoke; they would have to come back to the house, to be near enough to *Church's* house, for the triggers to be in close enough proximity to the central unit to work. That would be very hard indeed, but they didn't have to go inside. They could do it at night so they didn't see anyone.

"They'll worry," Terry said again, then paused. "You know it's far worse than that. They'll think we're dead. They'll think we've been killed."

"We talked about this," Tom said. They had. They could give an excuse of going away to Spain to work for several months, or *anything* ... but they would have to have those same excuses after every Overlay, have to see the faces of the listener, give the story to people they knew to be dead.

That life was over.

Terry opened his mouth to say something else, and then didn't. He set his jaw, nodded, and got into the car. Tom did the same. They put on their seat belts in silence. Terry put the keys in the ignition.

"You rang Mister Church," he said. It wasn't a question.

"Yeah. I told him," Both young men pondered this, knowing that they would never see Mister Church again. The Mister Church of each Overlay would find the Terry and Tom of his world when he realised all was lost, and begin the process himself, just as he had done the very first time. Tom and Terry One would never have to watch him die before their eyes again. That was something. They would be spared that. It was one more person to miss, but at least they could eventually remember him as the man who taught them how to peel potatoes, or showed them how an old mangle used to work. Not as the scared, dying aspect that had become their defining image of the man. In time, the real Mister Church would come back to their memories.

Not just Church. All of them.

But it was little comfort, sitting on Terry's driveway in his old Mondeo.

"Do you think the others are doing this?" Terry asked, looking up at the house.

"Who?"

"The first ones we sent back. And the ones after that. The ones who are nearly as old as we are now. Do you think they've reached this point too? Or are about to?"

"Probably," Tom said. "They're us."

Silence. Then Terry turned the keys in the ignition.

"Do you ever think, *why us?*" Terry asked, quietly. Tom was surprised. It wasn't the kind of thing Terry usually said, and it made him realise just how long it had been since they'd had a proper conversation.

"How d'you mean?"

"Why did we get to be the last?" Terry said, looking at his bedroom window. "Why did *we* get to live? We didn't deserve it. It's not exactly *living*, I know ... but it isn't being dead."

"No," said Tom. "We didn't. But this is what we were given. And we do with it as best we can." He remembered the same Christmas day for eleven years, many times a year, like living inside a memory. "And we should consider ourselves very lucky. But ... it's time to go, man." He tried to sound more convincing than he felt. All the same, Terry wiped his face with his hand and put the car into reverse.

"You want the radio on?"

"Yeah."

"Any station?"

"Something playing oldies."

"Aren't they all?"

There was a pause, and then they both started laughing. There was nothing else to do. The laughter didn't last long; thoughts of their families waking up and finding them gone, their loved ones first calling their friends and asking if they'd heard from the boys, and then waiting until night fell to call the police. The torment that was about to befall those people was mighty, and the only comfort to be had in the boys' minds was the knowledge that the people they knew had died long ago, swallowed by cataclysm at the end of the world.

But they'd laughed. In the face of Armageddon, that was a start.

*

4. The Man On Table Ten

Before everything changed, Lisa had been at work.

"Do me a favour, Lisa, and you'll be my favourite for the day," asked Kim, using her cutesy, I-need-a-favour voice as she came around to the staff side of the bar. It was unnecessary; she owned the place. "I know you're due a break, but couldja go and do table ten for me first? I've just got to sort out some change. Would you mind?"

"No, it's okay," replied Lisa, tired but happy to help, as ever. The bar had been quieter than usual that day—the rain had kept people away, even during the lunchtime rush—but Lisa's late-night studying the previous evening was taking its toll. Despite several coffees, she could barely keep her eyes open; if she tried to recall anything about the intricacies of the endocrine system now, all she got in return was an impenetrable fog. She began to wonder if the last-minute study session had just been a waste of time … but could she be blamed for wanting to get some extra time in with the books? The exam was on Monday, and she'd known that she'd be working all weekend; it had been her only chance. Paying the rent was one thing, but it meant nothing if she couldn't pass this module. *Final year, final chance*, that was the mantra she kept repeating to herself every time an opportunity to party (or drunk friends) came calling.

"Thanks," said Kim, already taking the tray out of the till. "Have an extra five minutes on your lunch. I appreciate it." She disappeared into the back office, tray in hand, and Lisa again found herself wondering if maybe, just maybe, she was a little bit too soft for her own good.

She sighed, and grabbed an order pad and pen. Her eyes fell on Chris at the other end of the bar, who was looking after any drink orders that came in. There hadn't been many so far during that dreary, quiet afternoon. The small, dark mahogany-effect tables that were dotted along the narrow, olive green coloured walls of the bar were pretty much empty; the only other patrons in there were a young couple, lost in the middle of finishing off their beer-battered cod and chips, and a slightly sweaty man in a grey suit that hadn't gotten off his phone in the entire time he'd been in there, along with two women who were simultaneously nursing orange juices and newborn children.

There was also, she now saw, the man on table ten.

He was surprisingly well dressed for the middle of the day; a three-piece blue suit and tie which, despite its inherent smartness, looked as faded and old as the man wearing it. He looked about sixty, with thinning silver hair that was slicked back upon his head. His thin right hand was nervously caressing a cup of tea, turning it around and constantly passing its handle back and forth between his fingers. His gaze flicked around the room, his eyes darting here and there as if he were watching a fly performing aerial acrobatics. He looked decidedly uncomfortable, and despite her usually caring nature, Lisa found her tired mind rolling its imaginary eyes with mild annoyance.

Great. I have to deal with the crazies again.

She hadn't seen him come in, hadn't seen him order his tea; she must have been doing the stock check in the cellar at the time. But there he was now, tucked away at the corner table like a frightened mouse, his seat wedged right into the valley of the two walls as if he were trying to disappear into them. It was also the table (Lisa would realise this when she thought about it all later, when she thought about it during the first of what would become an unending number of mental visits back to that shocking day) that gave him the best view of the whole bar, and the one that was furthest away from the glass wall that ran along one side of the building.

His head came up immediately as she crossed around to the public side of the bar itself, her movement instantly catching his attention. *He looks like a frightened mouse*, she thought again to herself, and then checked the thought almost as soon as it came; the description was inaccurate. He didn't look like a frightened mouse at all, but rather like an animal with a precious meal, an animal that has seen another creature appear in the near distance. Watchful, cautious, ready to act. His eyes were a shockingly clear, crisp blue; she could see that even from the other side of the room as she made her way over. Forcing herself to smile, Lisa raised the pad, feeling an odd compulsion to telegraph her intentions.

"Hi, are you ready to order?" she asked, as brightly as she could manage through both her tiredness and her discomfort around the man. He just radiated alarm.

He regarded her face for a moment, steely blue eyes staring intently at her as if she were someone to be vetted, someone who may harbour hidden intentions. His gaze then dropped, and he actually began to look her up and down. Despite the fact that she was already unnerved by the man, something about the way he did this didn't make Lisa think that he was being a pervert; this wasn't a lustful gaze, and Lisa would know one when she saw it. She was twenty years old and had lost the extra ten to fifteen pounds that she'd put on by drinking her way through her first few years of university (losing them due to living like a nun through the last six months of her current year) and her pretty face and long, thick brown hair drew enough unwelcome attention from the various lunchtime drunks—and evening wannabe Romeos—for her to have almost a sixth sense when it came to knowing if she was being checked out or not. No, this was a calculated examination, his eyes flitting from her hands, to her pockets, to her collarbone, then back up to her face. The whole process must have taken no more than two seconds, but this odd man had unsettled Lisa. The examination seemed far longer.

"Yes ... please," he said, finally, his face still expressionless as he nodded gently, his wide eyes still maintaining their intense stare, even when they dropped back to the menu in front of him. He raised his right hand—his left was under the table, presumably resting in his lap, and in fact Lisa was dimly aware that she hadn't seen that arm move even as much as an inch in the time she'd been watching him—and pointed to an item on the menu. "Sausages ...

please. Sausages and chips." Then he did something that freaked Lisa out almost to the point where she asked him to leave; he closed his eyes and sighed deeply, nodding slowly and with great certainty. Lisa's mouth dropped open at this, and she didn't even know it. A few moments passed, the pair of them locked in an almost comic tableau; the old man sitting and nodding in silence, Lisa standing there with her mouth gaping like a captivated child. Eventually, he opened his eyes again, and this fresh reminder of their startling blueness jolted Lisa back to her senses.

"Yes," he said, a faint smile beginning to play around his lips as he looked up from the menu and back at her. "The sausages. And the chips. And do you have any vegetables? Oh, and *parsnips*. Do you have any of those? I could never get them to grow." He leaned forward in his seat as he asked this last question, the idea occurring to him and bringing urgency to his eyes. His voice was strong and clear but slightly hoarse at the same time, like an old rock singer. His tongue briefly darted out, very slightly, and he licked his lips nervously. It was an action that he didn't seem to be aware that he was performing.

Lisa was stunned. This had gone from an ordinary customer interaction to her being ready to get Chris to take over; she was now *incredibly* uncomfortable around this man, and the change had happened in under a minute. Plus, the guy had *a presence* ... it was hard for her to put her finger on.

"Uh ... we have vegetables, but no parsnips," she mumbled, and watched the old man's face fall slightly at her words. Her reflex response to seeing an older person even slightly upset overcame her discomfort, and she found herself babbling. "But I'll double check with the kitchen, they might have some left over." The old man's eyes softened for a moment, and this time a proper, gentle smile spread across his face. He appreciated the thought, but there was a sadness in his expression.

"Thank you," he said, and just like that Lisa's revulsion was gone, if not her intrigue; his sincere thanks had humanised him, but hadn't dimmed his aura. There was just something *different* about him.

"No problem," replied Lisa, nervously returning the smile. "Would you like some more tea?" There was a pause whilst the old man seemed confused as to what she was asking, before he looked down at the cup on the table like he hadn't seen it before. He shook his head, still looking at it.

"No, thank you," he said, speaking slowly and deliberately, "but I would like a pint of beer. Any ale, I don't mind. And some whisky. And some schnapps, if you have it."

Lisa's eyes darted to the clock on the wall. It was 3:00 p.m.

"All at once?" she asked, in a surprised voice that made the old man look up. The blue eyes were now shiny, covered by a very thin, very slight sheen of water.

"Oh, yes," he said, "three glasses. Ice for the whisky. On the rocks, as I believe they say in America." He might have started to smile again, but at that moment Chris dropped a coffee cup behind the bar. The cup didn't shatter, but it did make a clattering noise on the tiled floor. Even so, the old man slammed backwards in his seat like he'd been shot, but it wasn't a motion of panic. He'd reacted with a controlled instinct, looking prepared to move again; that animal-with-food look was back in his eyes as his head craned around Lisa to see the source of the sound. His eyes were wider, but not *wide.* They were assessing, weighing things up once more. His shoulders slowly came down once he was satisfied that it was, after all, just a cup.

"Are you all right?" Lisa heard herself asking. The question had come out all on its own, gentle and sincere, but she was embarrassed as soon as the words were out. She needn't have worried; the old man didn't even look at her as he nodded without a word. He turned back to the menu once more, eyes scrutinising it the way a lawyer would examine a contract. Realising that she was dismissed, Lisa turned and made her way back to the bar, wondering what the hell to make of the exchange.

"Are you all right?" asked Chris as she returned, unwittingly repeating the same question Lisa had asked only a few moments before. He couldn't help but notice the unusual expression on Lisa's face. "Got a live one, have we?" Lisa looked at Chris, wondering what she could actually say about their elderly customer. What had happened? Nothing. Nothing at all, really.

"No, he's harmless," she said. "Just a little bit odd, but I think he'll be off home for a sleep after drinking what he's just ordered." Chris smiled, and went back to fiddling with his phone. After Lisa had rung the order through to the kitchen upstairs, she began to pour the old man's drinks whilst feeling a little shaken, choosing a pint of Pedigree as his beer. She scolded herself, wondering why she was allowing herself to be rattled by a slightly weird old man. Odd old drunks were nothing new to her, nor was taking a multi-drink order for them that included hard liquor ... but wasn't there something different about this man? Something in those electric blue eyes of his? As unusual as he was, he didn't *seem* like an old drunk; he spoke in a clear, well-intoned voice, like something from a better, classier age. She looked over at table ten as she loaded the old man's drinks onto a tray. He was still sitting there, of course, deeply engrossed in the menu like a reader with a captivating novel, looking like an old, strangely neat scarecrow.

With a sense of reluctance, Lisa transported the drinks tray over to table ten. As she placed it down on the table and took the glasses off it one by one, she tried not to catch the old man's eye whilst still wanting to observe him at the same time. Out of the corner of her eye, Lisa saw his head come up from the menu and intently follow each drink's path from the tray to the table, like a dog watching the descent of its food bowl. That sealed it; he was just an old drunk, after all. *No, he's not,* said a voice in her head. She ignored it, but still turned away from the table without a word and hurried as nonchalantly as possible back to the safe haven of the bar. As she decided to busy herself emptying the glass washer, her gaze was drawn back over to the table in the corner.

What the hell is wrong with you? she asked herself. *Jesus, haven't you got enough on your mind to worry about at the moment without getting hung up on the wino of the day over there? Get a grip!* But she still looked, and was

173

fascinated by what she saw.

The old man had laid all three drinks out in a straight horizontal line in front of him, and now sat staring at them, taking slow, deep breaths. Eventually, he slowly raised his right hand—the left still hidden beneath the table—and picked up the pint of Pedigree, eyes locked on it like a cat prepared to pounce on a small animal, the prey now become hunter. He lifted it as if it were the Holy Grail, slowly and reverently, and held it before his clearly misted-over blue eyes, considering it. Closing his eyes just as before, he gently put the glass to his lips, tipped it, then pulled it away, keeping his eyes shut and the glass held in midair. His hand was shaking slightly.

These were not the actions of any old drunk that Lisa had ever seen, even the alcoholics. The reverence with which he performed these movements was almost religious. She would have kept watching, but Kim chose that moment to return to the bar and ask Lisa to run some mail to the post office. Of course, Lisa complied, but as she grabbed her phone and began to leave, she kept one eye on the old man. He was now actually clutching the pint glass to his chest with a gentle grip, looking at the table with half-closed eyes.

Once outside, though, her head seemed to clear. The rain, whilst it still threatened to return from the grey sky above, was temporarily at bay, and the day now felt warm. The town centre street was full again, and the people that would have previously been trying to make their progress by moving from the dry safety of one shop awning to the next were now filling the pavement. Despite the still-ominous clouds, the mugginess that had been in the air had lifted thanks to the clearing rain, and the air felt comparatively fresh. With good timing, Lisa's friend Carla's name appeared on her phone; Lisa had taken her phone with her to call Carla in the first place, wanting to see how her coursework was going. The recognition of her friend's name onscreen interrupted Lisa's mild obsession with the old man, temporarily putting it out of her mind. The degree was *everything* this year, for Lisa if not for Carla. Carla liked to party, no doubt about it, but even she seemed to have knuckled down now. As a result, Lisa used Carla as her benchmark; if Carla wanted to party, she would say no. If Carla was studying but going out afterwards, Lisa *definitely* said no.

"Ah, come on," said Carla, using the jovial-but-pleading tone that Lisa had come to know so well; Carla, on this occasion, wanted to party. "You've done loads. You're already totally ready for the exam! Think about it, if you're stressed out come Monday, you won't be able to remember *anything.* You need to let off some steam. A night out would be good for you! Plus, Mick's mate is coming. He's supposed to be hot." Lisa was already smiling, the old man completely forgotten. If Carla was partying, she began to tell herself, then the study situation wasn't *too* serious ... but that didn't mean she would say yes. *Final year, final chance.* Even so, it was nice to at least entertain the idea of a night out with some potentially attractive company, but there was plenty of time for that once she reached the summer. *Ah,* the summer, the great, study-free, shining goal ... but she already knew that she'd be applying for post-grad placements. Still, there was bound to be a *bit* of partying, wasn't there?

"Maybe next time," she said, chuckling slightly but sighing at the same time, feeling mild regret about her circumstances but also amusement, knowing what was coming next from her friend.

"Lis*aaaaaaaaaa,*" whined Carla, knowing that the attempt was fruitless but trying anyway, "you're so boorinnnnggggg ... we haven't been out in aaaaaaages ... don't make me be a bad student all on my own!"

On her end of the phone, Carla laughed, then let out a sigh of her own; she knew that Lisa had the right idea. Monday's exam was so important, but she just needed to get out; she got the urge sometimes, the call of the wild intensified by catching increasingly regular glimpses of the impending spectre on the horizon ... *responsible adulthood.* "Come and get ready around mine! We'll get some tunes on, tart ourselves up, have a few drinks, do a few shots; hey, I've got a bottle of Archer's in, we can get onto that."

Carla's last sentence snapped Lisa out of her good mood. She'd been pouring a bottle of Archer's earlier, getting the old man his schnapps. The image of his line of drinks leapt into the forefront of her mind, laid out in front of him like troops for inspection. His hand reaching for the Pedigree, almost caressing it ... what the hell was it about the guy that bugged her so?

"Lisa ...?" Carla was saying, in the impatient voice of one who is testing to see if the connection on their phone is still good, and suspecting that it isn't.

"Sorry, Carla," Lisa said, snapping herself out of it. She started to rebuke herself, but then realised that she was wrong to do that. She wasn't an idiot, she wasn't wet behind the ears, and she'd seen plenty of ordinary weirdos at work to know that there was undoubtedly something different about the man on table ten. She wasn't being daft, and she had always trusted her instincts. Which meant that if there was something off about him, she found herself wanting to know what it was. "I've just been a bit weirded out since this old guy came into work."

"Yeah? What did he do?"

"Well, nothing really, but tell me what you think ..." said Lisa, her voice dropping to a whisper as she reached the post office and went inside, not wanting to be overhead as she stood in the queue. She quietly told Carla what had happened so far, pausing only whilst at the counter to say that she wanted the letters sending Recorded First Class. By the time she was heading outside with her errand finished, so was the story.

"Hmm," said Carla, sounding slightly distracted. "Sounds like a freak. Escapee from the loony bin."

"Car-la! Don't be so mean. But he was odd, no doubt. Something different there ... ugh, I have to go back in now as well," Lisa said as she began the short walk back to the bar. "I haven't relaxed since I spoke to him."

"I'm serious," said Carla, "he could be a legitimate psycho. The generally held opinion in psychological circles is that they're more charismatic than most people, you know. Something about them is more magnetic. That could be why he's gotten under your skin."

"Don't be ridiculous," said Lisa ... but what Carla had just said didn't *sound* ridiculous. It was, she supposed, perfectly feasible. The old man could be dangerous. She shivered slightly, but dismissed the thought. Possible ... but probably not likely. "I'll keep an eye on him, though; you can be sure of that."

"So..." said Carla, bored of the subject, and Lisa couldn't blame her. The guy really hadn't done anything to report, and so the report had been dull. "... Tonight?"

"You're breaking up, Carla, can't really hear you," said Lisa, smiling, as she approached the door of the bar.

"Bull*shit!*" laughed Carla, shouting down the phone. "You can hear me! Come on, partypartypartypartypart—" The tirade was cut off as Lisa grinned and ended the call, then opened the bar's outer door. Her smile died the instant she passed through the inner one and saw the old man still sitting at his table, a fresh plate of steaming sausages and freshly cut chips in front of him ... but all three of the glasses she'd brought to the table not ten minutes ago—two of them containing hard liquor at the time—were empty. The old man's eyes were closed, and he was swaying ever-so-slightly, moving gently from side to side in his seat.

Great, thought Lisa, her nerves dampened slightly by her annoyance. *Constant drunk or not, him banging down those like that is gonna mean I have a pain in the ass for the rest of the afternoon.*

The fact that his blue eyes were closed meant that she could openly stare at him as she made her way inside, and now she could see that he wasn't just swaying; his nostrils were working, and his chest was expanding and contracting in great, steady pulls of air. He was *smelling,* inhaling the aroma of his now-arrived dinner with great ceremony. As he did so, the door that Lisa had just used then finally swung to, the hydraulic closing mechanism having slowed its progress until the final click home. Lisa's soft-soled flat shoes hadn't made any sound as she walked in, but the door's closing did, and those shockingly blue eyes burst open. He didn't jump this time, but the old man's

177

right hand came up and gripped the edge of the table. On instinct, Lisa forced a smile to acknowledge him, her eyes caught by his superior stare. Without letting go of the table, the old man gave a slight nod in return, but his body didn't relax; in fact, his intense gaze followed her all the way back behind the bar, where Lisa actually felt compelled to stand out of sight behind the bar's supporting pillar.

Shaken, she decided that she'd had enough of it. She'd either ask Kim to get him to leave—she'd make up a reason—or she'd feign illness and ask to be taken home. She knew she wasn't being stupid; every instinct in her body was saying that *something wasn't right.*

Peering out from behind the pillar like a child, Lisa eventually calmed down enough to take a peek. The old man's head was bent again, those startling eyes out of sight once more as he lifted a forkful of food to his mouth. As he began to chew, the fork hovered before his face for a moment ... and then clattered onto the plate as he let it go, his right hand going to his face as his head began to jerk slightly. The old man had collapsed into tears.

He suddenly looked so pathetic, so crestfallen, that Lisa's intimidation vanished as her heart melted. An elderly person, alone, weeping ... Lisa was programmed to respond with kindness to the sight, whatever the situation. She still hesitated—who knew how he might react, and perhaps embarrassment would bring an aggressive response from him—but she looked to Chris at the other end of the bar, who'd also spotted the old man's distress. Predictably, he held up his hands, shaking his head and raising his eyebrows as if to say *don't look at me.* Chris was not one of life's Samaritans, believing that strangers can look after themselves or else find someone other than him to assist them. People outside of his social circle were not his responsibility. Chris pointed at Lisa, then made a fingers-walking gesture in the old man's direction, then waved at her with a smirk and turned back to his paper where it lay on the bar's surface. Lisa rolled her eyes, but stood twisting her fingers around each other as she wondered how best to approach table ten, or if she should even approach at all. Kim was nowhere to be seen; was she even still in? She looked back to table ten, where the old man now sat with his right elbow propped on the table, his right hand holding up his hidden, sobbing face. His left arm was *still* underneath the table, and for a mad moment Lisa wondered if he might not be holding a gun under there.

Don't be ridiculous, she told herself, *this is bloody Coventry, not downtown LA.* Which was true, but it didn't mean he didn't have a knife, and the man was clearly disturbed in some way or another. Perhaps he was a psychopath after all. Lisa took a deep breath, deciding to head over, but at the same time thinking that she'd keep table ten between herself and the man sitting there, no matter how much he might need someone to talk to or how distressed he might be. Lisa approached his table.

"Excuse me? Sir?" asked Lisa quietly, speaking as softly as she could to avoid causing the seemingly wired man any more reactionary surprise. "Is everything all right?" The man continued to cry for a moment; gentle, breathy gasps escaping from his mouth, but then raised his hand away from his face and held it up in front of Lisa, one finger raised whilst keeping his head down. *Just a moment.* He turned his face—still bent downwards—away to face the wall, then lowered his hand once. It went to his eyes, wiping them, and then laid flat upon the table top. Staring at the wall for a second, he began to take deep breaths, trying to compose himself. When he turned back to Lisa, his almost-otherworldly blue eyes were shining even more brightly than before, the ceiling lights reflecting off the water that was still in them. He managed a faint smile.

"No, no I'm afraid not," he said, his voice wavering. "Everything is, to use the parlance of the age, screwed. *Everything,*" he repeated, and let out a slight bark that was part laugh, part choked-back tears. He shook his head, and looked around the bar, that strange smile still on his mouth, and then something seemed to occur to him. He regarded Lisa once again. "But you asked," he said, the smile becoming slightly warmer, even if the sadness stayed in his eyes. "You saw me crying, and you came to help. That's something. That's really something." He shrugged. "It doesn't really change the main problem, I'm afraid—in fact, in many ways it makes it far, far worse—but that was nice to see."

"What's the main problem?" Lisa heard herself asking, the words coming automatically, but the old man was already shaking his head, holding up his right hand. *What the hell is in his left hand?* thought Lisa. *Is it a prosthetic limb or something? Is that why he doesn't move it?*

"Doesn't matter," he said, the dismissal instant and complete, as if even the idea of an explanation was something that he knew, from experience, was a waste of time. "You wouldn't believe it, and I didn't like being thought of as crazy when I was a *young* man; being thought of as a crazy *old* man would be even worse. But I appreciate your concern, I really do." He wiped the last of the moisture from his eyes, and pointed at his plate. "This will soon be going cold, something I certainly don't intend to let happen to this meal." This time, the smile reached his eyes, and Lisa found herself smiling back. There was kindness in him, that seemed clear.

"Okay, well as long as you're all right. Enjoy your meal," Lisa said, pretending to be happy to walk away, but secretly compelled to find out what this guy's story was. That was the point that the old man stopped her, and the point that Lisa would later come back to over and over again. If she'd turned away a bit faster, if she'd said nothing, if she'd just gotten out of there, hell, if she'd ran out of the door and never come back to the bar again ...

"Wait," he said, just as she'd taken her first step backwards, as she'd turned her head and her shoulders had begun to follow; in this manner, she'd looked away, so when she turned back she was surprised when she saw that the view before her had changed. The old man was leaning forward, both hands under the table now, his face deadly serious, but it was the eyes, the *eyes;* they seemed to burn inside, as if lit by a blue flame. It was a trick of the light, Lisa was sure, but despite this she shrank back slightly. The old man seemed bigger, filling the space between them. He didn't speak for a moment, as if he were weighing the situation up, and Lisa felt a sudden and intense sense of gravity. Something very important was here, some news of great weight and relevance, and she *knew* in that moment that the old man was not crazy in any way at all. He knew something, something very big indeed, and if she waited, if she behaved correctly, then he would tell her. The rest of the bar seemed to fade away, Lisa's world focused upon those blue, blue eyes.

"If you *did* think I was crazy ... that would be better ... " he said, speaking as if he were working it out in his head as spoke, but still staring at her. "You're a good person. I can see that. It's all over your face." He began to nod gently, becoming more sure about his planned course of action. "You're one of the good ones ... but even you won't believe it. And that's good. It means you won't worry. And I ..." He trailed off, and Lisa realised as his nostrils flared and his eyebrows wrinkled that he was about to cry again. She opened her mouth to speak, but the old man sniffed hard and then carried on talking, his voice now cracked and full of emotion. "I haven't told anyone about this for fifty years. It's been my secret. But it's been so hard ... all I need, all I *needed* ... is for someone just to ... I had to keep away from sight, you see. I couldn't be known as the local crazy, as that would bring *people,* and *risk,* and more important than anything, most of all, I had to stay safe. That was the most important thing in the world, even if I didn't want to do it. It was a duty. A terrible, terrible ... " His bottom lip started to tremble, and he squeezed his lips together and shook his head. "I'm sorry, I don't think I've spoken to anyone in person, at least conversationally, for ... well, at least ten years..."

Reacting instinctively, Lisa reached out and took his hand, wanting to tell him that it was okay, but the minute that she did so she let out a very faint shriek and pulled her hand away. The old man's hand was so hot that it had burned her skin. It had been like trying to take a fleshy plate out of the oven. Even whilst she looked at her hand in horror and surprise, she turned to the bar to see if Chris had noticed. She didn't want him barrelling over and upsetting the old man, didn't want Chris involved, and half her brain was checking on that whilst the other reeled and tried to deal with this new revelation. *His hand burned you! Touching him burned you! That isn't normal! That's impossible! But ... maybe it was a static shock? Just a little electric surprise, and hey, is your hand* actually *burned? There's no mark there, and you have been nervous ever since you started talking to the guy, and hands burning other hands is impossible unless one of them is on fire, right? His hands could be hot, but not burning hot ....* In this babbling manner, using the madness of the sane person, she rationalised it away even as the old man confirmed that something *had* just happened.

"Sorry, I should have warned you ..." the old man said as he wiped his eyes again, talking about the incredible temperature of his skin as if it were an embarrassing inconvenience, like a dog that had growled at her, or a baby that had just been sick upon the person holding it. "It gets like that sometimes, and I'm afraid I don't even know about it anymore when it happens. I'm completely used to it. It can be as cold as ice too, and I *mean* as cold as ice, cold enough to burn. I picked up a glass once and watched it begin to frost slightly in my hand; I'd had no idea before then. Of course, it doesn't happen all the time ... and never, of course, when I consciously want to use it as proof. Sometimes it doesn't happen for months on end. I tried to convince people once, in the early days, but I think, somehow, it knows when I want it to do it, and it won't. I'm *different,* you see. The hand thing ... that's just a side effect, I suppose. I don't understand it, even after all this time."

But that's not possible! That's not possible! He just had very hot skin, hell, don't people get almost too hot to touch when they get a fever?

"Do you ... do you need some ice ..." Lisa said dumbly, her brain trying to find ways to respond to what had just happened. The old man shook his head.

"It's not a problem. It's not *the* problem," he muttered, looking annoyed with himself. "I'm sorry, the booze isn't helping. I shouldn't have had so much. I wouldn't even be telling you any of this, I think, if not for that, but ... I need to.

I've needed to talk about this for fifty years, and most of the time I can handle *not* doing that, but ... I forgot about tolerance. The mind exaggerates your past drinking ability as the years go by, you know. I thought that my drinks order there was an amount that I used to be able to handle, easily, but then I haven't touched a drop of booze for five decades, either. It's all hitting me rather heavily."

Lisa looked at her hand again. There was no mark there. The knowledge seemed to fortify her, to root her once more in easy reality.

"Why, ah ... why haven't you had a drink in fifty years?" A thought followed on the heels of the question. "Should you be drinking now, I mean, is it a health thing—" The old man suddenly roared with laughter at this, shaking his head and wagging his right index finger. Lisa watched, shocked.

"Well, if that just doesn't take the biscuit," he said, chuckling gently now as his booming laugh subsided. He looked at her, and sighed. He seemed younger in that moment, lighter, the previous invisible weight on his shoulders seeming to dissipate. He cocked his head slightly to one side, regarding her again. "You really want to know? I'm finding myself rather wanting to tell you, although I think I shall rather regret it when I'm sober." He was right about the booze; *I'm* and *sober* had slurred ever so slightly together, coming out as *Amzober.* The look in his fiercely blue eyes was mischievous. "You won't like it, you know. You really won't like it ... and that's why you won't believe it." He'd changed again, from weakened, saddened old man to mischievous, scheming imp, dark intent on his face, a wrinkled Puck in a blue three-piece suit. Lisa shrank back again, a slight step backward that the old man noticed; the smirk turned into concern. "Please, trust me, you won't. You really won't. It's all right. I'm sorry, I get quite bitter about all this sometimes, you would too if you were me. It makes me act a little odd now and then. And I ... I need to talk. I've earned it, don't you see? I've earned this, and you can help me feel better. You really can." The eyebrows rose in the middle, an old man's attempt at puppy dog eyes, and Lisa thought that yes, she'd been right, the old man wasn't crazy ... but it still didn't mean that he was *completely* sane. Not all the time. *It makes me act a little odd now and then.* Lisa believed that part, at least, believed it a great deal, just as she believed the old man probably wasn't even aware that he was doing it ... but what the hell had happened to him, or rather, what did he at least *think* had happened to him?

Lisa remembered that she was actually overdue a break, and had been about to take it just before she'd been asked to deal with table ten. That seemed like it had happened yesterday, in a different time before she knew that this strange old man existed. Looking over her shoulder, she called to Chris behind the bar.

"I'm taking my break now, Chris. Tell Kim if she comes out of the office." Chris looked up, saw her still standing by the old man, and smirked. He then lifted his hand in a wave of acknowledgement, and went back to his paper. Lisa felt an uncharacteristic surge of hatred for Chris and his smug, self-satisfied ways. She knew too many just like him; cynicism as a defensive weapon and smugness in toeing the safe lifestyle-line more than anyone. They were everywhere, and their influence on the psyches of others was all-pervasive. Well, she wasn't going to let him influence her.

Pulling out the chair opposite the old man, she sat down and forced a smile. Relief seemed to wash over his face, and he went to pat her hand. She flinched, and he remembered in time.

"Sorry, goodness me, sorry," he muttered, putting his hand to his mouth. "I forget, I don't realise, as I said, and that doesn't help ... but it's been such a long time since I allowed myself to talk face-to-face to anyone. To be in company." He sighed, and leant back in his chair, looking into her eyes and shrugging. "I haven't left my house in decades." He looked at her, waiting for her reaction, but Lisa's wide eyes just waited. She didn't know what the hell to make of all this. After a while, he nodded, and turned his head to look at the window. "You won't believe me," he said again, quietly, as if he were talking to himself. "You won't believe me anyway ... so it's all right to tell it ..." He seemed so fragile in that moment, his face illuminated grimly by the grey light from outside. The burden was all over his expression, brought to the surface as he scanned through his story, remembering it all faster than he could ever tell it.

"I was born into money in 1933," he began. "I have no shame about that, and I've never understood those that have. My father had made his fortune in the paper trade, and Mother's family were already as rich as creosote. Her family would have preferred it if Father's family line had been of slightly higher stock, but he was such a mover and shaker in society, and a man of great means with it, that they eventually accepted him as one of their own. We were relatively untouched by the war, and after I moved back home from evacuation, I grew up in the suburbs of London. I was mainly homeschooled, my father adamant that I wouldn't be attending Eton. He'd missed me terribly during my time in the countryside, as had I him, and I was happy not to go. Plus, my father detested schools, and would often ask what the point was when I would inherit the family business anyway. He could teach me all I needed to know. Eventually, my mother gave up arguing with him about it, and home I stayed. I had no siblings, but I had a dog, sprawling grounds to play in, and a father that let me get away with murder. It was a very happy childhood." He looked back at Lisa, seeming to think for a moment, and then asked her a question. "Do you have any siblings?"

The question didn't go in for a moment, any more than the rest of what he'd just said, as Lisa's brain was still reeling from the shock; the guy was *eighty?* He didn't look a day over sixty, tops! Whatever his secret was, he could bottle it and make a fortune ... but then association brought her back to the present situation. What had he just said? The war, a fortune, his fortune, his family history, he'd asked a question ... she was back in the room.

"Uh, no," she answered, thinking the question unusual, coming as it did from out of the blue, and he smiled sadly as he noticed her surprise; he realised that she'd been away somewhere, and why.

"Yes, I look younger than you might think," he said, nodding and examining the back of his hand, opening and closing it, flexing the fingers and turning it back and forth. "Clean living ... nothing but clean living. *Constant clean living.*" The hand closed tightly into a fist as his jaw clenched, and then he shook his head. "But I'm getting ahead of myself. Before all the health-conscious times for me, there was a time consisting of exactly the opposite first. Anyway. Mother died in 1954 as the result of a horrendous bout of pneumonia, and Father followed a few years afterwards, due to lung cancer contracted as a result of a near-lifetime spent as a cigar smoker. He was sixty-three, Mother just forty-nine. He was ready to go by the end, keen to see Mother again— he believed in that kind of thing—and I was left alone at the age of twenty-one, with no family of my own and holding sole ownership of an internationally strong company, even in those days. Mother and I had never been close—I think she saw me as something to keep Father happy, and I never resented that, not knowing any better—but Father's death destroyed me. I had lost my dearest friend and ally, and wasn't ready to take over the reins at such abrupt notice.

"I'd expected to be eased in over time, even though I already had the know-how, and here I was with the livelihood of hundreds of workers thrust into my hands at a time when I had been emotionally shattered into pieces. I know that I should have been stronger. I know that I should have honoured my father's memory and faced up to my responsibility. But then I couldn't take it, I couldn't even begin to grasp the task at hand ... and so I ran. I appointed Nathan Spring, my father's second-in-command, to the head of the company. He would have guided me through it, it's so clear now, but at the time I was just a mess. I was a young man desperate to get away from everything around him, everything that was a reminder of that which was lost, and bought a ticket to France with no further plans than that. Nathan ... I let him down too. He and my father were like brothers, and he needed me to help him get through that time. He would have struggled just as much as I had, but his loyalty to the family meant that he would not let me, or my father, down. He was a good man. A

186

stronger man than I." He sighed, and drew a slow circle on the table with his finger.

"This was my punishment, you see," he said, staring at the grain in the table's surface as his fingernail skimmed along it. "I often see it that way. I ran in cowardice from one burden, and ended up with one bigger than you can comprehend, one nearly impossible to live with." The fingernail stopped, and he smiled slightly, exhaling as he did so. "Doing it again. I'm sorry. I'll try and keep the story more linear."

"It's okay, it's okay," muttered Lisa, leaning forward in her chair and not realising that she was doing it. The old man shrugged—*if you say so*—and continued speaking.

"Europe in 1954 was an easy place for a young man with money to lose himself, especially one that had never really travelled all that much, despite privilege. Whilst my debauched lifestyle was, at first, an attempt to forget everything via the bottom of a bottle or the same of a young woman, I'm ashamed to say that, over time, it became something else. It became a lifestyle that I revelled in. After a while, even Nathan stopped bothering to send his regular telegrams. I was merely a silent company figurehead to them eventually, and thoughts of home rarely even crossed my mind outside of occasions when I needed fresh funds wired over to me. I had friends, or at least, companions—money brings good-time friendships, and I knew them for what they were and that was fine by me—and I rarely slept in a bed alone at night. I don't know if I was happy, but I do know that I thoroughly indulged and even enjoyed myself; that is happiness of a kind, I think. I lost myself entirely in a haze of wild nights and regretful, hungover days, and whilst I travelled extensively throughout the continent, it was mainly to find new avenues for pleasure and hedonism, not to take in the sights of the luxurious and historical cities that I caroused around. I often feel like I saw very little of Europe, despite covering most of it over a period of six years."

Lisa's eyebrows raised, and the old man smiled and nodded. "Why stop?

The inheritance alone that I had received more than covered my expenses, even before I touched any of the company money. I didn't find love—I wasn't looking—and so I had no one else to consider. I had long put my father's death behind me, perhaps not ever fully facing up to it but finding a way of smothering it in my mind. Even though that had been the trigger that had fired me into my life of excess, I continued it purely because I saw no need to look deeper, no inclination for reflection. It was adventure, was it not? But adventure without consideration, without pause, is ultimately a dish only half-consumed. So I kept going, not knowing how, or desiring to do, anything else." He tapped the table with his finger, and sighed, lost in a moment. "But of course, over time, I grew tired of it. Not because of any kind of moment of clarity, or a lust for anything more substantial, but merely because I was physically exhausted. I needed a break from it, some time away from the screaming hangers-on and the constant mental haze. And so I returned to London—I didn't even inform Nathan, so completely removed was I from the workings of the company—intending to take a relaxing holiday and to spend some time figuring out my next move. A few weeks perhaps. But London was the worst place I could have been, the hustle and bustle of the place being the exact opposite to the respite I was seeking, and so I travelled to the family retreat in Stratford. The transition was a shock to say the least, moving from an almost constant whirlwind of noise to the near-total silence of the Warwickshire countryside. At first, I went through a kind of mental cold turkey, compelled to seek out the nearest burlesque club. Of course, there weren't any for a hundred miles, hence my choice to go there in the first place. I needed the rest, I told myself, to prepare for another go-around. I viewed it as a recharge, like an athlete nursing an injury before he returns to the rigours of his chosen sport. And so eventually, after a few days of near-madness and pacing the floor of the small, rural cottage (my skin seeming to crawl with restlessness) I spent the next few weeks reading (there was, of course, thanks to my father, an abundance of books present) listening to the radio, sleeping, taking long walks through the fields and villages surrounding my temporary home, and even fixing up some of the more run-down parts of the cottage. I found myself enjoying the solitude, taking time for myself and myself alone. Savouring the silence and the relaxed, steady nature of it all. I found a new kind of happiness, the *other* half of it, as I began to reflect on myself, on my future, and as more weeks passed I began to realise how hollow the past six years had been. There was no doubt that it had been a lot of fun, but ultimately, there was a lot missing. Back then ... back *then* ... I loved the cottage. Not that my new life was any more complete than my prior one, but at least I was discovering the other half of the puzzle. Weeks became months, and it truly *was* another kind of happiness; I began to think about how I could put both halves together and live a life of adventure *and* meaning, even how I could use my considerable fortune to make a difference to the world. It was an exciting thought. Such potential ..."

The old man sighed again, and was silent for a good minute. Lisa said nothing, having already come to accept these pauses as part of the old man's tale. When he looked up again, his blue eyes seemed to burn more fiercely than before; she thought that if she'd touched his hand in that moment, she would have been scarred for life.

"I was wrong," he said, his voice low and wavering. "I had made a terrible, terrible mistake. I wish I had never left Europe; I wish it as strongly as I have ever wished anything in my entire life. I think of those days the way a thirsty man in the desert thinks of a cool, ice-cold pitcher of water. I don't care if it was shallow or meaningless. It was *life,* an abundance of life. I would rather have drank myself to death and be found on the floor of a Berlin bier keller than have that which I do now. My time in the cottage was a rose-tinted taste of what would become the rest of my life, and I wandered into it smiling like a fool." His fist clenched again, his gaze drifting away from Lisa's eyes and into a past occasion that only he could see. She waited again, patiently, thinking how his time in the cottage actually sounded quite nice. What had gone wrong, she wondered?

Still lost in thought, the old man licked his lips again and spoke to Lisa without looking at her.

"I would like another drink, please," he said, firm in intent if not in speech. "Whisky. Double. Laphroaig if possible. I am having another blasted drink. And do you sell cigarettes?"

"Uh, no," mumbled Lisa, wide-eyed, "we don't. You can't smoke in here anyway. Or anywhere, really. You can smoke outside though." The old man shook his head gently.

"Ah yes ..." he said, quietly. "I forgot. As you've probably gathered, I've been detached for quite some time. Never mind. But the whisky, please. I *will* have that."

Lisa thought about asking if that was a good idea, and then thought better of it. Plus, she had to remind herself, the old man wasn't her concern. If he wanted to get blind drunk after a fifty-year layoff, then it was his choice. She did hurry back to the bar a little more quickly than usual, however, ignoring Chris's sarcastic questions about her lunch date as she filled the old man's glass. She hurried back to table ten and placed it there, re-taking her seat as the old man grasped the vessel and stared at it. He began to speak again without looking at or thanking her, his eyes locked on the glass in his hand.

"It was a Friday evening in December," he said, his voice even darker now, his mind having moved onto another point in time that he clearly did not like to revisit. "I knew no one in the nearby village that I would call a friend, but on my many trips down to the local shop there I had grown to know a few faces, people that would greet me as I passed and that I would greet in return. You know the kind of thing I mean. One or two of these occasions had even developed into brief bouts of small-talk, good-natured chitchat during which we would exchange pleasantries, and of course the inherent British village nosiness would come out; was I staying at Brandy Cottage? For how long was I there? What brought me there, and what was my background? They were inquisitive, but friendly, and I was happy to oblige them with answers, and so it was in this manner that I received more than one offer to join them in the local pub for a Christmas drink. These offers were partly out of good-natured kindness, and partly out of trying to score the privilege of being the first one to bring the new fellow down from his home on the hill. Again, I didn't mind. I found such small-town intrigues to be quite charming. I'd resisted for a while—drinking with strangers in a busy bar sounded too much like my other life, and too soon—but eventually I decided that if I were to capture that magic balance, I had to at least be prepared to dip my toes back into the water now and then. It was the Friday before Christmas, after all, and I would be lying if I claimed that I hadn't suffered my fair share of loneliness from time to time up in the cottage. It was time to pay The Bear and Staff a visit." His eyes moved back to Lisa, and she was shocked by the sadness she saw in them. They spoke of a lifetime of sorrow.

"I think they knew about my money," he said, his voice faint and hard to hear. "I think that's why they picked me. It may sound impossible, but think about the very nature of the experiment. Think about how impossible *that* is in itself, the power that would take; knowing about my money seems entirely plausible by comparison. They knew I would have more options than most. They wanted someone with no restrictions, someone with all options available to them. And the timing was perfect, just when I was ready to reconnect with the rest of the world, with people. Just when I'd started to care." He looked frightened, on the verge of re-experiencing something terrible, and Lisa's mind was racing. Who was he talking about? The people in the village? Had they set him up somehow? What had they done to him?

"It wasn't late when I set off," said the old man, "perhaps around five p.m., but the December sky was already starting to darken in the way that early winter nights will do at that time of year. Even so, I remember quite relishing the idea of a winter's stroll, all wrapped up in many layers with a cosy fire and a warm welcome waiting at the other end. I pictured myself removing my coat and scarf in front of the hearth and being handed a freshly poured beer. It was a lovely thought, and one that I never got to realise." He lifted the whisky to his lips, his hand shaking, and took a sip. His eyes closed, and he let out a sigh that was full of both satisfaction and nerves. He looked at his plate, having barely touched it since he started speaking, then hurriedly picked up his fork and plunged it into the pile of chips, scooping them up and shovelling them into his mouth where he chewed them like a hungry dog. He swallowed, breathing heavily through his nose, and then continued to speak, occasionally lifting food to his mouth at a more normal speed as he did so.

"It was a good twenty-minute walk from the cottage to the village, and it was one that I'd slowly gotten used to over time. My fitness had decreased dramatically during my time on the continent, and I'd put on weight while I was at it. I viewed my regular walks down to the village as a purification process, even taking heavy bags with me from time to time to make it more of a chore. I had a car, of course, but seeing myself—in my arrogance—as a proper man of the country, I used it as little as possible. The road to the village was a winding, pleasant journey, ideal for throwing the Jaguar around the bends on a weekend as the hills rolled away to either side of you. It was a place so seemingly isolated that one could convince oneself that civilisation was hours away, instead of merely the distance of a medium-length walk. On foot, at that time of day, with dusk coming in, it was a lonely looking trek, but so atmospheric that I was excited by the opportunity. Other people may have found it an unsettling prospect; seeing the darkening skies and growing shadows as ominous, their imaginations taking hold and wondering what might be coming out of its lair to stalk unsuspecting walkers once it became dark. I had never been a person to wonder such things, being a lifelong realist. Now, I know better." Lisa felt her skin prickle as goose bumps spread across her arms. She was captivated, scared to speak in case she broke the spell and ended the old man's story. Her eyes flickered as she glanced out of the window, looking at the sky as it darkened once more with the heavy threat of rain, and she found that she could picture the scene all too well.

"I was about five minutes removed from the cottage when first I saw it," the old man said, jaw stiff as he breathed steadily and cut himself a piece of sausage with his knife, one-handed, then swapped utensils, taking up his fork again as he skewered the meat and raised it to his mouth. He then spoke around it as he chewed. "I should have been able to see it as soon as I stepped outside, which leads me to believe it wasn't actually *there* until just before I first caught a glimpse of it. But there it was. In the clouds."

Lisa didn't breathe.

"The sky was *full* of clouds that evening, like a blanket. I'd brought an umbrella with me, certain that I would be caught in the rain along the way, even though none of them were really all that grey looking. But now there was one that *was* dark. One that was almost jet black. And square." He glanced at Lisa, as if to see whether she was paying attention as he got to the crux of his story, then back at his plate, picturing the scene. "It looked impossible, hanging above the field to my right and sitting amongst the other clouds, as if someone had spilled ink upon a thick sheet made of cotton wool; this fuzzy-edged square of black cloud placed slap-bang in the middle of the sky. People often talk about the clouds being black. They don't mean like this. They mean dark grey. This was *black,* impossibly so, and it was nothing to do with the fast-encroaching twilight. This was not natural, and I was almost too amazed by what I was seeing to feel any sense of fear. Almost. That only happened when I began to hear the sound, coming from all around me. That's when I began to feel terrified."

He shuddered, and looked around himself instinctively, a quick safety check.

"It was quiet at first, but got louder very quickly, growing like an approaching wave," he said, and now his voice was almost a whisper. "I remember turning on the spot, startled out of my amazement at the black cloud above me, spinning and trying to see where it was coming from. The closest thing I can compare it to is the sound of pouring sand. Pouring sand that grows louder with every second, except the sand is made of metal and it's being poured into a cardboard box. And I am surrounded by nothing but greenery and trees and hedges, and the sound of endless metal sand pouring onto cardboard is filling my ears in all directions, and now I'm almost mad with fear. And worst of all, I look ahead to where that huge black inkblot in the sky should be, and it's gone. I look directly up, already knowing that it's silently moved to hang right above me, casting me in shadow. The moment is surreal in its juxtaposition, though I'm too lost in terror to appreciate it; to my left and right, nothing but fields and beautiful landscape. Directly above, sheer blackness fills my view, swallowing my world. My bladder lets go, and I can feel the hot wet warmth running down my legs and plastering my trousers to my skin. The sound is deafening, each trickling grain like sadistic mocking laughter in my ears. I stumble backwards, holding my arm up before me impotently to ward off the black cloud as I fall to the floor, but it doesn't go away." The old man's arm raised up slightly before him, the fork abandoned, seemingly unaware that he was doing it as he relived the moment.

"It stays there, impossible and undeniable, and I feel my brain being jabbed at. My mind is being pickpocketed, and then all of my ribs break at once, and I scream. The feeling in my brain goes haywire as they analyse my response, gauge my reaction to the pain in what is no doubt their final few pieces of assessment, my selection already decided long before this encounter. Then there is nothing except the noise and the cloud and the pain from my ribs for several minutes, and all I can do is lay there and whimper, lost in fear and total confusion. Then I can feel mud under my fingers and rain on my face, the pain gone, and I am lying on the edge of a field."

The old man let out a long sigh, and again drank from the whisky glass, deeper this time, more of a swig.

Lisa felt like a simpleton, blinking dumbly and sitting in silence. He stared at her from over the rim of his glass. What he was saying was impossible, but said with such total conviction that she couldn't dismiss it. This time, she couldn't resist an urge to look over her shoulder again at Chris, to see if this was all some sort of team setup. She expected to catch him looking away quickly from watching her, his enjoyment of seeing her suckered in not being hidden fast enough. But there he was, still engrossed in his paper behind the undisturbed bar. The other patrons were all gone now except for the two women with the newborns, but even they were busy strapping their children into ridiculously and unnecessarily complicated looking strollers, preparing to leave. No one else in the bar appeared to be in on the gag, not openly at least. When she turned back to the old man, he smiled slightly, taking this as confirmation of his earlier prediction; she didn't believe him, and that was, as he'd already stated, good.

"My hands immediately went to my stomach," he continued, the smile fading as he returned to 1960. "My ribs were all intact once more, although one thing was immediately clear. The prominence of said ribs was such that I knew straight away that I lost a considerable amount of weight. They may have broken and then healed me, but they had clearly done something else. I felt my cheeks, felt the backs of my hands, felt my legs and gasped at the muscle wastage that had occurred. I was nearly emaciated. I was still dressed, but my clothes were so loose that it felt like I had been draped in a sheet. I vividly remember sitting up and seeing the way my trousers draped over my skinny thighs like a tablecloth. My shoes were missing, but despite the muddiness of the field, there wasn't a speck of dirt upon my bare feet. It was then that I began to vomit uncontrollably.

"This went on for some time, and the colour of the contents of my stomach was blue. A bright, burning blue; the same unusual blue that, no doubt, you have noticed in my eyes." He tapped the side of his head gently with the edge of his whisky glass, at eye level. "My eyes had been a deep, rich brown all of my life until that point. I still have a family painting I could show you that would prove it, one that I sat for at seven years old. My mother's were the same colour. But I digress."

Lisa sat very still.

"The blue substance that I'd produced disappeared into the mud almost straight away, so much so that I found myself plunging my hands into the earth in an attempt to dig it up again and look at it. The brilliant colour of it had alarmed me greatly, and as I'm sure you can understand—along with my general state of shock and confusion as to what had happened to me—I was almost hysterical in my motions. Giving up, I got to my shaking feet and looked around me. Immediately I could see that I hadn't travelled far, and was merely at a higher point to where I'd been when I first saw the cloud. I was now looking down from the top of the distant hill that the road from the cottage ran past, and was perhaps half a mile from where I'd seen that terrible black square of cloud. The thought almost paralysed me with fear again, and I looked skywards in terror; all I saw were grey rainclouds, but none any darker than that. A quick scan of the horizon also confirmed that the black cloud was gone. This assessment of the sky also confirmed something else; though the clouds were dark, the sky around them was relatively light. It was an earlier time of day, perhaps mid-afternoon. My brain had no clue as to how this could be possible. It had been dusk when I'd left home.

"I realised—now that my nausea, if not my confusion and alarm, had passed—that I was ravenously hungry. My legs were so weakened that they could barely support me, but I surmised that if I got back to the road, then I could find my way home again where food and warm clothing would be found. Then I could take stock properly, and that thought brought me comfort. I wouldn't have to deal with the madness of it, the *whys* and *hows* of any of this for a while whilst I attended to my immediate needs. Operating almost on instinct, I set off for home, my clothes and hair sticking to me, my body freezing cold and doused in rainwater. My bare feet were like blocks of ice. I assumed that this was the doing of the elements, and maybe it was, but perhaps it was the doing of that strange, temperature-changing side effect of mine. But I digress again. That isn't really important to the story." Another forkful of chips was shovelled into his mouth, and his hand shook once more as it carried the fork upwards.

"I nearly fell through the door upon arrival, as weakened as I was by the effort. It had taken me nearly an hour. It should have taken perhaps twenty-five minutes at full health. Even thoughts of dry clothing and warmth, however, were forgotten in my shambling dash to the pantry. I gorged myself like an animal, tearing chunks of ham and cheese free with my mouth and biting chunks of bread straight off the loaf. Sated, I then staggered into the kitchen and drank from the tap for probably a full minute. Almost weeping with relief, preparing for stage two of addressing my physical needs and still not allowing myself to consider what might have happened, I made it into the bathroom on my last legs and undressed. There I received two more enormous shocks; the first was from the naked appraisal of my sudden and extreme weight loss. I looked like something from a concentration camp. Looking down at my stick-like arms and legs and painfully defined ribs, I let out a wail of horrified dismay. Dashing to the mirror to investigate my face, I received the second and more severe shock; that of seeing my new and almost frighteningly blue eyes. My horror at this was so great that I barely even noticed my harsh cheekbones, or the fact that these new eyes of mine seemed to bulge in my skull due to the paper thin skin around them. The terrifying lack of muscle or packed flesh made me look like a skeleton. It was too much. I got into the bathtub, turned on the taps and sat there weeping.

"Later, when I'd bathed and felt at least physically more like a human being, I stoked the fire in the hearth and tried to come to terms with everything. I had begun to feel very hot, though, and soon doused the log fire's flames. I didn't know that a feeling of either high heat or icy coldness would be with me, on occasion, for the rest of my life. I have no idea why that is even part of it all. A side effect perhaps, as I say. Underlying all of it, though, was a fear that this was not the end of my ordeal, that I would glance out of the window and see the black cloud on the horizon, making its way towards the cottage to carry out the next stage of whatever terrible process it had already begun. I closed all the curtains in a feeble attempt to shut out the outside world. I had been reduced to a gibbering wreck, but the one question that stood out the most was that of the change in time, strangely. Not of what the black cloud could be; for some reason, I found that the easiest part to draw a line under in terms of understanding. I decided that, whilst terrifying, it was an inexplicable, chance phenomenon that I had stumbled upon and that the more important matter in that moment was knowing what it had done to me. However, I now think—and have for decades—that it was not chance, as I've already said. I think that I was chosen. I know for certain, at least, that they have been watching me ever since that day in 1960, so why could they not have been watching and considering me *before* then? Regardless, I remembered a briefly glimpsed vision from my recent return to the cottage; that of a newspaper lying in the porch, the regular Sunday delivery that I'd arranged with the village post office going ahead as usual. I'd had to pay extra to get the delivery boy to come out so far, but the fee was of no consequence to a man of my considerable means. The thought of the paper being here startled me greatly, however. The delivery was only on Sundays, and I'd left the house on a Friday. Had I lost two days? A quick trip to the front porch confirmed it. The paper was dated two days after the day I'd set off for the village. I'd lost at least two days in that field, or elsewhere. It is the 'elsewhere' that I shudder to even think of. Whatever had been done to me, it had taken several days to do so; I later found out that I'd actually woken up in that field on the Thursday. I had lost nearly a week.

"But that day, at that point, I was nearly dizzy with the vague comprehension of it all. Surrounded as I was by the physical relief of freshly returned warmth (at least, that's what I dismissed it as ... soon as I would realise that it was an unnatural warmth, one that would often burn surfaces other than my own skin on occasion, as you know) and full belly, my body cried out for rest, for sleep, and I barely reached the living room sofa before falling into unconsciousness. At least, I think it was merely all of those factors. It's an equal possibility that they had a hand in wanting me to sleep. The first stage was over, you see, that of realisation, of absorption. There had hardly been enough time for my mind to fully process what had occurred, but I think they are impatient. Recent events have convinced me of it, their own experiment being hurried towards a conclusion. They know that our minds are fragile things, and had I woken up in that field so transformed and already knowing that which they told me next, I think I would have gone insane on the spot. Their whole experiment would have been tainted at the very beginning, a complete waste of time. Either way, as I slept, they implanted the knowledge that would destroy the rest of my life. Thus, when I awoke, I knew the enormity of their plan, knew what they had done ... if not who they were."

His incredible blue eyes began to film over with tears once more, and his shaking hand went to his mouth. Lisa, with a surety of motion than belied her inner shakiness, nudged the whisky glass towards him with her hand. He nodded gratefully, and sipped from it once more. The question *Who were 'They'* that she'd been wanting to ask had already been answered—she could read between the lines—even if she didn't consciously believe him. As excited as she was by it all, the majority of her was seriously doubting his story ... but the other part of her had total belief, and her attention to his every word was total. He was utterly convincing. He believed it so *much,* and spoke so *well* ... it wasn't a lunatic's rant. His sheer presence transformed the impossible into the possibly plausible. It was a gentleman's tale. But it was also ridiculous ...

"The second—the very *second*—that my eyes opened later that day," he said, anger breaking through his sorrow, his eyes boring into Lisa's, "I knew. I knew as if they'd shown it to me and said *There, this is your destiny, we've made it for you,* and then got on with spending the next fifty years seeing which way I would jump. They'd taken my freedom, and far worse, doomed us all for the sake of mere experimentation. The human race had been put before the firing squad for the sake of their own curiosity, as if we were vermin." The glass went down, and when he spoke next, he spoke towards the floor, unable to look at her. Lisa knew that he had come to the heart of it, and her own began to race harder, running through the seconds, charging towards the end.

"They had made me into the timepiece," he said, his voice dead and cold. "I was now the doomsday clock; it sounds like an impossible concept, but I knew that they had done it. They had shown me, in my dreams, in my abominable dreams, and had given me a comprehension of the sheer scale of their power. I knew things about their nature, but not of their origin. Whoever they were ... whoever they *are* ... they are so far beyond our abilities and knowledge that we are to them as frogspawn is to us. And they are terrible. They are unforgiving, merciless; the very concept of such characteristics is beyond them. They are purely comprised of a desire for advancement. They prize it above all else. That they would do this to us, just as a test, that they would *consider* performing this action just to satisfy a curious instinct ... that says everything about their natures and their vast ability.

"One thing that I knew everything about, however, was the task, and the burden, ahead. They had shown me the end, coming as it would in darkness, and had shown me the part that I was to play in it all. I was the lynchpin, the keystone, and was now the focus of their interest. For they are psychologists, or at least they want to be. Our minds are of infinite fascination to them, with our unknown concepts of love and excitement and fear and joy ... of selflessness. I can only assume that elsewhere, other people such as myself are under scrutiny, and they have set themselves a timescale for discovering all that they can from *them* before my task is complete, for mine is the most important examination. When mine ends, everything ends."

He looked up from the floor at Lisa, to see if she understood. Her unwavering gaze made it clear that she did not. He snatched up the whisky glass and drained its remaining contents in one gulp, then leaned forward, placing his right elbow upon the table.

"They had told me what their terrible experiment was, and the role I had to play. They told me that, when I die ... this world, our people, all six billion of us, our history and our triumphs and our tragedies, all of it ... ends." He paused for a moment, the words hesitating behind his lips; he could see that even now she did not understand. He clarified it for her:

"With my death ... comes the extinction of the human race."

Lisa blinked a few times, then furrowed her brow. She almost wanted to laugh in the old man's face, with his expression so serious and grave with these ridiculous words—the same face that had been quite frightening just a few seconds ago—now seeming almost comical. She'd been completely wrong. The old man was fucking *nuts.* She'd been taken in until that point, but the bubble had burst with this last claim, as it had been one level of lunacy too much. She suddenly saw it all: he'd wandered down to his village pub, gotten smashed on scrumpy cider, wandered off across the fields on the way home and passed out. He'd then thrown up a few times, wandered home and had a dream, and had probably spent the last five decades getting so pissed that he now believed his own bullshit story, telling it to sucker after sucker in bars up and down the country just like this one. She felt fresh pity for him, at his desperate and lonely need for attention, and annoyance at herself for being so taken in. She'd been scared, actually scared! Still, it had been entertaining, he'd told it well and it sure had passed her break time. She glanced down at her watch. She had another twenty minutes at least, and was comfortable in her seat.

You might as well hear the old guy out.

Anything that took her mind off worrying about her studies for a few minutes was a good thing, and at least he wasn't *trying* to trick her. He clearly believed what he was saying; one look into his haunted, crazy- blue eyes could tell you that. She didn't notice the cold sweat of relief upon her back, or the way the tension had dropped out of her shoulders; she didn't really know just how much she'd bought into his story.

Silly old sod. The trick of it is in those eyes ... they're the first hook.

He was nodding now, back in the present with a sad smile on his face.

"I haven't seen that expression on another face in a long, long time," he said, leaning back in his chair, even letting out a bitter-sounding chuckle. "It used to drive me mad, so much so that, as you know, I haven't told this story in decades. Not in person at least. But the truth haunts a man, rattling around inside him like an echo, amplifying itself until it must be heard or else shatter you entirely. Maybe this is why I sometimes have my ... moments. So it's good to tell it again, very good, and better for you that you don't believe me."

"Oh, no, I—" said Lisa, beginning to protest, but the old man shook his head, still smiling, and held up his hand.

"It's all right," he said, "I'm glad, very glad. But I must finish. I have some way to go before I do." Lisa tried to think of something else to say, but couldn't. He knew she didn't believe him and wanted to talk anyway, and she was happy to listen. She didn't want to patronise him, and he was harmless. Now she was seeing the story in all of its lunacy, she remembered her earlier thoughts about the poor state of his clothes as well. The suit *was* nice, she supposed, but wasn't it also poorly maintained? Bobbling here and there, and perhaps made of a fabric that was actually quite cheap. These were *not* the clothes of a rich man, and certainly not one as wealthy as he claimed to be; she'd been stupid not to see that. She smiled indulgently—perhaps a little too indulgently, as his expression seemed to darken—and motioned for him to continue.

"I shan't bore you with the details of my coming to terms with this new reality," he said, shrugging and looking away slightly. "Needless to say that the next few weeks weren't pleasant. Fortunately, a telephone had been connected to the cottage previously, at my request, and so I was able to order supplies from the village shop to be delivered to the cottage. My appetite had disappeared entirely upon seeing the revelations I'd had, and were it not for my famished body I think it would have stayed gone, but the stomach has desperate needs sometimes. In this manner—never leaving the house, ordering supplies reluctantly from the village—I spent weeks spinning between states of disbelief, sorrow, self-pity, pity for the world, and madness. The inner heat and coldness regularly returning, disturbing me when they did. It may sound strange, to wake from a dream and somehow know that what you saw in it is true, but I can't explain it any better than that to you. I knew it was all true the same way that I know that water is wet. Acceptance, however, was a great deal harder; I felt dizzy and light-headed a lot of the time, and often had a feeling of disembodiment, that I was detached from myself and watching from afar, my new life merely a movie with my soul as the only observer. And then I would return to myself, and the reality of my situation would hit me afresh, confirmed and undeniable, and the process would begin again. How I didn't go insane and remain so, I don't know, and I think my new masters had a hand in that. The experiment required me to accept my new role, after all, to understand it and be capable of responding to it with a clear head. An examination of the human spirit would be no good if the spirit was driven mad by the task before him, and I think they would already have known the limits of our capacity for understanding. Now they wanted to know the limits of our *endurance*, of our ability to sacrifice."

He really believes this, thought Lisa. *Fifty years later, he still believes this … so what the hell has he been doing all for all of the time in between?*

"I drank again, of course," he said, nodding towards his empty glass; not a hint for a refill, but a visual reference. Lisa thought that the old man knew he'd had enough, his speech now becoming slower and more relaxed, the slur even more pronounced. "It didn't help, but some days I headed towards oblivion the way a frightened rabbit might bolt into the path of an oncoming car, carrying out any kind of motion that instinct may wish to perform. The thought of everything being lost to oblivion was too much to take, of course. The more I pondered it, the bigger it became, and so I began to drink every morning until sundown or unconsciousness, whichever came first. Naturally, after several weeks of this, even when I'd put weight back on due to binge eating and all the extra calories from various forms of alcohol, the body rebelled, and I began to wake to the most crippling migraines and continued bouts of vomiting. No blue substance this time, merely the half-digested remains of the previous night's bedtime snack. I kept going anyway, not knowing what else to do and being too immature to begin planning a course of action. I only stopped the day that I saw blood lying brightly on top of my vomit as it sat steaming on top of the rear garden's frosted-over grass.

"The sight had a profound effect on me. That streak of crimson, splashed before my eyes as if it had spurted from a freshly opened vein, seemed to symbolise the fragility of the human body. Of human *bodies,* of humanity's own life force ready to be spilled once and for all. Children, newborns, each one receiving less and less time on this earth the closer they were born to the time of my death. As I stared at that red streak, I realised—and not without a large degree of despair on my part—that fairness, and comprehension of reason, were irrelevant. My own desires and dreams were also irrelevant, not rendered so by my choice but by forces far, far in excess of my own. I had to live. I had to live *as long as possible,* and take as much care as was within my power to see that my mission was carried out.

"Fighting back would be a waste of time, and perhaps even disastrous. Do the maggots in a fisherman's creel have any power to prevent themselves from being impaled upon the hook? Any attempt at sabotage—not that I would know where to begin, and have not thought of a way in fifty years—could end in the experiment's early termination. After all, the worst element of their nature made it likely that they would do so; this whole enquiry was of the smallest interest to them, a distraction, a diversion. Should it become more trouble than it was worth to them, they would simply pull the plug. And who could I tell in a position of power that would listen to me? I was not without my contacts in various circles, if not those of my own then those of my father's. But they would think me a madman, with no proof except my own rambling account. And with my resources, I could afford the best physicians, surgeons, and dieticians in the world anyway, so what help could my acquaintances provide that I could not receive on my own, with a minimum of fuss? No. There was no need to take this to anyone outside of myself."

How convenient, Lisa thought cruelly, but kept it to herself. She felt bad for thinking it. It wasn't the old man's fault.

"I sat down in the frost that morning, my head pounding, and wept for a long, long time. I'd seen my future, and the misery to come, and I would not even be able to end it all when it became too much. With everything at risk, I couldn't even take one last holiday before I began my new life of total purity. A plane crash? Food poisoning? Any kind of foreign disease? All unlikely ... but when there was even the slightest risk of damage to my health, I would have to avoid it. I couldn't even go to the nearest pub for one last night of revelry, because it would only take a bar brawl or a drunken fall to kill every human being on the face of this planet. The stakes would the biggest imaginable when taking even the most infinitesimal gamble.

"I would have to become the world's biggest hypochondriac, and its most disgusting coward. I looked at the cottage, and saw how, again, like my finances, it was perfect for their enquiry; detached from the world, but not too detached, easily within an ambulance ride should there be an emergency. It was, to my immense dismay, almost custom built for the task. A sturdy construction, for sure, but already my eyes were wandering over its surfaces, assessing, finding weak spots. The beautiful windows would need to be barred, of course, to keep out any intruders that may attempt to burgle the place and cause me harm in the process. Hard or sharp edges on furniture would need to be either removed or covered in padding, and so on and so forth, my mind already busy with the problem as my soul died. Such thoughts were automatic, sealing my tomb around me even as I wept for the loss of my freedom.

"Eventually, I would create a set of rules for myself, one that I vowed to live by on an *absolute* basis. If ever I was uncertain on a course of action to take, I would refer to my list. I have done so for the last fifty years until today, barring one day that came not too long after the experiment began. That list that has kept me alive, and kept me well, for a long time; as you've already noticed, I look far younger than I should thanks to my own rigorous care. Again, that could also be my masters playing a part, rewarding my efforts and wanting the experiment to continue as long as possible, wanting to see my mind's dance play out for decades. I have never seen the black cloud again in all of that time, and only on one occasion have I ever had any definite sign of the experimenters at all. I have no wish for that to ever happen again. So ... the rules. It is a short list, and a straightforward one, but it covers most necessary angles."

He raised his hand, and extended a finger as each item was recalled from memory, his blue eyes not wavering from Lisa's as he did so.

"One: No alcohol.

"Two: No leaving the cottage grounds unless absolutely necessary.

"Three: Two hours of exercise every day.

"Four: One hour minimum outside the cottage each day, even in winter, for sunlight on the skin and the production of vitamin D, but ALWAYS with maximum factor sun cream in any weather.

"Five: No travel by car unless absolutely necessary."

The fingers retracted, and then the counting began again, continuing on the one hand. "Six: Full checkup by visiting private doctor once a fortnight.

"Seven: Two hours of reading every day, minimum, to maintain a healthy mind. (Not just fiction, either; I have learned a great deal about medicine and survival over the last few decades. I dare say that now I could give myself as good a check as any doctor, and perhaps better than most, in theory, but with very little practical experience I have to get all my opinions checked.

"Eight: Two hours of puzzles and crosswords every day, minimum, to maintain a healthy mind. (I used to have books and books of these sent to me, and eventually had to pay to have mine compiled specially. I became so skilled at them that most examples became too easy.)

"Nine: No visitors unless absolutely necessary. (Visitors meant a possibility of inward-bound disease.)

"Ten: A diet rich in fruit, vegetables, and protein every day, based upon the advice of medical professionals and updated as and when new research arrives. NO fried foods." The old man's hand returned to the table, and Lisa found herself wondering if the old man even noticed that Rules One and Ten had flown straight out of the window. "The updating part was, as you can imagine, almost impossible in later years once the Internet came into use and I had it installed in the cottage. Every day there was new and contradictory advice, and so I had to trust my own instincts at first. However, soon after, I had dieticians working for me, and I decided that I would be best listening to them and them alone. Recently, I have given up gluten and dairy products, and life has become the most unbearable that it has been since I was first adjusting to my new life." He sighed again, and fiddled with the now-cold food on his plate, using his fingers and occasionally breaking off a piece of sausage or picking up a chip, gently popping them into his mouth as he spoke.

"The radio was a big comfort, of course, as was the television, later, and the Internet far later than that. I would hide myself in another room of the house when professionals came to install any new invention that needed outside expertise to do so, then I would go around the building wearing a face mask and disinfecting every surface, the windows flung wide open to get new, clean air in. I was able to sell my stake in the company with a minimum of fuss, carrying the matter out via my solicitor and, I'm both glad and ashamed to say, without having to face Nathan Spring. This set me up to be comfortable for the rest of my days, and ironically, there will be a sizeable amount leftover after my death ... useless, of course. The worst thing is that I can't even put it to good use, as again, any chance that I might need such large funds in a case of life-saving emergency or extended specialist care, however unlikely, means that I cannot risk giving it away.

"I did have visitors, of course. I had a handful of English friends, both from my time in Europe and at home, that became so concerned by my sudden disappearance that a handful of them managed to track me down over those first few years. These weren't part of the hangers-on lot; these were good people. I wouldn't answer the door, but would at least talk to them through the

207

closed window. It could be said that it was a risk, perhaps drawing greater attention to the crazy recluse in his cottage of lunacy, but it is a policy that I have stuck to for the last fifty years and it has worked. All visitors have been addressed through that window, from maintenance men to campaigning politicians to salespeople, all of them finding themselves unnerved. It was my release valve, though, my protection against going completely insane. That terribly slim vestige of human contact became so precious and essential. The advent of chatlines and easily accessible pornography were God's own blessing to me, and it was indeed very useful that I was a rich man, I must say." Lisa blushed, looking away and feeling very uncomfortable, and the old man held up his hand once more.

"I apologise. Not appropriate talk for a young lady. Anyway, the first few times old acquaintants came by, I said nothing about my situation and merely pretended that I didn't recognise them. It was heartbreaking, but they didn't return after that. It was only with the first of the last two visiting friends that I broke down in front of them, descending into hysterical tears, and told them everything after swearing them to secrecy. They thought, of course, that I was mad, and when they talked of doctors I threatened to have them and their families killed. Yes, I really did. It destroyed me inside, but what else could I do? However, I was so despondent those first few years, that even during the very next—and last—closed-window exchange with a concerned, visiting friend that I broke down again and told my story to them as well, and the following scenes were almost a carbon copy of the first. I vowed to never tell a soul again after *that,* but later, I would. Just not in person."

"But on that last occasion at the cottage, after seeing my dear friend Mary through the glass, seeing the tears in her shocked and wide eyes, watching her trembling hand loosen on the bottle of wine that she'd brought ... seeing the bottle fall and shatter on the paving slabs outside, but having to keep my furious face and raised finger present, lest the illusion of fury also be shattered whilst my heart was secretly breaking ..." He paused, falling silent for a moment. "After that," he continued, speaking softly, "I snapped for the first and last time. I rebelled. Well, again ... the last time until today, but today is ... a different kind of rebellion."

He shifted in his seat, and began to tug at the sleeve of his left arm, the arm that had been hidden beneath the table throughout the conversation. Lisa stared, fascinated again, wanting to know what he had to show her; a birthmark that he would claim was a message from beyond? Or perhaps the arm was missing, her suspicions of a prosthetic limb about to be confirmed?

"I began to rage," he said, taking great care as he worked at the sleeve beneath the table. "Of course, I had raged many times, but always with an element of reserve. I felt like my masters would tolerate *vocal* rebellion, the way a parent ignores a child's tantrum, but despite my knowledge of their cold natures, I felt that they were not above pride, and not above punishment should that pride be offended; I had no wish to see the black cloud again. But that day was different. That day I had reached my limit. I was still relatively young, and had not learned full restraint. I began to drink again, relishing the taste of the two remaining bottles of wine in the cellar and to *hell* with my liver, getting blind drunk and screaming my rage to the sky. I hoped that my distant observers would hear it, and I went on in this manner for some time. Eventually, I snatched up a knife in the kitchen, and began to cut into my arm, yelling into the air that I didn't care, I didn't care either about the world or myself and that they couldn't stop me doing anything, that I would show them. Empty threats, but I was reacting without thought, in a state of near-lunacy. I wanted to damage myself, to provoke a response. Looking back, I wondered if this was exactly the sort of thing that they wanted to see."

Ah, thought Lisa. *That's what. I'm about to see his arm scars from where he cut drunken rants into his skin. If he does that, I'm leaving.* But she continued to stare at the still-covered arm as the old man talked.

"The pain was almost sweet, coming to me like an old acquaintance that represented a happier, warmer time. A joyful memory from another life. I don't know what I planned to achieve by this, but in that moment it felt like a true, honest way of sticking two fingers up at my captors. But even now, I think: were they truly my captors? The only force actually keeping me inside the cottage and bound to a life of the highest self-preservation was me, after all, and inside myself, as *part* of myself, lay my only constant companion: guilt, and I do not believe that there is a stronger force on this earth. Yes, they had put that upon me, that total responsibility, and all that came with it, and I was parent now to every child on earth, doomed as they were, their bodies in my hands. But it was I who actually chose to bound myself so. But then, that was the whole point of their test, perhaps. What would I *choose* to do? How would I choose to live? And I chose total isolation."

He paused in his fumbling motions at his sleeve for a moment and rubbed at his face, then returned to his adjustments.

"Anyway. I awoke some time later, on the kitchen floor, and my entire forearm was missing," he said.

Lisa couldn't stop a gasp escaping her lips as he completed his motions. The old man raised his other arm above the edge of the table, the sleeve now loosened enough to remove—she'd been right—his prosthetic forearm and hand. *Prosthetic* was perhaps too generous a word for it though; it looked like it had been taken from a department store mannequin, the skin-tone paint chipped and faded in a great many places. The forearm ended in a roughly cut edge where a rubber lip, looking as if it had been removed from a tyre or suchlike, was taped against it, presumably to protect his skin. But it wasn't the crudity of the limb's design that made Lisa gasp in shock. It was the state of the limb to which the prosthetic had been attached.

Not that it was a gory mess, either; it was the *perfection* of the amputation. Lisa had seen images of amputated limbs as much as the average person had, but she had never seen anything like this in her entire life. The limb ended in a slight taper, just above the elbow, and the end was covered with skin in much the same as any other long-term surgery. But where it entered into the realms of the insane—what made Lisa recoil and suddenly feel very, very frightened indeed because the old man's words suddenly didn't seem so crazy—was the fact that the edges of the limb's end looked like you could have used them to iron creases into cloth. They were so sharply defined, so perfectly even and crisp, that the limb almost gave the impression of a striking blade. It looked like someone had cropped the rest of his arm away using some kind of reality-based photo-editing software. The old man turned it back and forth, and even gently ran his finger along its edge. Lisa flinched, almost expecting him to cut himself on it. "Excuse the false arm," he said, missing the point entirely, and speaking airily. "I made it some time ago, in the days just after the 'amputation' and before I'd really finalised my rules. I still believed those early days that eventually I would somehow go out now and then, my denial keeping me sane, and so I had a department store dummy delivered." He chuckled, darkly. "I still never went out though, even when I'd constructed the arm. With great despair, I came to accept that other people brought an infinite number of minor but still world-threatening risks. I wasn't sure that I would even be able to find the arm today, but I did. I wanted to finally use it if I was leaving the house. Plus, I didn't want to stand out any more than was absolutely necessary. I've never shown anyone this, actually," he said, *actually* now coming out as *achsually,* the booze really starting to settle into him now. Lisa found herself wildly wondering if he would even be showing her his arm if he wasn't as drunk as he was.

"But anyway; this is what I awoke to find had been done to me in my sleep," the old man continued. "For a mad moment I wondered if I had done this to myself in my drunken rage, but one look at the impossible neatness of it soon availed me of that idea. Plus, it was already healed, looking as if it had been that way for years. You'd think the skin would split constantly, wouldn't you, being pulled around such an edge in this way, but it never has. It's impossible, but here it is. They can do anything they want, after all. They had given me a reminder, a little glimpse of what was at stake, telling me that, whilst my actions within the experiment were my own, I was to leave them out of it. I was to think only of the rest of my race and whether I cared to save them or not. They knew where my rage was directed; they wanted me to know that I was missing the point. As if that wasn't clear enough, I found *this* lying on the floor a few feet away from me. It was further clarification."

Before Lisa's goggling eyes, as she still reeled from the insanity of the photoshopped limb before her, he reached into his jacket pocket and produced a small, reddish brown object, paper-thin and cut into a rough rectangular shape. In almost direct contrast to the limb, the edges of it were rough, but the geometrically accurate shape was still perfectly clear. It was somewhere between a business card and a postcard in terms of size, and from what Lisa could see it was covered in a series of black swirls, random and uneven, some sitting in neat lines, others spraying chaotically here and there across its surface. It didn't look like it was made of paper; it reminded Lisa of parma ham in terms of texture. The old man placed it on the table and pushed it across to Lisa.

"Try and read that," he said, dropping his strange, razor-sharp stump of an arm back below the table. "What does it say?"

Lisa stared dumbly at the swirls on the 'card', her eyes almost hurting to look at the crazy design. What the hell was this? Read it? She could barely even bring herself to keep looking at it. It was horrible, repulsive. It spoke to her of dark things, of coldly malevolent intent. She wanted to swipe it off the table, or better still, to burn it.

It's making *you feel that way, isn't it? There's something about it. Just like him, just like you knew something was wrong when this crazy conversation started. What does it say? It doesn't say anything! His arm ... his impossible arm ...*

She looked up at the old man, who stared sternly back at her. Lisa could only sit there with her mouth agape, shaking her head slowly.

"I didn't think so," said the old man, picking the card back up and putting it into his inner pocket once more. "The others couldn't either. I've showed a few people on webcams before. Good lord ... webcams. What a blessing, even if I mainly only watch other people's, rather than display my own. It's even the perfect medium for telling my story, on the very rare occasions that I have. People *expect* other people online to be mad ... although, as I have said, I have seen that disbelief on several other faces; I don't tell the story often, only when I feel as if I must before I go genuinely insane. Plus, there is always that slight hope of finding someone else who is involved in their other ... experiments. If only to find another soul on the entire planet who could share, to some degree, my experience. But anyway ... the parchment. The few that have seen it—those online individuals—all saw different things. One saw it as a series of scratches. Another saw it as a sequence of concentric shapes. Another saw it as depicting the points of a constellation—"

"Squiggles," blurted out Lisa, interrupting and looking pale. "I saw it as a load of squiggles." The old man's head nodded towards her heavily, the physical carelessness of the drunk coming forth.

"Squiggles," he repeated, nodding some more, as if in slow motion. "Some see it as squiggles. There you are. For my part, however, it is clear as day; I see it in my mind less than I read it, if that makes sense." He sat back in his chair, and held his hand before him, as if to suggest he was looking at a large banner or billboard. "It's a series of images, showing how it will happen. How the end will come, immediately after the exact moment that my brain ceases to produce any activity. First, the black cloud will come again." He paused, and Lisa shivered involuntarily at the mention of it, as if the warmth around her had already been swallowed by the cloud's arrival.

"This time it will be far larger, growing to smother the earth and blot out the sun," the old man continued, his shocking blue eyes growing distant, "then we will all begin to wither, and not slowly, like a plant denied sustenance; we will wither like leaves on a hot griddle. And not just our bodies. All of our works and edifices, crumbling to dust, clearing a path for whatever purpose the experimenters may deem appropriate for our lands, should they decide that they want them. And we shall turn to dust and blow away, along with any memory that we ever were, and of any dreams that may have once existed." He sighed, heavily, and almost seemed to wither too, folding slightly in his seat as he looked down at the table. Lisa shivered in her seat as dread seeped crazily into her belly, and she couldn't resist a glance over her shoulder, feeling distant eyes observing her movements.

"*Terminatione Pares Exstinctio,*" the old man intoned, without looking up. "The only words upon the parchment; you don't see them, but I do. They haunt my dreams. Latin. *Terminatione pares exstinctio.* Termination Equals Extinction. Says it perfectly. I have never drank again since that day, until today." He chuckled, the lazy, guttural noise of the comfortably drunk. "Guilt, it seems, has its limits after all, just like love. That, and a fifty-year expiry date." He shook his head, a silly smile on his face, and patted his jacket where the "parchment" would be. "This, however, has never expired; you'd think it would have, made as it is from meat and bone. But again, they can do as they please, and what better way to make a reminder more relevant than to give me one that is a part of me?"

Lisa's skin crawled, her whole body wanting to bolt for the door as the physical origin of the parchment set in. Her head began to pound with conflicting thoughts as her only weapon—denial—proved to be less and less effective. The old man seemed to sense her discomfort, and made a loose, waving motion with his good arm.

"Don't worry," he said, a sadness in his voice even as he adopted a lighter tone, "these are all the words of a madman, after all. The more time passes, the more you will remember that. Tonight, perhaps, it may stay with you, but in the morning, it will seem half as impressive. Then even less so as that day wears on, and by the next, it may even be a funny story that you share with others, the one about the day you met the man who held the world to ransom with the beating of his heart." He gazed out of the window again, and Lisa saw a tear run down his cheek. "It wasn't all bad ..." he said, his voice cracking. "... it was, at least, a leisurely lifestyle, and I ate well for the most part. And as technology improved, things became easier, too. Why, in the last fifteen or so years I have spent most of my time online, making friends around the world and learning, learning. I've learnt, and read, so much. It almost ... *almost* ... makes up for not really living, for a lifetime spent inside the same four walls. I've made the best of it, I think, but how can one call a life devoted only to extending itself and maintaining complete isolation be called a life? Especially when one knows what happens when it ends? Can you imagine how it is to exist with such a burden? When knowing that one will be not be thinking in one's final moments *I have lived well* but instead *I have failed, I could not manage another day for them.* I have filled my time as best as I can. I can play six instruments, you know. I always dressed well, even when stuck indoors, because I felt that if I allowed my appearance to decay, so would my mind. I ordered in new clothes, but this suit, the one I'm wearing now, was my father's. I wanted to wear it on my trip out; I know it's a little shabby, but I felt wearing it gave the day a greater sense of occasion. D'you know ... I would have dearly, dearly loved a pet. Even that much of a companion would have been heavenly ... also, my cooking, you know, even with an absolute minimum of oil, is as good as it could possibly be ... " The tears ran thicker now, faster, and he did not wipe them away. "None of it even as good as a simple, fatty, fried-up meal like this," he said, flicking a hand at the plate of half-eaten food on the table. "I hate to think of the impact that it will have on my insides, though. I see many days stuck on the toilet, perhaps. Perhaps not. Can I have another drink?" he said, suddenly turning his gaze fully towards her.

Another drink? thought half of Lisa's mind. *Are you insane? You need to be back inside, back at the cottage! Your liver, at your age! And your arteries, suddenly having to deal with garbage like that after fifty years? Why not just snort a few lines while you're at it!* The other half told her that she was a complete idiot, being taken in by the rantings of an old soak, but even that half couldn't forget the image of that impossible arm, and the feeling she got from that terrible parchment. The doubting half was a very quiet voice indeed now, barely audible. All her trembling voice said, however, was: "Why ... aren't you ... at home?"

The old man seemed confused for a moment, his eyebrows furrowing in lost thought, and then he got it. "Ah ... you mean, why today? Why, after fifty years of rules, have I left the cottage?" he smiled, and wagged a finger at her. "You think that I should still be there? Still inside in my terrible solitude, unable to break it in any meaningful way? Have I not earned this holiday?"

"No ... no ... I mean, yes, you have, but why ..." The old man held up that hand again, his blue eyes twinkling—if fire can twinkle—but it may have just been the tears catching the light.

"I know. Excuse the mischief of a drunken old man," he said, and started to dry his face with his hand. "You mean, what specifically made me pick today? Well, I must confess that it is something that has perhaps been building for some time—even the immense power of guilt is finite, as I say—but then two things have happened at the same instant. It is so much of a coincidence that I suspect that, possibly, my old friends have played a hand in things. I think they have tired of the experiment now, or have at least gleaned enough information that they wish to introduce a new element to see which way I would jump. I've lived my solitary existence for all this time, what else is there for them to learn? I don't know. But either way, the first of the two things.

"Yesterday was my birthday. Eighty years to the day that I was born. And over the last fifty of those years, I have watched the world, first only hearing and then *seeing* the terrible news that came in. The damning examples of humanity at its worst. And the same question has rattled around in my head over and over and over ... do you remember what I said about the bouncing echo of thought, how it amplifies in your mind? Well, this one, time and again, was always the loudest: *why am I bothering?* Whether the world is only as bad as it's always been, whether it's worse, or whether it's just the amplification in my head over the years ... every day, every minute as I grow older, the question is more present than ever. Maybe I am mad, after all. Maybe I'm just bitter. Or maybe I just want to die, and am looking for an excuse." His face was expressionless, his cheeks slack.

"However, the answer has always been the same; the children, the innocent ones who play no part in the madness. That answer has *always* kept me in line. But yesterday—my birthday—as 'chance' would have it, I *had* to leave the cottage for the first time in decades; my doctor had advised me to do so for the first time. I always covered my arm when doctors visited, by the way, dismissing it as a childhood injury that never went on record, thanks to our private family doctor. It's never really been questioned. Obviously, I've had a few illnesses over the years, but far less than most people, of course, thanks to my lifestyle, although once I had an eye infection that became quite severe; I didn't worry too much though, because in the worst instance I would lose the eye. Hardly life threatening. Anyway, I'd had a cough for a long time, and I presumed that I'd managed to catch it off my doctor on his last visit. Doctors have always been, after all, the only people to see me face to face inside the cottage in all of my time there. Now I think about it, I see another piece of evidence of the experimenters' hand in it all; it was blood that brought my mission home to me that time in the garden, many years ago, and blood now that signals the closeness of its end. You see, a week or two ago I saw something in the latest piece of phlegm that I'd coughed up, splashed across it the same way it had lain atop my pool of vomit all those years ago; a streak of red.

"Of course, I rang my doctor immediately, and he said that I would need to go for a chest X-ray at once, and that he would refer me to the hospital. What a dilemma! Break rule number two, or risk further illness! I had to cover the greater risk; to ignore the advice of my doctor would be, clearly, the larger of two evils. With shaking hands, I called a taxi to the cottage to take me into Coventry, the quickest place my private cover could get me into. Can you imagine my nerves, excitement and fear? Of course, you cannot. You simply cannot.

"I shan't bore you with the details of my amazement at the changes in the scenery around me; I was aware, at least, of technological advances in the world thanks to films and television, but to be amongst it in person was a different thing entirely. I told myself to keep my acknowledgement of such things to a minimum, so as not to be become hooked on the rush of it all ... but I fear that despite this the glorious barbs of modern society have placed their hooks in me. I have become obsessed from only that brief excursion, and I think that too has played a part in leading me here today. But I digress.

"There were, of course, white masses on the X-rays of my lungs. It isn't confirmed—I have to have a scan or two to be sure—and they may be benign, but I think not. All the signs point to lung cancer. And diagnosed on my birthday, of course. And that it would be found in me, someone who has never smoked a single cigarette in his entire life, not even at the height of my hedonism; it can only be a push, a nudge from the experimenters. Would I continue my solitude, hiring home care and undergoing chemotherapy in whatever manner I found to be the most effective, perhaps turning my home into some kind of medical centre, replete with all the equipment I could need? Spending the last of my days prolonging my already-long life in deep discomfort? Or would it be the straw that broke the camel's back, leading me to decide that my responsibility had been carried out enough? Would I decide that the world was already burning, and that to merely try and hold back the flames in the face of Armageddon was pointless?"

He burped, out of nowhere, breaking the solemnity of the moment, and chuckled again.

"Excuse me," he said, patting his stomach. "I should really finish this meal before it turns into ice, I suppose." He picked up the fork again, and once more began to talk around mouthfuls of food. "The honest answer is that I don't know. How long would I have anyway, realistically? If not *lung* cancer, then surely some other form at my age, especially if the observers are wanting this wrapped up reasonably soon. With chemotherapy, I could prolong my life by what, three to five years? Ultimately, after a life of sacrifice, should I not be allowed a year or two of freedom, without undergoing such horrendous radiation treatment, free to do as I please, and *then* succumbing to the hereafter? Would I be doing anything other than letting nature take its course? And truly, would an extra two or three years really make a difference to the rest of the world? What goal are they trying to reach that they would manage to obtain within that extra time? I don't see it. They *wanted* me to be tempted, and I have been, and I am also very, very tired. You may even think it surprising that I would be so glib about such matters, after a lifetime spent acting in the opposite manner. I would disagree. Sometimes there come moments in life where there isn't a revelation, the skies do not open up, and instead you merely realise a different perspective. One that feels like it's always been there. And let it not be overlooked ... I have not yet decided what I am going to do. Guilt is an unfathomable power, but when it is in you less and less with every act of genocide that you see on the evening news, you find that after fifty years it suddenly has even less of an effect at long distance." He shovelled in the remaining food greedily, tapping a finger on the table as he chewed.

"But *today*," he said, "*today,* at the very least, I decided that I would eat, and drink. Last night I decided to stay in a fine hotel in the city. I found myself quite delirious with the possibilities after my medical news, although I imagine most people feel the opposite way. It was a terrifying experience nonetheless—I awoke screaming five or six times—sleeping and residing in different surroundings being a greatly unsettling thing for me. But despite my tiredness, I awoke feeling energised, thrilled. I made up my mind to spend a day out, to better get my head around the issues at hand, and whilst it took me some time to be able to set foot out of the hotel, the thought of a drink, and a fried meal, eventually propelled me out of the door. I asked the taxi driver to take me somewhere good to eat, and here I am. I don't know if I will return home today. I may even take some more time. And I think ... I *think* ... that I *may* never go home again. I don't know." He breathed heavily through his nose, and then thought of something and chuckled drunkenly. "But I *would* like another drink," he finished, his eyes blinking slowly, slightly dazed. He smiled at Lisa.

"You see? I'm just an old man who likes a drink, after all. I'm harmless. You wouldn't keep an old man from his only comfort, would you?" He managed a one-handed shrug, but Lisa felt like crying herself, now. She was deeply confused, but her brain latched onto this new question with eagerness; his request was something that she had an answer for.

"I'll get you another drink …" she said, slowly standing on autopilot, her legs shaking. "Whisky …?" The old man nodded, gesturing theatrically and swaying in his seat as Lisa found her feet. "Are you … finished with that …?" she asked, as if in a trance, and began to reach for the plate with its few remaining morsels, but the old man scowled slightly and grabbed for it.

"No, no," he said, shaking his head rapidly, "I'll have this finished by the time you come back though. Then I can have that other drink, and tell you all about life in the cottage. That'll be interesting for you …" This last part was meant as a joke, and the old man started to chuckle. He then considered it again, and chuckled some more, seeming to be amused by his own laughter in the way that only a drunk can. The chuckles turned into a throaty laugh, and the old man stretched both his good arm and his stump as he did so, stretching out his spine, letting his head fall back with a grin.

It makes me act a little odd sometimes.

"Ha! *Life!*" he cried, and Lisa noticed the tears were running again as his laughter continued, echoing around the walls of the now-empty bar. Still laughing, he bent and began to scoop the last few bits of food into his mouth. Lisa backed slowly away, dazed, and made her way behind the bar thinking that she certainly wasn't going to sit at table ten again, that she would perhaps never talk to another customer again, that maybe she would find another job. Her hands shook as she picked up the whisky bottle, and it clattered against the metal measure as she poured the liquid. She could still hear the old man's drunken, bitter laughter, of course, muffled by the last of the food. Chris's back was to her as she upended the measure into the glass, and the idea of telling it all to him flashed across her mind. She quickly dismissed it. Chris was not the person to share this with, if she should share it at all. Not Chris, not anyone; they wouldn't ever understand.

She looked back over to table ten, where the old man seemed to have stopped laughing, and was now tapping out some sort of strange rhythm on the table, rocking back and forth in his chair. Lisa stopped what she was doing, and watched; the rhythm was uneven, but the old man's eyes were closed in deep concentration. A moment later, his eyes flew open, looking brighter than before and bulging in his skull, and that was when Lisa realised that he wasn't tapping the table, he was weakly banging it; eating whilst drunk and laughing had proved disastrous. He was choking.

Lisa froze, and dropped the glass onto the floor where it shattered with a loud bang. Chris spun round at the noise, startled, then caught a glimpse of Lisa's expression and looked in the same direction that she was staring. Immediately, Chris was off, dashing around the bar and running over to table ten. He pulled the old man and his seat away from the table, and grabbed his shoulders with both hands as he got his arms around the old man's neck from behind in order to perform the Heimlich manoeuvre. That didn't happen, however; Chris's arms recoiled as he let out a yelp of pain.

"*Fuck!*" shouted Chris, grabbing at his arms as the old man fell forward across the table, banging it harder now and catching Lisa behind the bar with his blue, terrified eyes. "Like a fucking *oven!*" Chris immediately tried again though, not having time to wonder why the old guy was like a human hot plate, and recoiled in pain once more. Lisa was back in herself now, grabbing two bar towels and frantically soaking them under the cold tap in the bar sink.

"Here!" she shouted, running out from behind the bar now, carrying the soaking and cold towels to Chris. He got the idea immediately, wrapping them around his arms and gingerly pulling the old man back against his seat to give

Heimlich another try. Chris began to yank against the old man's chest, wincing as he caught other bits of his skin against the man's bare neck or ears, the head that they were attached to now starting to turn a light shade of purple. He was suffocating.

"*Come on!*" shouted Chris, as the old man spasmed in terrible silence. "*Cough it up!*" Chris was so lost in what he was doing that he didn't hear the first scream outside, or the second, but Lisa did; her ears had pricked up already, tuning in to the other sound coming from the street, the sound that was getting louder and louder by the second.

Like tiny bits of metal, she thought in that chaotic moment. *It sounds like tiny metal filings poured out in their millions into ... a ... cardboard ... box ....*

Lisa turned towards the window in a shell-shocked haze that made her look drugged. She managed to stay on her feet when she saw what was occurring, but only just.

The clouds above were boiling. They turned and spun on the spot, as the handful of people on the street outside gasped in terror. The grey masses above seemed to be turning around a central point, like water around the centre of a whirlpool, and something was emerging there. Lisa's blood turned to water as she watched, already knowing what that something would be. A darker, no, a *black* shape was appearing like smoke from a chimney, but already it was taking shape and, of course, forming a square. It then began to grow, expanding rapidly in all directions so quickly that, from Lisa's vantage point, the entire sky visible to her through the window had suddenly turned black. The bar almost became invisible in the gloom; none of the lights were on in the daytime due to the glass wall normally letting in all the light required. Now everyone outside was screaming, several of them running as if to get out from underneath the terrible blackness above them.

Lisa found her voice.

"*Chris!*" she screamed, but he didn't look up, and it was just as well; he might have stopped what he was doing, stunned by the view outside, and then he would have never freed the chunk of chewed up potato that was blocking the old man's windpipe. It fired onto the floor, its former victim whooping in a ragged gasp of air and falling onto the table's wooden surface, hitching in oxygen like a dying man, which of course he had just been. Lisa's legs finally gave way, and as she fell onto the floor, the light through the window—*the light, how is it back*—seemed a little too bright and dazzling, spots dancing before her eyes.

Where did it go, she thought crazily, and as she faded into unconsciousness she heard the old man gasping the words *I'm sorry, I'm sorry.* Then there was the sound of stumbling feet, and the slamming of the bar room door.

***

The next day, with her television off—the nonstop post-incident coverage was too much to take, the various theorists and religious crazies bringing it all back to her in vivid, terrifying detail—Lisa sat in her bedroom, her books surrounding her, open and ignored. How could she study? How could she think of books, knowing that the he was out there somewhere, making up his mind?

Chris had missed it, incredibly. The black cloud had disappeared so fast, and he'd been so engrossed in trying to save the old man's life, that he hadn't seen any of it. He'd *heard* about it, of course, as had everyone else in the world; the cloud, even in its brief appearance and expansion, had reached the edges of Europe, after all. Only two people knew the source of it, and one of them was Lisa. She supposed that fact made not one bit of difference in the grand scheme of things, but it certainly did to her. It meant, of course, everything.

Studying had been her first defence, her first attempt at doing something other than cry. That was the real world to her. Solid, irrefutable. It might help her forget and, as the old man had said, lessen her belief to fifty percent by the next day, and half again after that, and again after that. But all she could think of was that cloud as it spread—like a cancer, she supposed—and how the old man was exactly that: old. How long would he have left anyway, even after all of his efforts? How long—

She shook her head and slammed the book shut that she'd been failing to read.

The television was right. It was a temporary weather phenomenon. It was a solar flare affecting the ozone layer somehow. Something we don't understand passed in front of the sun. It was somehow an unregistered volcanic eruption of previously unseen magnitude. It was just an awful, awful coincidence.

But her hands still shook, and she'd still spent all of yesterday phoning her loved ones and friends in hysterics, telling them that she loved them, arranging to travel back home tomorrow to see her parents, unnerving everyone. She would see them *all,* she vowed.

Studying was out for the evening. She felt tears beginning again, but she slapped herself, hard, and then dug her fingernails into her arms. That had been working; she had the scabs to prove it.

That won't change anything though. Nothing will. Nothing can.

The clock on her desk said 7:03 p.m. In a moment of impulse, Lisa picked up the phone.

"Carla?" she said, trying to hide the tremor in her voice when her friend picked up, refusing to burst into tears and certainly not to scream. "Let's go out. Let's go out and get fucking smashed."

*

If you enjoyed this book, *please* leave a star rating on Amazon; the feedback that I've had is not only the thing that keeps me writing, but also means more people are likely to buy my books and that *also* keeps me writing. And if you do ... your name goes into the *Acknowledgements* section at the beginning of the whichever book I write next! You can also find out about my other available books while you're there. Follow Luke Smitherd on Twitter (@travellingluke or @lukesmitherd) or go to Facebook under 'Luke Smitherd Book Stuff'. Most importantly visit

lukesmitherd.com to sign up for the Spam-Free Book Release Newsletter, which not only informs you when new books are out (and *only* does that) but sometimes means that you get new short stories for *free!*

Plus: read on after the Author's Afterword for a FREE preview of Luke Smitherd's other book, IN THE DARKNESS, THAT'S WHERE I'LL KNOW YOU.

Author's Afterword:

(Note: at the time of writing, any comments made in this afterword about the number of other available books written by me are all true. However, since writing this, many more books might be out! The best way to find out is to search Amazon for Luke Smitherd or visit www.lukesmitherd.com ...)

Hi folks. If this is your first time reading my stuff, then I really hope you enjoyed it. If not, then you already know the drill; this is where I tell you a little about the book, but essentially beg you - my face smeared in my own feces and my clothes torn, body emaciated from starving for reviews, *reviews* – politely to leave this book a lil' star rating on Amazon. I can't stress enough how much of a difference they make to the sales of the books I write, and *every* one counts. Just like those pesky witness depositions. *Bastards.*

This is the second 'collected' edition of my work (the first being *In the Darkness, That's Where I'll Know You,* collecting *The Black Room* parts 1-4 ... which hey, might be a nice follow-up read eh? *Eh?*) and, as with that book, I'm a little nervous about releasing it. Will putting three of my existing novellas into one 'bargain' collection affect the sales of the books in their individual formats, effectively taking money and sales (which affect the visibility of my catalogue as a whole on Amazon) away from my feverishly grasping mitts? We'll see. I'll be interested to hear the feedback from you guys as to how these work together as a collection; for my money, *Weird. Dark.* is a perfect title for this collection. Plus, as long time Smithereens (the name that some asshole came up with for my regular readers/reviewers, and a title worn in much the same way as the Scarlet Letter was in days of yore) will know, all my books are referred to in discussion by acronyms of their titles. WD is, by a country mile, the easiest one to write now, which is a relief. I'm just glad I didn't call it *Weird. Dark. 40.*

The first of these to be written was TMOTT, way back in the early part of 2013. The most recent was The Crash, which was written for my Patreon subscribers (patreon.com/lukesmitherd) along with the accompanying downloadable audio 'discussion.' It's funny to think how completely my life has changed since the days of TMOTT, and -- I'd like to think – how my writing style has hopefully improved, in my eyes, if only because I've learned how to repeat myself less and not over-labour the point (if you think I'm still overly verbose, you're *really* lucky that you didn't read the very *first* draft of *The Physics of the Dead* (TPOTD) before it took an edit. That's the favourite of many Smithereens, however, so what do I know. I think it's still my own personal favourite too.)

These stories were written in Cambridge, New York, Derby, and Coventry respectively, with this afterword being written in Paris. That sounds like I am now some sort of globe trotting pornstar, and that isn't the case; I just know how to travel cheap, combined with being able to make a living solely off my writing. I look back to where I was in 2011, when this whole career started, and while my personal life has been through some tough ups and downs – some very much so – I consider myself *unbelievably* blessed to be able to do this, and have had some great times along the way too as a result. So thankyou. It's only possible because of you guys leaving your reviews, sharing on Facebook and Twitter, recommending me to your friends (*and if you stop doing it I cease to exist so you have to keep doing it forever and ever ...* are you buying this?) so that thank you is as sincere as I can make it. A special thankyou has to go to my Patreon subscribers; eventually the stories they get months before everyone else will be published (although they are the only ones that get the audio. The unlucky buggers) but *The Crash* was theirs only a few weeks ago. I wanted to include it here as a little bonus story, but didn't want them to feel ripped off, so I asked their permission. Yes, it's my work, but I want to look after those guys. The warm response I received was genuinely delightful. So thanks a lot Patreon people, and for your support as well obviously.

In a way, now that I think of it, this collection kind of marks a bit of a milestone along the way for me. Do long time Smithereens remember when I said, all the way back in the afterword of TSM, that I was going to write a book of short stories? That, uh ... never happened? Well, in a roundabout way ... here it is.

And now for the now-traditional-prediction-of-what-I'm-going-to-do-next-that-never-actually-happens: the plan for the rest of 2015 is to continue the *Tales of the Unusual* series (that HOUYFB and MNIMG were originally published under, and techincally, TMOTT should be retconned and labeled as the first one of these, but for some reason I didn't quite feel right doing that) and then, at the start of 2016, go away for a little while and write a full-length novel that ... whisper it ... I'm going to start shopping around to 'traditional' publishers. Thanks to you guys, I now have a career. The next logical step is – without sacrificing the integrity of the writing in *any* way – is to try and take it to the mainstream. Watch this space.

Long time readers will know that this probably won't happen and I'll end up back in Vegas with a handle in my hand instead. But I'll at least *try.*

As always, join in the bullshit over on the Luke Smitherd Book Stuff facebook page, follow me on Twitter @travellingluke and @lukesmitherd, and more importantly sign up to the Spam Free Book Release Newsletter over at lukesmitherd.com to not only be alerted when new books come out, but also to sometimes to get FREE books! And you ONLY get emailed at those times; this has been the case since day one.

Oh, and PS: the Smithereen Title requests continue to arrive. Only this week we crowned Captain Toronto; if YOU want to be just like The Hero of Hogtown himself, drop me a line at lukesmitherd@hotmail.co.uk saying the place of which you want have Smithereen superiority; the only rule is (I think) it can't be a state, province, country, or county. Wait, is Toronto a province? Ok, I just checked. It isn't.

See you next time folks. If you do decide to quickly leave a star rating before you forget ... (:-D) that'd be a much bigger help than you possibly realise. Sincere thanks if you do. And thanks anyway, as ever, for choosing to read my stuff.

Stay Hungry.

Luke Smitherd,

Paris,

September 3rd 2015

Luke Smitherd Book Stuff on Facebook
@travellingluke
@lukesmitherd
lukesmitherd@hotmail.co.uk
patreon.com/lukesmitherd

And now for that exclusive free preview of one of Luke Smitherd's other books, IN THE DARKNESS, THAT'S WHERE I'LL KNOW YOU.

IN THE DARKNESS, THAT'S WHERE I'LL KNOW YOU

Chapter One: An Unexpected Point of View, Proof That You Can Never Go Home Again, and The Importance of the Work/Life Balance

***

Charlie opened his eyes and was immediately confused. A quick reassessment of the view, however, confirmed that he was right; he suddenly had breasts. Not very noticeable ones, perhaps, but when he'd spent over thirty years without them, even the appearance of a couple of A-cups was a real attention grabber. As he continued to look down, the very next thing to come to his attention was the material covering them; a purple, stretchy cotton fabric, something he had never worn, nor had he ever harboured any plans to do so. As he watched his hands adjust the top, he came to the most alarming realisation of all; those weren't his hands doing the adjusting. The giveaway wasn't in the slenderness of the fingers, or the medium-length (if a little ragged) fingernails upon their tips, or even in the complete lack of any physical sensation as he watched the digits tug and pull the purple top into position. It was the fact that, while they were clearly stuck to the end of arms that were attached to his shoulders (or at least, the painfully skinny shoulders that he could see either side of his head's peripheral vision; his shoulders were bigger than that, surely?) they were moving entirely of their own accord.

He was so stunned that he almost felt calm. The bizarreness of the situation had already passed straight through *this is crazy* and out the other side into the utterly incomprehensible. Charlie stared dumbly for several seconds as his mind got caught in a feeble loop, trying and failing to get its bearings (*What ... sorry, what ... sorry, WHAT ...*) While, in that moment, he never really came any closer to coming to terms with the situation, his mind did at least manage to reach the next inevitable conclusion: this wasn't his body.

The loop got louder as these unthinkable, too-big-for-conscious-process thoughts instantly doubled in size, but got nowhere (*WHAT ... WHAT ... WHAT THE FUCK*). All Charlie was capable of doing was staring at the view in front of him as it moved from a downward angle, swinging upwards to reveal a door being opened onto a narrow hallway. A second doorway was then passed through, and now Charlie found himself in a bathroom. He wanted to look down again, to see the feet that were carrying him forward, to help understand that he wasn't doing the walking, to aid him in *any* kind of conscious comprehension of his situation ... but he quickly realised that he couldn't affect the line of sight in any way. The viewing angle was completely out of his control. Instinctively, he tried to commandeer the limbs that were attached to him, to move the arms like he would have done on any other minute of any other day since his birth, but there was no response. There was only the *illusion* of control; the moment when one of the hands reached for the door handle at the same time that he would have intended them to, as he reflexively thought of performing the motion simultaneously. What the fuck was going on? *What the fuck was going on?*

The crazy, unthinkable answer came again, despite his crashed mind, even in a moment of sheer madness—what other conclusion was there to reach?— as he saw the feminine hands reach for a toothbrush on the sink: he was in someone else's body—a woman's body—and he was not in control.

Incapable of speech, Charlie watched as the view swung up from the sink to look into the plastic-framed bathroom mirror, and while he began to notice the detail in his surroundings properly—tiny bathroom, cheap fittings, slightly grubby tiles, and candles, candles everywhere—the main focus of his concern was the face looking back at him.

The eyes he was looking through belonged to a woman of hard-to-place age; she looked to be in her mid- to late-twenties, but even to Charlie's goggling, shell-shocked point of view, there was clearly darkness both under and inside her green eyes (physically and metaphorically speaking) that made her look older. Her skin was pale, and the tight, bouncy, but frazzled curls of her shoulder-length black hair all added to the haunted manner that the woman possessed.

All of which Charlie didn't give a flying shit about, of course; thoughts were beginning to come together, and his mind was already rallying and coming back online. While Charlie would never describe himself as a practical man, having spent most of his life more concerned with where the next laugh was coming from rather than the next paycheque, he had always been resourceful, capable of taking an objective step backwards in a tight spot and saying *Okay, let's have a look at this.* While he was beyond that now—had he been in his own body, that body would have been hyperventilating—he was now aware enough to at least think more clearly. As the woman continued to brush her teeth, Charlie watched, and thought the one thing to himself that instantly made everything else easier:

This is probably a dream. This is fucking mental, so it's got to be a dream. So there's nothing to worry about, is there?

While he didn't fully believe that—the view was too real, the surroundings too complete and detailed, the grit and grime too fleshed out and realised—it enabled him to take the necessary mental step back, and put his foot on the brake of his runaway mind a little.

Okay. Think. Think. This can't actually be happening. It can't. It's a lucid dream, that's what it is. Calm down. Calm down. That means you can decide what happens, right? You're supposed to be able to control a lucid dream, aren't you? So let's make ... the wall turn purple. That'll do. Wall. Turn purple ... now.

The wall remained exactly the same, and the view shifted downward briefly to reveal an emerging spray of water and foaming toothpaste. The woman had just spat.

Right. Maybe it's not quite one of those *dreams then, maybe it's just a very, very realistic one. Don't panic. You can prove this. Think back. Think back through your day, think what you'd been doing, and you'll remember going to bed. What were you last doing?*

He'd met the boys, gone for a drink—excited about the prospect of one turning into many—the first night out for a little while. Clint's mate Jack had been over from London too, which was both a good excuse and good news for the quality of the night. They had ended up on a heavy pub crawl, and somebody had said something about going back to their place ... Neil. That guy Neil had said it. And they'd gone to Neil's, and then ...

Nothing. Nothing from there on in. And now he was here. As he felt hysteria start to rise, escalating from the panic that he already felt, Charlie frantically tried to put a lid on it before it got badly out of control.

You passed out. You had some more to drink and you passed out. That's why you can't remember what happened at Neil's, and this is the resultant booze-induced crazy dream. So wake up. Wake your ass up. Slap yourself in the face and wake the fuck up.

Charlie did so, his hand slamming into the side of his head with the force of fear behind it, and as the ringing sting rocked him, he became aware that he suddenly had a physical presence of his own. If he had a hand to swing and a head to hit, then he now had a body of his own. A body inside this woman's body? Where the hell had that come from?

There'd been nothing before, no response from anything when he'd tried to move the woman's arms earlier. He'd been a disembodied mind, a ghost inside this woman's head, but now when he looked down he saw his own torso, naked and standing in a space consisting of nothing but blackness. Looking around himself to confirm it, seeing the darkness stretching away around him in all directions and now having a body to respond to his emotion, Charlie collapsed onto an unseen floor and lay gasping and whooping in lungfuls of nonexistent air, his body trembling.

His wide, terrified eyes stared straight ahead, the view that had previously seemed to be his own vision now appearing suspended in the air, a vast image the size of a cinema screen with edges that faded away into the inky-black space around him. Its glow was ethereal, like nothing he'd ever seen before. How had he thought that had been his own-eye view? It had clearly been there all along, hanging there in the darkness. Had he just been standing too close? Had something changed? Either way, there was no mistake now; there was just him, the enormous screen showing the woman's point of view, and the black room in which he lay.

Charlie pulled his knees up into a ball and watched the screen as he lay there whimpering. That slap had hurt badly, and instead of waking him, it had added another frightening new dimension to the situation. He was terrified; he lay for a moment in mental and physical shock, and for now, at least, everything was beyond him. The words that he feebly tried to repeat to himself fell on deaf ears—*it's a dream it's a dream it's a dream*—and so he lay there for a while, doing nothing but watch and tremble as the woman made a sandwich, checked her e-mails on her phone, and moved to sit in front of her TV. She flicked through channels, thumbed through her Facebook feed. As this time passed—and Charlie still watched, incapable of anything else for the time being—he came back to himself a little more. He noticed that, while he was naked, he wasn't cold. He wasn't warm either, however; in fact, the concept of either sensation seemed hard to comprehend, like trying to understand what the colour red sounded like. Thoughts crept in again.

You can't actually be in her head. You can't actually be INSIDE her head. People don't have screens behind their eyes or huge holes where their brain should be. You know that. You haven't been shrunk and stuffed in here, as that's not possible. So this ... HAS ... to be a dream. Right? You have a voice, don't you? You can speak, can't you? Can you get your breath long enough to speak?

Charlie opened his mouth, and found that speech was almost outside of his capabilities. A strange, strangled squeak came out of his throat, barely audible, and he felt no breath come from his lungs. He tried several more times, shaping his mouth around the sound in an attempt to form words, but got nowhere.

Focus, you fucking arsehole. Focus.

Eventually, he managed to squeak out a word that sounded a bit like *hey* and, encouraged by that success, he tried to repeat it. He managed to say it again on the third try, then kept going, the word getting slightly louder each time until something gave way and the bass came into his voice.

"Hey ..."

With that, the ability to speak dropped into place, even if getting the hang of it again took a real physical effort. He at least knew *how* to do it now, his mind remembering the logistics of speech like a dancer going through a long-abandoned but previously well-rehearsed routine. He looked out through the screen with sudden purpose, determined to find out if she could hear him.

"Hey ... *hey* ..." he gasped, his lips feeling loose and clumsy, as if they were new to his face. Charlie sat up, hoping to get more volume behind it, more projection. He thought he had to at least be as loud as the TV for her to hear him, if she was capable of doing so at all.

"*HEY*," he managed, but there was no external response. Charlie's heart sank, and he almost abandoned the whole attempt. After all, it was easier and more reassuring to resign himself to the only real hope that he had; that this truly *was* a dream, and thus something he could hopefully wait out until his alarm clock broke the spell and returned him to blessed normality. Things might have turned out very differently if he had, but instead Charlie found the strength to kneel upright and produce something approaching a scream.

"HEY!!" he squawked, and fell back onto his behind, exhausted. Staring at the glowing screen before him, dejected, Charlie then saw a hand come up into view, holding the remote control. A finger hit the mute button.

Charlie froze.

The image on the screen swung upwards, showing the white ceiling with its faint yellowing patches marking it here and there, and hung in that direction for a second or two. It then travelled back to the TV screen, and as the hand holding the remote came up again, Charlie realised what was happening and felt a fresh jolt of panic. Without thinking, he blurted out a noise, desperately needing to cause any kind of sound in an attempt to be heard, like a fallen and undiscovered climber hearing the rescue party beginning to move on.

"BAARGH! BA BA BAAA!" Charlie screeched, falling forwards as he almost dove towards the screen in his clumsy response to the images upon it. The hand hesitated, and then the view was getting up and travelling across the living room and down the hallway. It looked like the woman was going to look through the spyhole in her front door, and as she did so, the fish-eye effect of the glass on the huge screen made Charlie's stomach lurch. He still saw the fairly dirty-looking stairwell outside, however, and realised that the woman was inside some sort of apartment block.

Charlie stared, trying desperately to pull himself together, and assessed the situation. She could hear him then; but she certainly didn't seem to be aware that he was there. So she could be as unwilling in all of this as he was?

It'sadreamitdoesn'tmatteranywayit'salladreamsowhocares—

He didn't believe that though. He just couldn't. There had to be some sort of explanation, and he couldn't be physically *in* her head, so this was ... an out of body experience? Some sort of psychic link?

Charlie surprised himself with his own thoughts. Where the hell had all of that come from, all of those sudden, rational thoughts? True, he'd been confronted with something so impossible that he didn't really have much choice but to look at the available options, but ... was he suddenly adjusting again? When this all started, he didn't even have a body, but one quickly appeared. Was his mind following suit? He was still trembling, his shoulders still rising and falling dramatically with each rapid, shallow in-breath of nothing, but his mind was at work now; the shock had seemingly been absorbed and moved past far more quickly than it should have been, he was sure. Would he be this rational already if he were in his own body? Whatever was going on, being here was ... different. He felt his mental equilibrium returning, his awareness and presence of mind growing. He was scared, and he was confused, but he was getting enough of a grip to at least function.

You have her attention. Don't lose it.

He opened his mouth again, got nowhere, reset himself, then tried again.

"Lady?"

The view jerked round, then everything in sight became slightly farther away, very quickly; she'd spun around, and fallen backwards against the apartment's front door. The view then swung sharply left and right to either side of the hallway, looking to the bathroom doorway and then to the doorway of another, unspecified room. Charlie assumed it was a bedroom. He tried again.

"Can ... can you hear me?"

The view jerked violently. She'd clearly just jumped out of her skin, her fresh adrenaline putting all of her physical flight reflexes on full alert. It was a dumb question to ask—she obviously could—but even with his growing sense of control, Charlie's mind was still racing, his incredulity at the situation now combining with the excitement of finding that he could communicate with his unsuspecting host.

It was clear that she was terrified, and Charlie realised that he couldn't blame her. She was hearing a voice within the safety of her home when she'd thought that she was by herself, and Charlie could only guess what it sounded like to this woman. Did his voice sound as if he were right behind her, or was she hearing it actually coming from the inside of her head? Charlie couldn't decide which would be worse.

Get a grip, man. Of course she's going to shit herself when you start talking to her. Just … try and think, okay? Think straight. You have to get out of this. You need her to talk to you; you need her if you're ever going to get this sorted out. Get a grip, get control, and think smart.

"Please, it's—" He didn't get any further as the jump came again, this time with a little scream; it was a brief squeal, clipped short as if she were trying to avoid drawing attention to herself. Charlie jumped with her this time, startled a little himself, but pressed on. "Please, *please* don't be scared. I'm shitting myself here too. Please. Please calm down—" The second half of this sentence was lost, however, disappearing under a fresh scream from the woman. This time it was a hysterical, lengthy one that travelled with her as she ran the length of the hallway into the living room, slamming the door behind her. Charlie heard her crying and panting, and watched her thin hands grab one end of the small sofa and begin to drag it in front of the door. The scream trailed off as she did so, and once the job was done, the view backed away from the door, bobbing slightly in time with the woman's whimpering tears and gasping breath.

Charlie was hesitant to speak again; he knew that he simply had to, but what could he actually say without sending her off into fresh hysterics? The answer was immediate; nothing. There was no way to do it easily. She would have to realise that she was *physically* alone at least—and safe with it—and the only way to help her do that was to keep talking until she accepted that there was no intruder in her home.

Not on the outside, anyway.

"I need your help," he tried, wincing as the view leapt almost a foot upwards and then spun on the spot, accompanied by fresh wails. "Please, lady, you're safe—" The cries increased in volume, to the point where he had to raise his voice to be heard. In doing so, Charlie realised that he now had his voice under complete control. And wasn't the blackness around him a fraction less dark now, too? "Look, just calm down, all right? If you just listen for two seconds, you'll find that—"

"*Fuck ooofffff!!*" she screamed, the volume of it at a deafening level from Charlie's perspective. He clapped his hands to the side of his head, wincing and crouching from the sheer force of it. It was like being in the centre of a sonic hurricane. "*Get out of my flat! Get out of my flaaaaaaat!!!*"

"Please!! Please don't do that!" Charlie shouted, trying to be heard over the woman's yelling. "Look, just shut up for a second, I don't *want* to be here, I just want to—"

"*Get out! Where are you? Get out!! Get oooouuuuuttt!!*"she yelled, ignoring him, and as the view dropped to the floor and shot backwards—the living room walls now framing either side of the screen—Charlie realised that she'd dropped onto her ass and scooted backwards into the corner, backing into the space where the sofa had previously been. Frustrated, terrified, in pain and pushed to his limit (it had been one hell of an intense five minutes, after all) Charlie let fly with a scream of his own, hands balled into fists over his throbbing ears.

"*JUST SHUT THE FUCK UP FOR A SECOND!!*" he screamed, and whether it was from using some volume of his own, or because her own screams were already about to descend into hysterical, terrified and silent tears, the only sound after Charlie's shout was that of the woman's whimpers. The view still darted around the room though, trying to find the source of the sound, a source well beyond her sight.

Charlie seized his moment. At the very least he could be heard, and *that* hopefully meant he could start talking her down. She was more terrified than him—of course she was, at least he'd had time to get used to the situation whereas she'd just discovered an apparently invisible intruder in her home— but he had to get through to her while she was at least quiet enough to hear him. Hysterical or not, she had ears, even if he appeared to be currently standing somewhere in between them.

"Look, I'm sorry for shouting like that, I just need you to listen for a second, okay? Just listen," Charlie said, as soothingly as his own panicking mind would allow. "I'm not going to hurt you, okay? Okay? It's fine, you're, uh ... you're not in any danger, all right?"

"Where ... where are you? *Where are you?*" the woman's voice sobbed breathlessly, small and scared. Her thinking was clear from the confusion in her voice; she was finally realising that she should be able to see the person talking to her, that there was nowhere in the room that they could be hiding. Charlie thought quickly, and decided that it was best to leave that one for a minute. He'd only just got her onside, and didn't want to push her over the edge.

"I'll tell you in a second. I'm, uh ... I'm not actually in the room, you see. You're alone in the flat, and you're safe. You're fine. Okay?" She didn't reply at first. The sobs continued helplessly, but Charlie thought that they might have been slightly lessened, if only due to confusion.

"Wha ... what?" she stammered, the view swinging wildly around the room now. "Your voice ... what the fuck ... *what the fuck is going onnnnnn ....*" And then she was off again, the hysterical screaming coming back at fever pitch. Charlie stood in front of the strange, glowing screen, his hands at his ears again while she bawled, blinking rapidly as his mind worked. After a moment or two, his shoulders slumped and he sat down. There was nothing he could do but wait, and let her adjust. His own breathing was beginning to slow further, and he was finding acceptance of his situation to still be an easier task than he thought; while it was no less mind boggling, his panic was dropping fast, and unusually so.

It's being in here that's doing it. It has to be.

Either way, he let her have a minute or two to calm down. Eventually, he stood and began to pace back and forth in the darkness—illuminated dimly by the unusual light of the screen—while he decided what to say next. His frantic mind kept trying to wander, to seize and wrestle all the aspects of the situation into submission, and failed every time.

You don't like the dark. You don't like the dark! Don't think about it, don't think about it ... think about ... wait ... there's no breeze in here, no echo. It really is a room of sorts then, a space with walls on all sides?

He looked out into the darkness, looking for walls, and saw none; there was only seemingly endless blackness. Charlie thought it would be best not to go exploring *just* yet. Instead, he tried to control his breathing, and quickly ran through a mental list, double checking his actions and decisions of the previous few days before his night out:

Went to work. Did the late shift. Argued about sci-fi films with Clint. Helped Steve throw the drunk arsehole out that had started slapping his girlfriend. Went home, stayed up and watched a film because I had the Wednesday off. Met Chris in town—

And so it went on. By the time he'd finished a few minutes later—while he was no clearer about what had led him to be inside this woman's head—he told himself that he really *did* feel more capable of beginning to deal with things, and less frightened; in the absolute worst case, even though he didn't believe this to be the *actual* case, this situation was real, and had to be resolved. If he'd got in, then he could get out, and if this was the *best*—and more likely—scenario, where this was all just a dream, then he would wake up and all would be well.

Yeah. And if I had wheels, I'd be a wagon.

Charlie took a deep breath, and decided to speak again.

TO BE CONTINUED IN **IN THE DARKNESS, THAT'S WHERE I'LL KNOW YOU**, *AVAILABLE NOW ON AMAZON.*

Star ratings for WEIRD. DARK. can be left at the Amazon.com or .co.uk! ☺

Also By Luke Smitherd:

The Stone Man

The #1 Amazon Horror Bestseller

Two-bit reporter Andy Pointer had always been unsuccessful (and antisocial) until he got the scoop of his career; the day a man made of stone appeared in the middle of his city.

This is his account of everything that came afterwards and what it all cost him, along with the rest of his country.

The destruction, the visions ... the dying.

Available now on the Amazon Kindle Store, and soon in traditional book format

Also By Luke Smitherd:

An Unusual Novella for the Kindle

THE MAN ON TABLE TEN

It's a story that he hasn't told anyone for fifty years; a secret that he's kept ever since he grew tired of the disbelieving faces and doctors' reports advising medication But then, he hasn't touched a single drop of booze in all of that time either, and alcohol loosens bar room lips at the best of times; so on this fateful day, his decision to have three drinks will change the life of bright young waitress Lisa Willoughby forever ... because now, the The Man On Table Ten wants to share his incredible tale.

It's afterwards when she has to worry; afterwards, when she knows the unbelievable burden that The Man On Table Ten has had to carry throughout the years. When she knows the truth, and is left powerless to do anything except watch for the signs ...

An unusual short story for the Kindle, The Man On Table Ten is the latest novella from Luke Smitherd, the author of the Amazon UK number one horror bestseller *The Stone Man*. Original and compelling, *The Man On Table Ten* will leave you breathless and listening carefully, wondering if that sound you can hear might just be *pouring sand that grows louder with every second ...*

Available now on the Amazon Kindle Store

Also By Luke Smitherd:

The Physics of the Dead

What do the dead do when they can't leave ... and don't know why?

The afterlife doesn't come with a manual. In fact, Hart and Bowler (two ordinary, but dead men) have had to work out the rules of their new existence for themselves. It's that fact—along with being unable to leave the boundaries of their city centre, unable to communicate with the other lost souls, unable to rest in case The Beast should catch up to them, unable to even sleep—that makes getting out of their situation a priority.

But Hart and Bowler don't know why they're there in the first place, and if they ever want to leave, they will have to find all the answers in order to understand the physics of the dead: What are the strange, glowing objects that pass across the sky? Who are the living people surrounded by a blue glow? What are their physical limitations in that place, and have they fully explored the possibilities of what they can do?

Time is running out; their afterlife was never supposed to be this way, and if they don't make it out soon, they're destined to end up like the others.

Insane, and alone forever ...

Available now on the Amazon Kindle Store, and soon in traditional book format

Also By Luke Smitherd:

THE BLACK ROOM: A NOVEL IN FOUR PARTS

FROM THE AUTHOR OF THE AMAZON UK #1 HORROR BESTSELLER, 'THE STONE MAN', COMES A NEW MYSTERY TO UNRAVEL...

What Is The Black Room?

There are hangovers, there are bad hangovers, and then there's waking up inside someone else's head. Thirty-something bartender Charlie Wilkes is faced with this exact dilemma when he wakes to find finds himself trapped inside The Black Room; a space consisting of impenetrable darkness and a huge, ethereal screen floating in its centre. Through this screen he is shown the world of his female host, Minnie.

How did he get there? What has happened to his life? And how can he exist inside the mind of a troubled, fragile, but beautiful woman with secrets of her own? Uncertain whether he's even real or if he is just a figment of his host's imagination, Charlie must enlist Minnie's help if he is to find a way out of The Black Room, a place where even the light of the screen goes out every time Minnie closes her eyes...

Part one of a thrilling three-part novel, 'The Black Room, Part One: In The Black Room' starts with a bang and doesn't let go. Each answer only leads to another mystery in a story guaranteed to keep the reader on the edge of their seat.

THE BLACK ROOM SERIES, FOUR SERIAL NOVELLAS THAT UNRAVEL THE PUZZLE PIECE BY PIECE

Also By Luke Smitherd:

A HEAD FULL OF KNIVES

THE LATEST NOVEL FROM BESTSELLING AUTHOR LUKE SMITHERD

Martin Hogan is being watched, all of the time. He just doesn't know it yet. It started a long time ago, too, even before his wife died. Before he started walking every day.

Before the walks became an attempt to find a release from the whirlwind that his brain has become. He never walks alone, of course, although his 18 month old son and his faithful dog, Scoffer, aren't the greatest conversationalists.

Then the walks become longer. Then the *other* dog starts showing up. The big white one, with the funny looking head. The one that sits and watches Martin and his family as they walk away.

All over the world, the first attacks begin. The Brotherhood of the Raid make their existence known; a leaderless group who randomly and inexplicably assault both strangers and loved ones without explanation.

Martin and the surviving members of his family are about to find that these events are connected. Caught at the center of the world as it changes beyond recognition, Martin will be faced with a series of impossible choices ... but how can an ordinary and broken man figure out the unthinkable? What can he possibly do with a head full of knives?

Luke Smitherd (author of the Amazon bestseller THE STONE MAN and THE BLACK ROOM series) asks you once again to consider what you would do in his latest unusual and original novel. A HEAD FULL OF KNIVES is a supernatural mystery that will not only change the way you look at your pets forever, but will force you to decide the fate of the world when it lies in your hands.

Available now in both paperback and Kindle formats on Amazon

Printed in Germany
by Amazon Distribution
GmbH, Leipzig